# OPERATION STAGECOACH RED

# OPERATION STAGECOACH RED

## J. T. FITZGERALD

PENTLAND PRESS, INC.
ENGLAND·USA·SCOTLAND

PUBLISHED BY PENTLAND PRESS, INC.
5124 Bur Oak Circle, Raleigh, North Carolina 27612
United States of America
919-782-0281

ISBN 1-57197-052-5
Library of Congress Catalog Card Number 96-71067

Printed in the United States of America

# DEDICATION

This book is dedicated to all the men and women who served in Vietnam, the last romantic war. With a special tribute to the Agency personnel who gave their lives. No walls or monuments to show their names. Known only by God and family.

# ONE

The black sports car eased over into the right lane as the driver prepared to exit at the next ramp. He smiled as he read the big letters, CIA HEADQUARTERS NEXT EXIT.

When he had first seen the sign he wondered why the most secretive organization in the world would advertise their whereabouts right on the George Washington Parkway. He finally concluded that everybody knew what the big white building in Langley was anyway. Besides, the thousands of people employed there had to have directions to get to work.

Taking a quick glance at his watch, he saw it was exactly ten-thirty. He had to be in Mr. Fanning's office no later than eleven o'clock. "Damned Washington traffic," he mumbled as the cars in front of his slowed to a crawl.

It was stop-and-go for the next ten minutes before he reached the ramp. He was lucky it was the middle of the morning; there was no local traffic, and after flashing his badge at the gate, the guard waved him through.

It was two miles from the gate to the big white building. The winding road through the Virginia woodlands had twenty-five-miles-per-hour signs posted, but he was running a little late. With no one else on the road, he didn't figure anybody would notice if he stepped on it a little.

Driving into the visitors' parking lot, he spotted an open space in the front row. According to his watch, he still had fifteen minutes. Even with the long walk he should be there in plenty of time. Turning the rear-view mirror, he checked to make sure his tie was straight.

This was part of the Agency he didn't care for. He had spent the last three years in Vietnam in Special Forces camps along the Cambodian or Laotian border. There, you were your own man. You learned to survive from one day to the next.

But six months ago he had been recruited by the Agency to do a job. They brought him back to the States and put him through their training with a group of recent college graduates. He had to get up at the same time every morning, wash, shave, and, worst of all, wear a suit and tie.

He was going back to Nam anyway, and a coat and tie wouldn't help him there. He remembered being told once that the only times you wear a suit are the day you get married and the day your wife dies. Maybe that's what kept him single.

Reaching the main entrance, he walked across the shiny marble floor to the main desk where a guard was seated.

"Yes, sir, may I help you?" the guard asked.

"I believe you can," he replied. "My name is Burt Courage. I have an appointment with Mr. Fanning of Special Operations in his office."

The guard picked up a roster and ran his finger down the sheet until he found the name. "Ah yes, here it is," he smiled. "A Mr. Courage at eleven. If you'll sign here, I'll take you to the elevator."

The office was on the second floor. As he stepped out of the elevator, Courage was taken back by the decor. He had made a number of trips to the main building before, but he had always been on the first floor. There space was limited, small cubicles were used as offices, and everybody complained about cramped working areas.

But this was like another world. He could feel his feet sinking into the thick carpeting as he walked toward the door at the end of the hall. Oil paintings of previous directors lined the walls, and he sensed each set of eyes following him as he walked by. This was where all of the decisions were made, he thought to himself, as he stopped in front of a door with Fanning's name on it in big gold letters.

As he stepped inside, he again adjusted his tie, and checked his hair with the palm of his hand.

The clicking of the typewriter must have drowned out the opening of the door; he had to clear his throat before the woman behind the desk looked up. She stopped typing and looked over the top of her blue-rimmed glasses.

"I'm sorry," she said politely, "I didn't hear you come in. I presume that you are Mr. Courage?"

"You presumed right." He winked.

She looked to be in her early fifties, neat and attractive, with mostly blonde hair. There was enough gray showing that she wouldn't be able to hide her age much longer.

"Please have a seat and I'll tell Mr. Fanning you're here. He must be very anxious to see you. I was told that once you arrived I should hold all of his calls." Reaching over, she pushed the button on the intercom. "Mr. Courage is here, sir."

For the protection of all new agents and their families, the first order of business was to give them a new name. Using their real first name and the first initial of their last name, the Agency would give them a new identity that they would use as long as they were employed. As he read the code name Burt Courage, he laughed to himself. How appropriate, he thought.

"Tell him I'll be with him in a minute," the voice replied.

Picking up Courage's file, Mr. Fanning leaned back in his chair. He had read it a number of times, but he wanted to go over it once more to make sure there wasn't something he'd missed. They kept accurate records on all of their employees from the day they came on board, including their training and final evaluation—and Mr. Courage had quite a dossier.

He wasn't your normal Agency recruit. They usually took the very best from the top colleges and universities in the country. Courage had just barely finished high school. Then, after two years of busting his back in a coal mine, he must have figured there was an easier way of making a living and joined the Army.

After completing Special Forces training he had done three full tours of Vietnam. He was awarded two Silver Stars, two Bronze Stars, three Purple Hearts, and the Vietnamese Cross for gallantry. He was an expert in guerrilla warfare, he could fieldstrip any weapon in the dark, and there was nobody better with explosives. He spoke fluent Vietnamese and was familiar with the terrain where the operation would be conducted. At the Agency training center he had finished in the top ten percent of his class.

Those were the good points; now the bad. He had a quick temper that had gotten him in trouble a number of times. He was a womanizer, and when not on duty he would sometimes drink to excess. Jack Daniels on the rocks was his favorite; when unscrewing the top from a bottle he had been heard to say, "We don't need this anymore," and he would then toss the top in the trash. He would call it his cocktail hour and down the entire bottle. But, never on duty.

Mr. Fanning smiled and shook his head as he slid the file back into the folder. "Well, this was the man selected," he sighed. "He'd better be good. If he isn't, this will be his last trip to Vietnam."

Reaching over, he pressed the button. "Betty, you can send him in now."

When Courage stepped through the door, he had to look up at the man standing behind the desk. Burt was six-feet-one and a solid hundred and ninety pounds, but he was still a head shorter and at least sixty pounds lighter than Fanning. His dark, leathered skin, solid white hair, and thick white eyebrows reminded Burt of a billboard advertisement of a man selling suntan lotion. With every hair in place and his blue pin-striped suit, he looked more like an executive of an oil company than somebody working for the Agency. He seemed to be in his early fifties, but by the way he filled out his suit he could tell he took care of himself.

"It's a pleasure to meet you, Burt," Fanning said with a friendly smile as he pushed his hand across the desk.

When they shook hands, Courage couldn't help noticing how large Fanning's hands were. "It's a pleasure meeting you, too, Mr. Fanning."

"Have a seat and relax," he said with a slight New England twang. "I've just made some coffee. Would you care to join me?"

"No thanks, I'm not much of a coffee drinker. But I'd like to have a cigarette, if you don't mind."

"Go ahead," Fanning replied fixing himself a cup. "You'll find an ashtray on the table next to you. I used to smoke myself, but then I took up racquetball to keep in shape. I soon found out that they didn't mix. So, if I wanted to continue playing, I'd have to give up smoking. It was difficult at first, but it's been over ten years now and it doesn't bother me anymore."

He returned with his coffee, taking a sip before putting it on the desk. "Before we go any further, I'd like to congratulate you on how well you did in our training program. All of the people in your classes were college graduates, many of them the cream of the crop. You managed to finish in the top ten percent. Not bad for somebody who spent the last three years in the jungle. It showed us that you've got the brains. Your military record shows us you've got the balls—a rare commodity these days, especially in our business.

"Now, before we get into the operation you'll be involved in, I'd like to bring you up to date on where the Agency stands in Vietnam. We are primarily an intelligence gathering organization. Granted, we've had our share of little brush wars with the Communists over the last thirty years in hot spots all over the world. We've got the resources to recruit, train, and supply enough hit-and-run guerrilla armies to keep the Ruskies and

Chinese off balance. We've had our share of successes and failures. But that's part of the game."

Picking up the cup of coffee, he leaned back in his chair. "I guess our latest one was Laos. We thought that with the backing of General Vam Pao we could have won the war. But we underestimated the Pathet Lao and wound up losing. So we packed up and moved into South Vietnam, hoping we could help out to win there.

"We originally had the right idea. Use our resources to gather the intelligence and then turn it over to the military. They had the men and firepower to get the job done.

"Now, I've never had much love for the British, but they were the only ones who were successful in winning a guerrilla war. That was in Malaysia in the late fifties. They knew the only chance they had of defeating the Communist insurgency was to destroy the infrastructure at the lowest level. You start at the villages and the hamlets and cut off the enemy support and supplies. Without support from the locals, they had no chance of winning. So instead of running large-scale operations, they went after the support elements.

"When they dried up their support at the local level, it broke their back. They just faded into the jungle and withered away. The war was over in a few years. I hate to admit it, but we learned from them.

"The only problem is that when we provided the same type of information to our military, they weren't interested. All they're concerned about are body counts. The Generals are convinced that the war will be won on the battlefield. I had one tell me that he wasn't worried about no infrastructure. Just let him kill all of the enemy soldiers and there'll be nothing to worry about.

"I often wonder if some of these people ever read the history of Vietnam. They've been fighting for hundreds of years, and they've never run out of people yet. That's one commodity they have plenty of.

"Hell, they've been invaded by the Chinese more times than you can count, were made into a colony by the French, and were invaded by the Japanese during World War II, and then when the Japs were driven out, the French returned. They finally kicked the Frenchies out in 1954. War to these people is a way of life. I guess when we first came, we were just another foreigner trying to take over their 'country.'"

He finished his coffee and placed the cup on the desk. "This damned war," he said, shaking his head. "We allowed ourselves to get drawn into more than we can handle. From intelligence gathering, we initiated the Phoenix program. It provided the best intel in both North and South Vietnam, but the military wasn't interested in using it. So we decided to start running our own operations. Now we're running almost as many operations as the military. It's draining us of money and manpower, and there doesn't seem to be an end in sight.

"It's been an expensive lesson, but we've finally concluded that a military victory in Vietnam is not possible. Of course, if you tried to tell a bunch of Generals at the Pentagon that a country with an Air Force consisting of a handful of old Russian biplanes, a Navy of a couple of battered boats, and an Army equipped with a few East German tanks and fifty-year-old weapons could defeat the greatest superpower in the world, they'd think you belong in a rubber room. But unless there's a drastic turnaround, that's exactly what's going to happen. And that, Burt, is why you are here.

"For the past three months we've been working on an operation that, if successful, could turn the war around. We've put our best people on this and have worked it out to the last detail. There's a high risk factor, but with the right man we give it a fifty-fifty chance. We'd like to increase the odds, but time is our biggest enemy now. It's got to be done before the rainy season, and that's less than two months from now. That's the reason you'll be leaving for Saigon the day after tomorrow."

Reaching over, Fanning opened the desk drawer and removed a large envelope, held it up momentarily, and then dropped it on the desk. "This is it," he announced. "Operation Stagecoach Red. Being that you're the star performer, I'll give you a general outline of what it's all about.

"Let's see how good you are at current events. Who's the President of North Vietnam?"

"Ho Chi Minh," Burt replied quickly. "Hell, we used to have his picture on our dart boards, and whenever you searched dead NVA or VA bodies, they always had a picture of Uncle Ho to protect them in battle. But it wasn't thick enough to stop an M-16 round."

Fanning walked over and poured himself another cup of coffee. "That's right," he replied. "Now tell me who the Vice President of North Vietnam is."

Burt thought for a while, then looked over at Fanning and shook his head. "I don't know. If they do have one, I've never heard of him. I always thought Ho was the big honcho."

"Oh, they've got one all right," Fanning answered sharply. "And that's what Stagecoach Red is all about. You're going to snatch that son of a bitch right out from under their noses and bring him out alive. He'll be delivered to the Embassy in Saigon."

Burt looked at Fanning. They were testing him. He'd start laughing at any time and tell Burt it was a joke. But Fanning kept sipping his coffee, and he wasn't laughing. He was serious.

"You want me to put the arm on the Vice President of North Vietnam and haul his butt back to Saigon? Just walk in and take him? Somebody around here has to be crazy. I've been over there, I know what it's like. They've got security you wouldn't believe. These people just don't mingle with the peasants. They're well protected. You need an army, not just one man."

"Damn it, Burt," yelled Fanning, slamming his hand on the desk. "Look around you. This goddamned war is tearing this country apart. You can't look at television or pick up a newspaper without seeing it as the lead story. We're losing three to four hundred young kids every week, and it's draining this country of billions of dollars. We've got anti-war protesters at the Pentagon on a daily basis, and the movement is spreading like an epidemic through the colleges. And it's going to get a lot worse. There's a liberal media that doesn't want us to win, and a Congress that won't let us win. When you put the military in a no-win situation, it doesn't take an expert to figure out the end result.

"The President is under a lot of pressure to get out. But he doesn't want to come out a loser. Our people feel that if you succeed in getting our man back, we may be able to pressure the North Vietnamese into a negotiated settlement. That's how important he is to their cause. It may also buy us some time."

Folding his hands, he leaned over the desk and looked into Courage's eyes. "This is our last hope. I can't force you to take this assignment. All I can do is ask. You have every right to tell me to go to hell and walk out that door, and I wouldn't blame you. But you're the best shot we've got, and I'm asking."

Courage squirmed around in the chair. Fanning's stare made him feel uneasy. "Well," he replied, clearing his throat, "if you've got a good enough plan, maybe I could pull it off. Besides, I didn't have anything planned for the next few months anyway. It might be good to get back in the bush again."

Fanning smiled and took a deep breath. "Good, I'm glad we've got that settled. Now, what I've told you of the operation will go no further than this room. When you arrive in Saigon, somebody from the Embassy will be there to meet you. The Chief of Station in Vietnam is John Collins. He's the one that will be going over the details with you.

"Except for myself, the Director, the Ambassador, Collins, and a few others in Saigon, no one even knows about this. And that's the way it's going to stay. We're not even going to tell the military. One little slip and the entire operation could be compromised. We're not going to take that chance. That way if we screw it up, we only have ourselves to blame."

He pulled another envelope from his desk and tossed it to Courage. "Inside that envelope are papers identifying you as a civilian working for the Department of the Army. There is also a plane ticket and your immunization record. Check with the dispensary before you leave. I'd hate like hell to have you get all the way over there and then not get you in because you don't have your shots."

As Courage sifted through the papers, Fanning stood up. "Now," he continued, "there's something I want to go over with you before you leave. It's not a very pleasant subject, but you have the right to know.

"On your previous trips to Vietnam you were running around the jungle in your Army suit. If you got yourself captured, they'd toss you in a prisoner of war camp. It'd be a little rough, but you'd probably survive. This time you'll be wearing civilian clothes. You get yourself picked up and they find out who you are, it could be mighty rough. And, they have ways of making it very unpleasant. If for some reason that does happen, the Agency will deny even knowing you. So you watch yourself out there. I want to see your smiling face back here when you're finished."

When Burt had checked everything to his satisfaction, he looked up at Fanning. "It looks like everything is in order. I've already got my passport."

"I only wish that we had more time," Fanning continued. "I know you must have a thousand questions, but they'll all be answered when you arrive in Saigon. Is there anything I can help you with right now?"

Burt paused for a while. "There is one question. Where did you come up with the name 'Stagecoach Red?' I don't see the connection."

"Ah," Fanning replied with a laugh. "I thought that up myself. It may sound a little corny, but I think it fits the situation.

"When you latch onto our man and head for home, you're going to have the entire North Vietnamese Army after your ass. When I was trying to come up with a name for the operation, I remembered when I was a kid and used to go to the Saturday afternoon movies—you know, the old Westerns that cost twenty-five cents. There would always be a scene where the bad guys would be chasing the poor helpless stagecoach. You knew that no matter how badly outnumbered or outgunned they were, somehow the stagecoach would make it to a friendly town or a relay station just before the horses dropped.

"When we were reviewing the operation, I kept seeing the bad guys chasing the good guys, and it reminded me of the stagecoach in those old movies. Then, with the 'Number Two Red' in hand, we have 'Stagecoach Red.' Get it?"

Burt shook his head slowly and smiled. "You're right, it is corny."

They walked to the elevator together. Just before Burt pushed the button, Fanning put his hands on Burt's shoulders and looked into his eyes. "Burt," he said somberly, "you can be the difference between victory and defeat. It's a lot of responsibility for just one man. But we've got confidence in you. And I can assure you that this country is grateful. Godspeed, and I'll see you when you get back."

As the door slid open they shared a quick handshake. Courage disappeared into the elevator, and Fanning walked back to his office and slumped in his chair. The thought of his not being entirely honest with Courage started to bother him. After all, he had the right to know.

Why didn't he tell him that he was the only one on the committee who thought the operation had any chance of success? All of the others believed it was doomed from the start, a suicidal mission that would result in the loss of too many lives, with little or no chance of succeeding.

But when he challenged them to come up with something better in the short period of time they had, they reluctantly agreed that even a thousand-to-one shot was better than what lay ahead for Vietnam if nothing was done.

As he walked over and poured himself another cup of coffee, a smile came across his face. "I've got a gut feeling about that guy," he said to himself. "Something tells me that he's going to make it back. There's a survivor mannerism about him. He could have been tied to the anchor of the Titanic, and somehow he would have bobbed to the top."

He was sure he'd see Burt Courage again.

# TWO

It was hot for September as Courage boarded at Dulles Airport for the flight to Saigon. Better hot than cold, he said to himself, fastening the seat belt. Going from one hot climate to another isn't bad. But when you go from cold to hot, it takes about a week to adjust.

It didn't matter when you went to Vietnam, it was always hot. The flight would be sixteen hours, and most of it would be in darkness, with two stops for refueling and changing planes. To make it more complicated, he would arrive the day before he'd left, because the plane would cross the international date line.

It was always Burt's contention that whoever designed airline seats had it in for him. He could never get comfortable, regardless of how he twisted and turned. After his sixth double bourbon he finally dozed off.

He was sleeping peacefully when he felt a gentle push on his shoulder and heard a soft voice whisper in his ear. "I'm sorry to disturb you, sir, but we are preparing to land at Tan Son Nhut Airport, and the pilot has just turned on the seat belt sign. Please put your seat in the upright position and fasten your seat belt."

Awakening slowly, he rubbed his eyes and pulled up the seat. As he fastened the seat belt, he gazed into the eyes of the last American female he would see for a long time. His staring must have made her feel uneasy. She blushed and moved quickly down the aisle.

On the last refueling stop in Guam they picked up about fifty soldiers. The military craft they had been on had developed some type of trouble, so they'd been put on this flight. When they boarded and walked down the aisle, Burt scanned each of their faces. They were all between eighteen and twenty, and by their close haircuts he figured they had just finished training and would be used as replacements for those ready to rotate back to the States.

When the plane descended low enough that they could make out the ground below, the soldiers pushed their faces against the windows to see the place that would be their home for the next year. "Hellfire," a young voice with a southern drawl called out. "You see them rice paddies down there? That looks just like our place in Louisiana. They grow rice the same way we do. Shit, Vietnam will be just like being at home."

This drew a round of laughter and jokes, but it was a scared laughter. The soldiers were all scared, but no one wanted to be the first to show it.

"All right, people," a voice boomed. "Get back to your seats and stay put until we land."

Watching them scramble back to their seats, Burt wondered how many of them would be taking their next plane ride home in an aluminum box. He knew what he was getting into; he was well trained and knew how to survive in Vietnam. But these were just kids. Their only worries six months ago had been whether they could get the old man's car and who looked old enough to buy the beer.

Now here they were, ten thousand miles away from home in a country they had only seen on the tube at night. But this wasn't television anymore, this was the real thing. They'd be the ones in the body bags now. Maybe he couldn't do anything for this bunch, but if the operation was a success, they might not need any more planeloads of American youth to die in this hellhole.

Normal procedure for an aircraft landing, once clearance is obtained, is to make a slow descent to the runway. But normal procedures do not apply at Tan Son Nhut. When "Charlie" has nothing better to do, he likes to hide in a rice paddy and use approaching aircraft for target practice. Not wanting to risk a seven million dollar airplane and a planeload of passengers, all flights arrive at a high altitude and remain there until receiving clearance from the tower. Upon receiving permission to land, the plane goes into a steep dive, pulling up just before touching down on the runway.

Having landed there before, Burt knew the reason for the sudden roar of the engines and the steep dive, but the soldiers didn't. The joking and laughter turned quickly to silence as they tightly gripped the arm rests. Some squeezed them so tightly that their knuckles were white.

Realizing that some of the soldiers were frightened, a burly Master Sergeant unfastened his seat belt and stepped into the aisle, putting both hands on his seat to keep his balance. "All right, you people," he hollered in a deep, gravelly voice that was louder than the engines. "I want all you young troops to relax. There is nothing wrong with this aircraft. Let's just say we're taking a shortcut.

"Now, once we land, I want all you to stay in your seats. You'll remain seated until the civilians have departed the craft. Then, at my command, you'll move out in a column of twos."

When the door was opened and the hot air rushed through the plane's interior, one of the soldiers called out, "What the hell is that smell? Christ, it's enough to make you gag."

"Don't worry about it," the Sergeant said. "You'll get used to it."

As he looked around at the soldiers, some of whom were holding their noses, Courage took a deep breath. "Vietnam," he said to himself. "The only country in the world with its own smell." To these people it was strong and acidic, but to him it was home.

It took him almost two years to come up with what he figured was the reason for the country's distinct odor. For the last thousand years the main ingredient in the Vietnamese diet had been a sauce called Ncoc Man, a chopped mixture of rotten fish and strong spices. The smell would make your eyes water. The Vietnamese believe it's a health food and douse anything and everything with it. It's on their breath, their clothes, and even their sweat. Burt had almost walked into a Viet Cong ambush a few years back, but they were upwind and he had picked up the smell, so he'd known "Charlie" was waiting. It may be offensive to some, but it had saved his life.

Putting that together with the hot, humid weather and stagnant air, along with the thousands of motor scooters and cars polluting the atmosphere, you have the "smog capital" of the world.

When he reached the bottom of the stairs, Burt saw a Vietnamese customs official. "Please have your passports ready," he kept repeating in broken English.

Fanning had told him that there would be somebody to meet him at the airport, and it didn't take long to spot him. He was a tall blond dressed in slacks and a bright yellow shirt who scanned all of the passengers as they made their way to the customs area.

He looked to be in his early twenties. Courage shook his head and wondered if he knew how out of place he looked. With his blond hair, blue eyes, and tall, lanky frame, he wouldn't be hard to find in a crowd—not in Vietnam.

The man carefully scrutinized each of the passengers as they placed their luggage on the table. Burt, dressed in jeans, a tee shirt, a cowboy hat, and sunglasses, must have looked more like a construction worker than somebody from the Agency. The blond man gave him a quick glance and continued checking over the others.

When the last of the bags was on the table the man folded his arms, and his smile changed to a look of frustration. It appeared that the person he was waiting for must have missed the flight. As he was about to turn and leave, Courage held up his hand. "Excuse me, are you looking for me?"

Looking quickly across the table, the smile returned. "Are you Mr. Courage?" he asked, surprised.

"That's me," Burt replied. "I'm sorry I'm not wearing a suit, but my cleaner lost all of my clothes and this is all I had left."

"Oh no, that's all right," the man replied. "They just gave me the name of who I was to pick up. They didn't give me a description, and no one was sure you were even going to be on this flight.

"By the way," he said, pushing his hand across the table, "I'm Chris, from the Embassy. If you'll give me your passport and immunization record, I'll clear you through customs and you won't have to wait in line."

After a handshake, Burt gave him his records, and Chris disappeared into a small room at the end of the table. He must have known his way around. In less than five minutes they were out of the terminal and were headed for downtown Saigon.

He must have thought this was Burt's first trip to Vietnam, as he talked about the hot weather and foul smell. Pretending he was listening, Burt would give an occasional nod of his head. The traffic was getting heavier as they headed for the heart of the city.

"Yeah," Chris sighed. "This is it, Saigon. The Pearl of the Orient, the Paris of the East. I wonder how anybody could compare this to Paris."

Lighting a cigarette, he looked over at Chris and chuckled. "If the Frenchies left a name, that's about all they did leave. This was one of their colonies for over a hundred years. They were the masters. They bled the place dry until the Vietnamese had taken enough and kicked their asses out of here. The problem is that the ones doing the replacing were worse than the French."

"I see," Chris responded, keeping his eyes on the road. "I would guess that you are either a history bug or you've been over here before."

"Well, I guess you could say a little of both."

The jeep was now barely crawling in the heavy traffic. "This is one thing I still have a hard time adjusting to," Chris spurted as he slammed his hands on the steering wheel. "These people have no concept of traffic control. There are no traffic lights, no policemen; it's just one big congested mess. I mean today is Sunday; I thought there wouldn't be much traffic, but just look at this!"

"What do you expect?" Burt replied, shrugging his shoulders. "You've got a city swollen to four times its capacity with refugees trying to get out of the line of fire in the only safe place in the country. Then you've got every other one owning a motor scooter, with nothing better to do than drive around. It doesn't bother these people; they've got nothing else to do."

As they continued to move by inches, Chris started laying on the horn. It wasn't doing much good. Everybody else was doing the same thing. As a motor scooter squeezed by them, Burt tapped Chris on the shoulder.

"Now there's a typical Vietnamese family," he said, pointing at the motor scooter. "Six of them on one scooter. That's a feat in itself, and then to be able to balance it, without dumping anybody off when you're weaving in and out of traffic—that takes a certain talent. These people can put their entire family and all of their belongings on a bicycle and make fifty miles a day. Ten of them can exist on a pound a rice for a week. They've seen war, floods, famine and foreign invaders. But if you asked any of them what they would like changed, they'd tell you—nothing. Hell, it don't get no better than this."

As annoyed as Chris was with the traffic, he looked over and managed a faint smile. "That's very interesting," he replied, nodding his head. "I don't get out of the city very often. Maybe if I extend my tour, I'll get to know the place a little better."

Twenty more minutes of baking in the sun and breathing exhaust fumes finally took its toll. "Hang on, Mr. Courage,"

Chris cried out, driving over the curb and onto the sidewalk. "There's an alley just at the end of the block. It's a shortcut."

The street vendors scattered as the jeep roared past. Chickens and bamboo baskets filled the air, as well as a volley of shaking fists and screaming Vietnamese as the jeep turned into the alley.

"You'd better get the hell out of here," Burt laughed. "There's a lynch mob behind us."

Chris pushed the pedal to the floor, hoping there was nothing coming the other way. It was just wide enough for one vehicle and there was no way he was going to stop and back up.

Reaching the end of the alley, he made another sharp turn, forcing Burt to hang on with both hands. It was like they were in a different world. Giant trees lined the street and there was hardly any traffic. As Burt glanced at the houses behind the stucco walls, he knew this was the French section of the city.

He was still admiring the scenery when the jeep pulled over to the curb and stopped. "This is it," Chris said, pointing to the marquee on the front of the building. "This is the hotel where you'll be staying. Reservations have already been made. It's not the fanciest place in town, but there's a bar and restaurant. I've been here a few times—it's not too bad."

Reaching in the back and grabbing his bag, Burt looked up at the name. "La Duc," he said. "If my Vietnamese is up-to-date, that means 'The German.' It don't look too bad from the outside. Thanks for the ride." Burt stepped out of the jeep.

"Oh, by the way, Mr. Courage," Chris called, "You've got an appointment at the Embassy at eight o'clock tomorrow morning. There will be someone here to pick you up at seven-thirty sharp. He'll wait out front for you. It'll be a green vehicle with an Embassy sticker on it."

When Chris had left, Burt walked to the entrance of the hotel. There was an American MP and a Vietnamese guard in the small sandbag bunker. The Vietnamese who worked in the hotel had to be searched before entering, but when they saw Burt was an American they just gave him a casual glance.

As he walked to the check-in desk he took off his sunglasses and dropped his bag on the floor. The clerk had his back to him, so Burt cleared his throat to get his attention.

"Yes, sir, may I hep you?" the clerk asked in broken English as he stood up and hobbled over to the counter. Judging the ages of the Vietnamese was a very difficult task. For some reason they didn't have a middle age. You were either young or old. He figured the wrinkled old man standing in front of him was between forty and ninety.

"Yeah, I'm Burt Courage, I believe you have a reservation for me."

The old man smiled as his shaky hands nervously checked the ledger. "Ah yes, here it is. You sign here pweese and I give you key."

As he filled out the form, Burt glanced up at the old man who was still grinning. He didn't have any teeth and his hair stuck straight out. Burt also noticed his clothes. He was wearing a long-sleeved plaid shirt three times his size, plaid pants, and a wide plaid tie that hung to his crotch.

"Hey, you know something? Looks like you and I have got the same tailor."

With his limited knowledge of English, the clerk must have been told to agree to anything said to him by Americans. "Yes sir, yes sir," he replied, nodding his head in agreement. "You me same same."

When the form was completed, the old man handed him a key. "You room on number three floor. But elevator no work. You must take stairs."

Picking up his bag, Burt gave the man a disgusted look. "How in the hell do you people ever expect to win a war when you can't even keep an elevator running?"

"Yes sir, yes sir," he replied, nodding his head. "No problem, no problem."

"What the hell's the sense complaining to you," Courage grumbled to himself as he walked to the stairs. "There's nothing you can do about it."

The room wasn't that big, but it had everything he would need. There was a bed, a small bureau in the corner, and a shower. It was better than some of the dumps he had stayed in on his previous trips to Saigon. He didn't bother to unpack. The long flight without much sleep made the bed too tempting. Tossing his bag into the corner, he threw himself on the bed and was soon fast asleep.

# THREE

When Burt awoke the room was filled with darkness, but through the open window he could hear the street traffic below. Groping around, he found his watch. "Ten-thirty," he sighed. "I wonder if that restaurant is still open. I haven't eaten all day."

Burt pulled himself together and went downstairs.

"Damn it," he said to himself, as he read the sign that said the restaurant closed at eight o'clock. "Well, I see the bar is still open. If I can't get something to eat, I'll do the next best thing and have myself a few cocktails."

Located next to the restaurant, the bar must have been mainly for the hotel guests. It had only four stools, and there were two small tables in the corner. The room was dimly lit and it took a few seconds for his eyes to adjust to the darkness. "Not bad," he said softly, as he slid onto one of the stools at the bar. "Nice quiet place like this, a guy could do some serious drinking in here."

He was so engrossed in the quiet decor that he didn't notice the bartender placing a napkin in front of him. "May I help you, sir?" the bartender asked politely.

"Yeah," Burt yawned, "I'll have a double Black Jack on the rocks, with plenty of ice."

"I'm sorry, sir," he replied softly, "but I don't understand."

"Ah, I'm sorry," Burt answered quickly. "That's an American term. I want Jack Daniels Black Label in a glass full of ice. You do have Jack Daniels?"

The bartender thought for a second, repeating the name. "Yes, Jack Daniels we have."

As he watched the bartender walk away, Burt noticed how tall he was. While the average Vietnamese is rarely over five feet six, this one was over six feet tall. He was also darker-skinned and had perfect white teeth, another rare commodity.

Burt watched as the bartender meticulously measured the liquor and carefully poured it into the glass. Of course, he thought to himself. I should have known it, he's from the North. The North Vietnamese were always taller and darker-skinned than their brothers in the South. They were also supposed to be smarter. It had been a while since he had seen any North Vietnamese—the last ones were the four he'd left dead on some jungle trail in Phu Bon province.

"Here you are, sir, Jack Daniels on the rocks. That will be two hundred piasters, please."

Reaching into his pocket, Burt took out two crumpled dollar bills and tossed them onto the bar.

"I'm sorry, sir," the bartender said, "but I can't take American money. I can only accept piasters."

"Well, you're out of luck. I just arrived in country and haven't had a chance to change my money over. What the hell, it's only two bucks."

"That's no problem, sir, I'll just charge it to your room."

As the bartender moved away to write up the charge, Courage stuffed the money back in his pocket. "Well I'll be damned," he said to himself. "I wonder if I got off in the right country?" With the exchange rate of twenty Vietnamese dollars for one American dollar, the bartender could have made forty dollars on the deal. Most of the Vietnamese would kill their own mother for American green, yet he had turned it down. Burt also noticed that he spoke English with almost no accent, unlike the broken pidgin that most Vietnamese spoke.

As he sipped his drink, Burt watched the bartender at the far end of the bar holding each glass up to the light to assure it was clean. Now there's a guy that's got something going for himself. He's neat, speaks perfect English, and best of all, he's honest. But, Burt wondered, if this is an Agency hotel, what the hell is a North Vietnamese doing here?

After three more doubles, he signed his tab and headed for his room. He hadn't had a decent night's sleep since leaving Washington, and he had to be up early.

The following morning, after a quick shower to take the sleepiness away, Burt headed for the restaurant. It had been twenty-four hours since anything but booze had gone into his stomach, and he ordered the breakfast special of scrambled eggs, toast, and coffee. The Vietnamese had a knack for murdering American food, but maybe this place was different.

His wish was short-lived. When the waitress placed his order on the table, he took one look and pushed the plate away. The eggs were burnt on the bottom and runny on top. The toast was coal black and cold, and the coffee wasn't much better. The only similarity it shared with American coffee was that it was wet and black. "As hungry as I am," he grumbled, "there's no way I could eat that. I'd have to be mad at my stomach."

He forced the coffee down in two gulps and walked outside.

It was exactly seven-thirty when the green jeep pulled up to the curb. "I guess you're here to pick me up," he called out to the old Vietnamese driver as he jumped in beside him. The old man smiled and nodded his head.

It was Monday morning. Traffic was light and this would be the coolest part of the day. Leaning back in the seat, Burt closed his eyes and drank in the cool breeze as they headed for the center of the city.

As they pulled up to the main gate of the Embassy, a young Marine Sergeant in starched fatigues held up his hand for them to stop. "May I see your identification papers?" he asked sharply.

When he was satisfied, the Sergeant stepped back and waved to the guard at the gate to open up. As they drove around the circular driveway in front of the Embassy, Burt noticed there were a lot of people patching and painting the walls. As they got closer, he could see they were covering over bullet holes.

He had read that the Embassy was hit during the Tet Offensive and had suffered minimal damage, but that was over six months ago, and they were still repairing the building. As they drove around to the rear, the old man pointed to a small door. "You go."

Entering the building, Burt saw a long narrow hallway with more bullet holes in the walls and ceiling that had not been repaired yet. Minimal damage, he thought to himself. I wonder what they would consider major.

The guard at the front desk gave him directions to where Collins' office was located. JOHN COLLINS, DEPUTY AMBASSADOR, the sign said in big black letters. He wondered how many people knew he was the CIA Station Chief in Vietnam.

Stepping into the brightly colored office, he heard a typewriter being used at the desk directly in front of him. The typing continued until the young man felt his presence.

"Yes, sir, may I help you?" the man asked. He reminded him of Chris—young, in his early twenties, with the Ivy League look about him. He was about the same size, too, but he had brown hair and green eyes.

"Yes, I'm Burt Courage. I have a meeting with Mr. Collins at eight o'clock. Can you tell me where I can find him?"

"I sure can," he responded quickly, jumping out of his chair and extending his hand across the desk. "I'm Brian," he said cheerfully. "I'm Mr. Collins' secretary. I also handle all of the administrative work for our people in the country, as well as being in charge of making the coffee and keeping the office clean. May I officially welcome you to Vietnam?" They shook hands.

"Mr. Collins is waiting for you," he continued as he returned to his chair. "In fact, I was instructed to give top priority to your clearance when you arrived. As soon as you've been cleared, Mr. Collins will meet you in the conference room."

Courage lowered his head, shaking it back and forth in disbelief. "Cleared?" he asked inquisitively. "What the hell do you mean, cleared? When they recruited me, I had to fill out a background information form that was fifteen pages long. I had to list where my grandmother and grandfather were born, where my parents were born and went to school, where I was born and went to school, and who my friends were. They wanted to know how old I was when I stopped wetting my pants. When they were finished, they knew everything from the time the doctor slapped me on the ass up until the day they hired me. They did everything but sniff my socks. Believe me, there's nothing left to check. Now you tell me I have to be cleared!"

Brian had leaned back in his chair, laughing hysterically as Courage talked. "Sniff your socks, stop wetting your pants, that's a good one, I've never heard that one before," he blurted out between laughs. "Wait till I tell the other guys that one!"

Taking his handkerchief from his pocket, he wiped the tears from his eyes. "I'm sorry," he replied, trying to get his laughter under control, "but I've never had anyone explain it that way before. You've certainly got a way with words. Here, let me get you a fresh cup of coffee and I'll explain it to you."

Along with the coffee, Brian offered Courage a chair, then walked back behind his desk and sat down. "Now," he continued, folding his hands behind his head and leaning back, "you say that you are Burt Courage and have the papers to prove it. In most instances that would be enough. But not this time. We have to make absolutely sure that you are the same person that left Headquarters two days ago. We must have positive proof that Burt Courage was not kidnapped by the KGB and replaced with one of their men. They could easily find someone who could be your double. They've done this in the past. But even with all of the modern technology, there's one thing they can't do, and that's duplicate fingerprints. I'll take your prints here and forward the results back to Headquarters. When you've been confirmed, Mr. Collins will be notified, and he'll take it from there."

Burt nodded his head. "Very impressive," he responded. "You people don't take very many chances, do you?"

For the first time, Brian had a serious look on his face. "In this case, Mr. Collins isn't taking any chances."

As he rolled Burt's fingers over the ink pad and onto the card, he inquired about his accommodations. "They ain't too bad," Burt answered. "The room's okay, and there is a bar, but I'd have to numb my taste buds to eat in the restaurant."

Brian looked up and smiled. "Well, you've been here before. Most of the hotels have Nationals working as cooks. It's very difficult for them to prepare something they've never seen before. But I do know where there are some nice French places in the city. If you're going to be around for a while, I'll tell you where some of them are located."

Finishing with the last finger, he picked up the card and reviewed his work. "Okay, this should do it. I'll take this back and run it on the computer. With top priority, it should be back in about an hour. While you're waiting, you can go down to the cafeteria and get something decent to eat. With this being the Ambassador's residence, there is an excellent chef on the staff."

As Burt turned to leave, Brian added, "There's one thing I want to caution you about. With few exceptions, everybody believes that Mr. Collins is the Deputy Ambassador. Most people don't even know that we exist here. We would prefer that you don't talk to anybody. However, if it's necessary, be very discreet about who you are and what you're doing here."

Burt looked over and gave him a friendly wink. "Don't worry, they'll get nothing out of me."

Burt did draw a few stares in the cafeteria when he sat at one of the tables. All of the American civilians were dressed in slacks and ties, and the lowest military rank he saw was a full Colonel. He figured it wasn't very often that they saw someone in the Embassy dressed in jeans and a tee shirt. Screw 'em, he thought to himself. I'm not over here to win a fashion show. He finished his meal and headed back to Collins' office.

"Now that's what I call perfect timing," Brian called out when he returned. "I just this very minute told Mr. Collins that your confirmation had come through. He's waiting in the conference room for you right now. If you'll go to the end of the hall and take the elevator to the third floor, there'll be a Marine guard who will escort you to the room."

Three Generals joined him in the elevator and pushed the button for the second floor. When he reached over and pushed the button for the third floor, they all looked at each other. He knew what they were thinking. The third floor was the Ambassador's private quarters. This was for Presidents, dignitaries, and Chiefs of Staff. What the hell business could this guy have with the Ambassador?

When the door opened on the second floor, they gave him one final stare before they stepped out. "Assholes," he mumbled.

As the door opened on the third floor, a Marine dressed in class A blues snapped to attention. "Yes, sir," he barked. "May I help you, sir?"

"Yeah, I've got a meeting in the conference room. I was told you'd show me where it is."

Standing rigid, eyes looking straight ahead, the Marine did an about-face. "Yes, sir," he repeated in his military-trained voice. "Follow me, sir."

Following him down the carpeted hallway, Burt had to walk fast to keep up. Suddenly the Marine stopped, opened a door, and stepped inside.

"This is it, sir," he barked. After Courage entered, he stepped out and closed the door.

Conference room, he thought. Hell, there's enough room in here to have a hockey game. In the middle of the room was a large, dark table with fifteen to twenty chairs neatly lined up on each side. Hanging from the ceiling were an American flag and a South Vietnamese flag; these drifted back and forth in the cool breeze from an air conditioner that made it twenty degrees cooler than any of the other rooms he had been in. Along the paneled walls were more chairs, and there was a bar in the far corner. There were no windows. Only the soft hissing of the air conditioner broke the silence.

Preoccupied with his surroundings, Burt had not noticed the figure seated at the head of the long table.

"Mr. Courage," a voice echoed across the room. "I see that you are fascinated with our meeting place."

The owner of the voice stood up and walked towards Burt. "You know, I've been here over a year, and this room still mystifies me. I'm John Collins," he added, extending his hand, "Chief of Station here in Vietnam."

As they shook hands, Burt looked at his new boss. He wasn't as tall as Fanning, and had black hair with a few tinges of gray. He looked to be in his early fifties. He and Fanning had one thing in common: they both had the CIA look about them—the hard eyes, the square jaw, and the air of being all-business.

"Let's move to the front where we can be more comfortable," Collins said. Returning to the head of the long table, he sat down and motioned to Burt to do the same.

"Let me start off by saying that I sure hate jerking you around like this. Normally when someone arrives in country we give them at least a week to get acclimated and settled in. But as you've already been told at Headquarters, we're fighting the clock on this operation and there's no time to waste. One day could be the difference between success and failure.

"The first thing I want to go over with you is that Stagecoach Red will only be discussed in this room. The reason is that this is the only sterile room in the country. It is checked on a daily basis for any electronic surveillance. And it's not only the enemy we have to worry about. I'm sure the South Vietnamese would like to know what's being said in here, along with the U.S. military and a few others. So outside of this room, nothing is said. Any questions?"

Burt shook his head.

"Another reason for this is that with the exception of the Ambassador, myself, one other in country, and the people back at Headquarters, no one knows of the operation. We're not even telling the military what we're up to, and after the briefing, you'll understand why.

"But before we get started," he said, pushing himself up from the table, "I have some fresh spring water that just arrived from the States that has been chilling since this morning. Would you care for some?"

Contemplating the offer, Burt rubbed his face. "Well," he finally answered. "I don't like drinking that stuff straight. If you've got a little bourbon you could mix with it, I think I could force it down."

"Sure thing," Collins replied with a laugh. "And if I read your file correctly, it's Jack Daniels Black Label. I believe we have that."

Handing Courage his drink, he sat back in his chair. "I used to like that stuff myself back a few years, but those days are gone. Only in moderation now. Bumps," he said, as they touched glasses.

Finishing the last of the water, Collins put his glass on the table, walked over to the wall, and pushed a number of buttons. The lights dimmed and a large movie screen slowly descended from the ceiling, stopping when it touched the top of the table. Reaching to the floor, Collins pulled up a slide projector and placed it in front of the screen. From his pocket he produced a slide and inserted it into the projector, then flicked on the switch.

"Now, Mr. Courage, I'm going to see how good you are at history." The picture was out of focus and it took a few turns to get it corrected. As Burt looked at the photo, he knew he had seen the image before, but couldn't remember where or when. It would have to be from a history book. There were a bunch of men seated around a large table. He could tell by the uniforms on the Caucasians that they were French Generals. The Orientals in the baggy uniforms and pith helmets were Vietminh.

He continued studying the photo. "Well," he finally replied. "I know I've seen it before. It looks like the French and Vietnamese in some type of get-together. I think I saw it in a history book."

"Very good," Collins replied, seemingly impressed. "You're right on target. This is the signing of the peace treaty between the French and Vietminh, after the Frenchies got the hell beat out of them at Dien Bien Phu. This was taken at the signing in July 1954. They love to take pictures of the vanquished, and naturally they wanted to rub the French's nose in it. Of course, the French said it was just a peace treaty, but everybody else knew it was their surrender. They picked up and left right afterward.

"Now, as you look at the photo, forget about the French Generals and the Caucasian civilians. They aren't important. And of course the old man seated in the middle with the long straggly beard is none other than Ho Chi Minh. Seated next to him, in the Vietminh uniform, is General Vo Nguyen Giap, the military genius credited with defeating the French. He'll be discussed later.

"If you'll look at the man standing between where he and Ho are seated—let me see if I can focus this a little better." Collins zoomed in on a figure wearing glasses and a large white Panama hat that covered most of his facial features. Courage moved up to the screen to get a better view.

"You won't be able to see him much better up there. It's an old picture, probably taken by some soldier who didn't know very much about photography. But it's one of the few we have. That, Burt, is the man you're going after. His name is Minh Nguyen Huy, Vice President of North Vietnam and head of the NVIS, the North Vietnamese Intelligence Service—the most powerful man in the country under Uncle Ho."

Collins walked up beside Burt and stared at the picture. "We're going to get that old goat," he hissed, as he poked his finger into the screen.

After turning the lights up and shutting off the projector, Collins freshened their drinks and motioned for Burt to have a seat.

"Before we go any further I'll give you a little background on our man. I've been in the intelligence game a long time. The first rule is, always know what the other guy is doing. As good as the KGB is, we've penetrated it a number of times. That, along with the defectors we get, gives us a pretty good idea of what the Ruskies are up to.

"In fact, we've never had much difficulty in penetrating any of the European Communist bloc countries. All you do is offer them money or asylum. If they want out enough, you've got 'em.

"But we've had very little success with any Asian country. We've tried for years to get someone inside the North Korean and Chinese communities, and we've struck out every time. The North Vietnamese are the same way. They structure their intel forces differently. You can't buy them off because they have no use for money. Every member is so carefully scrutinized that if they are even suspected, they are liquidated. So here we have a third of the world's population, and we can't even find out what the weather is like.

"About two years ago we got lucky, and I mean real lucky. We finally penetrated the NVIS. One of the members decided that he'd had enough and wanted to live the good life. He initially wanted to defect and asked us if we could get him and his family out.

"We needed somebody on the inside, not a defector. It took a lot of negotiating and promises, but we finally convinced him to stay in place under the condition that at the first sign of trouble, we'd get him out and provide enough money for him and his family to live comfortably. We couldn't pass up a bargain like that.

"Of course there was always a chance it was a North Vietnamese setup right from the start. But everything he has sent us for the past two years has been one hundred percent accurate. It has been very damaging to the government up North.

"It's lucky for us the Vietnamese are sticklers on paperwork. They document everything on paper. Now, the French had a dossier on Huy up to 1954. From what we got from them, along with information from our plant, we've pieced together his life up until a few weeks ago. There were things we never dreamed of. I believe we've finally found out what really happened in the North.

"There isn't much to know about his early life. He was born between 1900 and 1905 to a peasant family in a small village near Hai Phong. He became a Marxist early in life, and was jailed in the early 1920s with his newfound friend Ho Chi Minh. After their release from prison they founded the Lao Dong Party. He was jailed a number of times by the French, but he was gaining power, and they released him after a short time behind bars.

"He made a number of trips to Moscow as Ho's spokesman, but our information is a little sketchy on how long he was there.

"He must have received a good deal of military training. When the Japanese invaded in 1942, he was made a Division Commander. By the time the war was over, he was second in command of all military forces.

"After the departure of the Japanese and the return of the French in 1946, Ho made overtures to the United States that his country did not want the French back, that they were an independent country. But the U.S. was in no position to tell the French that they couldn't have their property back. After all, we were allies, and it was theirs before the war.

"Ho then sends Huy to Moscow to ask his Russian comrades for help. The Ruskies, thinking this would be a good chance to get a foothold in the Far East and embarrass the United States and France, jump at the opportunity. What the hell, it's not going to cost them any people, just a bunch of guns.

"To lead the war, Ho picks Van Giap. He is an expert in guerrilla tactics, just the type they'll need against the French. But the French proved to be a lot tougher than Ho or Van Giap thought. From 1946 until 1952 they fought to a stalemate. One of the reasons was that with Ho being the spiritual leader and Van Giap being the military commander, they had their disagreements on how the war could be won.

"Enter Mr. Huy, who had support on both sides. He is put in charge of the war effort; by 1954 the French are on the ropes, and by the end of the year they're gone. Van Giap receives all of the credit, but that's the way Huy wanted it. It turns out he is a very private person and shuns the limelight, but he's always waiting in the wings.

"After the defeat of the French, Ho is proclaimed President. During the war the people were united behind him, but after the departure of the French there were a number of political factions that, although united in hating the French, were not sold on Ho and his Communist doctrine. He was on pretty shaky ground after the war, and there was enough political unrest that something had to be done.

"Huy is put in charge of silencing all opposition, a job he is well suited to do. His first target is the Catholics. They're creating the biggest problem. They want freedom of religion and that doesn't fit in with Huy's plan.

"He goes after them with a vengeance. He charges them with everything from treason to being capitalistic sympathizers. In the beginning he rounded them up and put them on trial. After they were found guilty of some trumped-up crime, they were promptly executed. But that wasn't fast enough, and there were too many Catholics.

"Then he switched to mass roundups and mass executions. Those who were lucky fled to the South. Out of a population of over two million Catholics, less than a million made it there. When he was through, there weren't enough of them left to have a good Sunday afternoon bingo game.

"After he finishes with the Catholics, he goes after Ho's other enemies. More arrests, more executions. 'Enemies of the people,' he calls them. By 1957 he's exterminated between a million and a half and two million people, about fifteen percent of the population. That would be about the same as slaughtering thirty million Americans.

"When it comes to mass murder, this guy ranks right up there with Stalin and Mao. But his work was effective. When he was finished, there wasn't an enemy to be found, and Ho was in full control.

"As a reward for his services, Ho offers Huy the number-two spot. After all, he's a few years younger than Ho, and who could better carry on his policies? But Huy turns it down. He says being a member of the Politburo is reward enough. There, he could keep an eye on what was going on. He then forms the NVIS to make sure there are no traitors.

"Then, sometime in 1961 or '62, he disappears. I mean, whammo, he's gone. There were rumors that he resigned from the Politburo because of poor health. There were others that he had died and the party did not want the outside world to know. There was one story that Van Giap had him assassinated.

"Now, we can put all of those aside. He's alive and well. Our source tells us that he was taken out of retirement sometime in 1967 and put in charge of the military. Contrary to what the North Vietnamese put out on their propaganda films, the war is not going very well. Air strikes in the North are having a devastating effect. There are food shortages and they're having a hard time keeping the supply routes open. There's not much dissension at home, but they've lost a lot of men in this war for the little territory they've gained. The high command in Hanoi finally came to the conclusion that a new strategy and a new field commander were needed.

"Huy is an expert on the United States and the American way of thinking. He knows that one virtue we lack is patience. When we do something it has to be done yesterday. He also knows that he doesn't have the firepower to defeat the Americans in a conventional war. But America would be fighting on his terms.

"He reads everything that is being written about the war, especially in the American newspapers. He waits while the military says that the war is winding down and that there is finally a light at the end of the tunnel; that the South Vietnamese are improving, and are now taking the war to the enemy; that a Communist defeat is imminent.

"When he figures they've put their foot in it far enough, he hits with the Tet Offensive. Because it was a Vietnamese holiday, it was never expected. Many of the South Vietnamese troops were on leave from their units. Our source told us about it two months before it happened, and we informed the military. They told us we were crazy. Their order of battle figures showed there were not enough NVA troops to conduct a large-scale offensive. So much for telling the military.

"The Tet Offensive was their biggest gamble of the war, and by looking at the outside of the Embassy, they did have a few limited successes. It took a while to roust them out of Huy. But when the smoke finally cleared, it was a complete disaster for them.

"When it was all over, they didn't control one more inch of territory, and confirmed body counts had them losing over two hundred thousand men. God only knows how many were killed by air strikes, where it was hard to get a body count figure.

"According to our figures, and the military agreed, which is a rarity, they lost one third of their army. Anybody who knows anything about strategy will tell you, to lose a third of your army in one battle is a disaster. The only one I could think of with a higher percentage than that was Custer.

"So why does Huy send his troops to be slaughtered in a battle he knows can't be won?" Collins looked deep into Courage's eyes, as if he should have the answer. "Because," he called out, slamming his hand on the table, "he got what he wanted. He won the battle that had to be won. He had his media victory. So what, he lost a couple hundred thousand people. What the hell, lives are nothing to him. If he can grab the American headlines, what's a half million people?

"The Americans and the South Vietnamese did a good job considering they got caught with their pants down. But that isn't reported. The media turns the greatest victory of the war into the biggest defeat. Using the 'light at the end of the tunnel,' they tell the American people that they've been lied to by the White House and the Pentagon. Anytime they can stick it to the military they usually do. And in this case, they went for the throat.

"So here we have a bunch of Generals with egg on their faces, still without any answers as to how the offensive could have happened. You've got the White House that doesn't know who's telling the truth, and a wishy-washy Congress that will go any way the wind blows. Stick a microphone in their faces and they'll tell you anything you want to hear. The same spineless bastards that got us in here in the first place now want us to pack up and go home, to take our losses and forget about it.

"Could you picture it if we had the same thing going on during World War II as we have now? I mean, just picture the major networks covering the Normandy invasion, hearing on the six o'clock news that over six thousand Americans had been killed that morning securing the beachhead. There would have been such an uproar, there would be Congressmen standing on the Capitol steps demanding an end to this senseless killing. Roosevelt would have been on the phone the next day to Hitler, and Europe would still be under the Nazis. It's amazing how things change, isn't it?"

Collins grabbed his glass, filled it with spring water, picked up the Jack Daniels, and returned to the table. "Here," he said, placing the bottle in front of Courage. "You can pour your own. That way I won't have to keep running over to the bar."

Slumping in the chair, Collins took a long drink and then a deep breath. "As it now stands," he continued, "the military has everybody believing that with the casualties the Communist forces suffered, it will be at least two or three years before they can put together a viable fighting force. They hope by that time the South Viets will be strong enough to defend themselves. With a lull in the fighting, the anti-war protesters will get tired of marching, and things will go back to normal.

"A few months ago we received information from our source in the NVIS that the old man is one step ahead of us. His troops aren't sitting back licking their wounds. They are being brought back up to strength by new replacements and are preparing for another offensive. We don't have the exact date, but it will have to be before the rainy season—we figure in about a month.

"Huy knows that another offensive, regardless of the outcome, would be the final straw. It would tell those bureaucrats back in Washington that the military don't know what the hell they are talking about. With the opposition mounting every day, and the military having lied twice, the President would have to admit that the war could not be won and would have to start withdrawing American troops. With the Americans gone, the Viet Cong would sweep right through the country.

"The only chance we have of preventing the offensive is to take Huy out of the picture, which is going to be your job."

Collins dimmed the lights again, and after he pushed more buttons, a large map of North and South Vietnam descended from the ceiling. Collins then turned on a smaller light, shined it on the map and picked up a pointer. "This," he said, pointing to an area, "is where Huy operates from. It's in the province of Vinh Long, in the village of Dien Ban, just across the South Vietnamese border. He couldn't find a more secure area. It's where the Ho Chi Minh Trail enters the South, and it's been a Communist stronghold for the past thirty years."

Collins stared at the map and then chuckled. "I can see why the old fox feels safe there. It's the most inaccessible area of Indochina, right where North and South Vietnam join with Laos. It has high mountains on three sides and a snake-infested jungle to the south.

"Dien Ban is the main staging area for all men and supplies going south. Huy likes to be where the action is, and what better place to be than where the Ho Chi Minh Trail starts? This will be the type of terrain you'll be going through. But I'll be going over that later."

Courage held up his hand to get Collins' attention. "John, this may seem like a dumb question, but if you know where he is, why don't you just take a B-52 strike and turn the place into a dirt pile? Wouldn't that solve the problem?"

There was an immediate smile on Collins' face, as if he knew that would be asked. "Good question," he replied quickly. "And I may as well answer it now. The primary reason is that we want to get him out alive if possible. Not only would they have to postpone the next offensive, but he has the name of every agent, double agent, and government spy from the hamlet to the Presidential Palace. With that information we could set them back thirty years.

"The other reason is that he doesn't know that we know he's in Dien Ban. He also makes trips back to Hanoi. Our information takes a few days to get here. If we blew the place apart and he wasn't there, he wouldn't feel safe there anymore. That's one chance we don't want to take. There are also rumors that there are Russian SAM missiles in the area. Furthermore, the Air Force would be a little reluctant to risk a seven million dollar plane on a target we selected without being told why. And as you've already been told, not even our own military is being informed.

"We've got to be so very careful on this operation. Huy has spies everywhere, even in some of the American units that hire the Nationals. One piece of paper left on a desk, or a slip of the tongue—if this ever got out, you'd never get within a hundred miles of that place."

Collins turned up the lights, walked over to his briefcase, and returned with a large brown envelope. On the front it read in black letters, TOP SECRET EYES ONLY JOHN COLLINS— STAGECOACH RED. After breaking the seal, Collins removed the contents.

"I want to go over this with you now. That way I can put it through the shredder when we're finished. Now, I want you to remember this operation was put together in a hurry. There are a few things that we may want to change. Let me go through it quickly. Hold your questions until I'm finished.

"'Agent Burt Courage,'" he read, "'accompanied by four North Vietnamese Privates and one North Vietnamese Lieutenant, who have already been cleared by this office, will be flown at the opportune time from Saigon to Danang. There, on the first moonless night, they will be flown by an Air America helicopter to an area northwest of Danang. There, at a selected site close to or behind enemy lines, they will depart the aircraft. Agent Courage will be wearing the uniform of a

U.S. Army Captain, with identification that shows he is the Commanding Officer of a unit deployed around the Danang area. This officer will be said to have been captured by local forces in the act of poisoning a village water supply and spreading germ warfare. As a result, he has been ordered to be taken to Hanoi to be tried as a war criminal.

"'The North Vietnamese officer will have forged documents from the Twenty-sixth Division Commander that the prisoner in custody is a war criminal, and all unit commanders will cooperate to assure that the prisoner arrives safely in Hanoi.

"'They will then proceed in a northwesterly direction until they reach the area of Dien Ban. Upon their arrival they will procure a casket and truck. (Latest reports are that, with the amount of activity in the area, these are readily found in abundance.)

"'At an opportune time, Huy's headquarters will be penetrated. He will be sedated, placed in the casket, and loaded onto the back of the truck. Then they will proceed down the Ho Chi Minh Trail to a designated area in Quang Nhai province approximately twenty miles from Special Forces Camp 127. At this point they will leave the trail and proceed on foot towards the camp.

"'On leaving Dien Ban, Courage will change into civilian clothes. His identification will state that he is an East German journalist being escorted to the front. If they are stopped, the casket will be said to contain the remains of a party official being returned to his native village for burial. The subject will be sedated at all times.

"'To prevent any chances of compromising the operation, the Special Forces camp will be alerted ten days after the drop near Danang. Upon recovery of personnel, they will be expedited to Saigon by private carrier.'"

Collins studied the document for a few more moments and then handed it to Courage. He watched in earnest as Burt read each word, digesting each part of the operation. He could see by Burt's expression that there were doubts about the operation.

Pushing the report back to Collins, Burt shook his head. "I don't know who's crazier, the guy who thought this up, or me for taking it. I could think of a thousand things that could go wrong, and any one would be fatal."

"I could think of two thousand," Collins quickly interrupted. "But it's the only game in town, and we've got to go with it. You've been over here a number of times, what do you think of it?"

If he was waiting for an immediate answer, it didn't come. Picking up his glass, he walked to the bar and filled it with ice, returned to the table an filled it with Jack Daniels and slumped in the chair, still pondering the question. It was a long two minutes before he answered.

"It could work," he responded. "The Vietnamese are fanatics about germ warfare. They've been telling the world and their own people that the Americans have been using chemicals to poison their water and food supplies. Of course, they've never been able to prove it. If they could get their hands on somebody who was caught in the act, they'd jump at the chance to put him on trial for all the world to see. That part I think we can get by with. And if we keep the old man sedated in the casket, we should have plenty of time. They don't have the best of communications; it sometimes takes weeks for messages to get to the South.

"But the thing that has me a little confused is, why is it so secretive that Headquarters won't even let the American military know? Yet at the same time, there are five former North Vietnamese soldiers going along. What if somebody gets homesick?"

Collins leaned back in his chair and took a deep breath. "That is one of the areas in which I really believe we've done an excellent job. The four North Vietnamese Privates were draftees who deserted just after they arrived in the South. The government has an amnesty program called Chieu Hoi, or 'Open Arms.' Anybody giving themselves up can spend the rest of the war in a nice, safe place with enough to eat. The Viet Cong haven't been very receptive, but there have been good results with the North Vietnamese. I guess there are a lot of their soldiers who don't want to fight, but they don't have a Canada to run to.

"The ones who have come in are hated more than the Americans. I've seen directives from Hanoi that if they are caught, they are to be shot on sight.

"We had a big list, but the four selected were young farm boys from an area close to the border, all of whom have families. They were told they would be going back into North Vietnam, but not where or when. They were also told that if they were successful, they would receive fifty thousand American dollars upon their return and relocation to anywhere in the world, along with their families. That's more money than they could make in ten generations. We got their families out and have them at a compound just outside the city. They were allowed to meet them, just to show we can keep our part of the bargain.

"They were also told that if there is one slip, a screw-up of any kind by any one of them, all bets are off. They don't get the money and their families will be turned over to the South Vietnamese Secret Police. That's another death sentence. I think that scared them the most.

"We originally were only going to use two, but with four armed escorts, everybody along the way will know how important a prisoner you are. Plus, it's going to take that many when Huy's casket has to be carried from the trail to the camp.

"Like I told you, they're just a bunch of uneducated farm boys, but they know that fifty thousand dollars and relocation is better than dying in some stinking jungle.

"Now," he continued, "I want to get to the man who is as important to the operation as you. Without him, you wouldn't get two miles from the drop-off point. He'll be the one doing all of the talking. You make damned sure that you take care of each other. If anything happens to either one of you, the operation won't succeed. And we don't want that to happen.

"His name is Van Nguyen Thao. He's about your age, twenty-nine or thirty. He was born somewhere around Hanoi to a very prominent family. His old man was a big wheel with the Vietminh and was a decorated hero in the war against the French. But he had one thing against him—he was a Catholic.

"After the country was partitioned in 1955 he saw the writing on the wall. He managed to get his wife and daughters to the South, but the border was closed before he could get Thao and his brother across. He knew he was on Huy's hit list and was able to hide out for a few years. They finally found him. Thao was in the hospital at the time, so only his brother and the old man were killed. As long as they got those two, they must have figured that was good enough.

"He changed his name and lived in the streets until joining the North Vietnamese Army, the NVA, in 1964. He said this was the only way of escape. When his unit was sent into South Vietnam, he deserted, but not before killing the propaganda officer.

"He was picked up by the Marines and worked for them as a Kit Carson scout for about a year. We stole him away about three years ago and he has worked for us since. He's been on three missions to the North, and his information has been right on target. We fed him sensitive information that we would have recognized, had it been passed. It never was.

"He was the one who gave us the information about the Tet Offensive three months before it happened. I mean, he gave us dates, places, and troop concentrations. But who was going to believe a former enemy officer?

"The reason I'm going into the details about Thao is that you may be thinking he could be a double agent and this is all a setup. I can assure you it isn't. I'm risking my career on him."

He could tell by the expression that appeared on Burt's face that this was the wrong choice of words. "I know," he added, clearing his throat, "that you're risking much more. But if I thought for one moment that Thao wasn't totally loyal, I'd scrap this operation right now.

"There is, however, one area that concerns me. He holds Huy personally responsible for the death of his father and brother, and the millions of others he's eliminated. He is a firm believer in the Oriental code of justice, an eye for an eye. If something should happen to you, he might go ahead and kill the old man to get his revenge. I'm not saying he would, but it's something for you to remember.

"While we're on that subject, I want to go over something that was not included in the text of the operation. This was sent to me from the Director himself. If for some reason Huy cannot be taken out alive, he is to be killed. But this will only happen if you've exhausted every means of getting him out. God knows how much we need him alive.

"If it comes down to that, you will personally do the job. Thao will be carrying a false canteen. Inside will be syringes and enough medication to keep him sedated during the journey. There will also be a small-caliber pistol with a silencer in case of an emergency.

"If you are forced to make the kill, you shoot him twice through the heart. We don't want any head shots. You'll be taking pictures of his face and they don't want any, how should I say, messy photos. Then you are to cut off his middle and index fingers from the right hand. They have some of his prints, but those two are the only identifiable ones they have. They want to make damned sure they've got the right man."

Collins looked at his watch. "Damn, I didn't know it was this late." Standing up, he stretched his arms and straightened his tie. "I think we've covered about enough for today. Be here tomorrow morning at eight o'clock sharp. Thao will be here with an overlay of the area. We've got to put our heads together to come up with a plan to get into the compound. The one we have now is still up in the air."

He walked over to his briefcase and handed Burt a map. "Here, I want you to go over this and pick out a route from Danang to Dien Ban. You're familiar with the terrain. Chart out what you figure to be the safest and quickest route.

"And one more thing. I wouldn't wash or shave anymore. If you're going to be a prisoner of war, you'd better have that grubby look."

Courage finished what was left in his glass, which was mostly water, and placed it on the table. "So tomorrow I meet that famous Mr. Thao," he said ponderously. "I'm looking forward to this. Here, the same guy I would be out to kill under normal circumstances, I'll be walking into North Vietnam with. This should be interesting."

Collins reached in his pocket and tossed Burt a set of keys. "Here, there's a jeep outside you can use. You'll be doing a lot of running around in the next few days. You'll need it."

As Burt turned to leave, Collins called after him. "Before you leave, I want to ask you something."

"Sure, what is it?"

"One question I thought for sure you would ask is, why take a risk using North Vietnamese, when we could just as easily have recruited five South Vietnamese? Didn't that pop into your mind?"

Burt looked at Collins. "John," he said smugly, "you forget I speak the language. There's a difference in the dialect. Sending one of these Southern boys would be like sending someone from New York into Georgia. Their accent would give them away in a minute."

"Very good," he replied. "Before this operation came up, even I didn't know that. Now I see the reason you were selected. That's the kind of stuff that will keep you alive."

When he got back to the hotel, Burt studied the map. From Danang to Dien Ban was just over one hundred and fifty miles.

They would be going through rice paddies, thick jungle, elephant grass, and then the mountains. He estimated that with
the terrain and the heat, it would be at least ten days. If they
ran into trouble, it could take longer. Then, if everything went
according to plan, two days after leaving Dien Ban they would
be in friendly hands.

When he finished tracing the route, he tossed the map on
the dresser and stretched out on the bed with his hands
behind his head, staring at the slow-moving ceiling fan. "If
everything goes according to plan," he grumbled. "If anything
goes according to plan, it will be a miracle."

Turning out the light, he lay still in the darkness. He tried
to get to sleep, but there was a tingling in the palms of his
hands and in the pit of his stomach. It was the same feeling he
used to get on his previous tours just before they would go
into the bush or spring an ambush. It was his "ultimate high."
God, he thought to himself, I think I'm looking forward to this.
He liked the idea of the challenge, the gamble. And this would
be the biggest of his life.

# FOUR

Three cups of strong French coffee stimulated his circulation the following morning and he arrived at the Embassy at eight o'clock sharp. When he entered the conference room there were two figures bent over the table. One, he knew, was Collins; the other had to be Thao.

Collins looked up when he heard the door close. "Ah, Burt," he called out. "You're right on time. Thao was just showing me the overlay of the district."

As Burt drew closer, Thao looked up. "Hey," Burt said quickly. "I know you. Aren't you the bartender at the Duc?"

"Yes," he answered, with a smile and a bow. "And you drink Black Jack on the rocks."

Collins laughed as he put an arm around each man's shoulders. "I should have known if he was a bartender, you'd know him. So, let me formally introduce you two."

As Courage shook Thao's hand, he was still mystified by his size. He was the biggest Vietnamese Burt had ever seen.

"Now," Collins continued, "the reason we used him at the Duc is that it keeps him off the street. If we didn't have a safe house to keep him in, the South Viets would either pick him up and draft him into the Army or throw him in jail for some reason. It's a nice place to stay, and he makes a few bucks running the bar.

"Before you got here, Thao was briefing me on Dien Ban and the District Headquarters where Huy stays. This is going to be the sticky part of the operation. Getting in and out is going to be touch and go.

"Move over here, Burt, and Thao will start from the beginning."

In the middle of the table were small buildings made of clay. Thao stood close by with a pointer.

"How about the lights," Collins asked, "do you want them dimmed?"

"No, that's okay," Thao replied. "This is Dien Ban," he said, pointing. "I have tried to remember all of the buildings and where they're located. But, not being able to use a camera, I had to work from a mental picture.

"There are many Army units camped in and around the district, but they are of no importance. This," he pointed, "is the District Headquarters. This is where Huy eats, sleeps, and conducts all of his business. The only time he leaves it is when he makes a trip to Hanoi. And then there is an armed escort.

"The Headquarters is located in the southwest part of the village. It also serves as the province capital. The compound was an old French fort built about seventy years ago. There are a lot of them around Vietnam and they are all basically the same. This one takes up, in American terms, about ten acres. There is a ten-foot-high wall all the way around. The top of the wall is approximately a foot across, and there is broken glass embedded in the cement.

"There are four corners and the main gate. There are guard towers at each corner, manned twenty-four hours a day. But with no enemy forces within a few hundred miles, the guards sleep most of the time.

"The only way into the compound is through the main gate. It is also manned day and night by four guards. But again, with not much to worry about, they are very lax. They go through the motions of checking people, but they're more interested in gambling or eating.

"Just inside the gate is the District Headquarters. It's the largest building in the compound. It was where the Governor stayed when the French were here. This is where Huy meets all

of the dignitaries, but he doesn't live there. Behind this building is a soccer field and track. As soccer is not very popular
with my people, the field is now used for parades and cere-
monies.

"Along the inner walls to the north and east are Army barracks. This is where the units that protect the area are housed.

"Now, back in the southwest corner behind the soccer field,
in a remote area, is a small house hidden in the trees. There
are no buildings anywhere nearby. This is where he lives. He
could have it a lot better in the main building, but he prefers
his privacy, and lives there.

"I was never able to get very close. When I walked around
the soccer field, I did notice that there was a four-foot wall
around it, and a bunker near the side.

"I watched the place for two weeks. The only people who
ever came in and out were an old man, who is the cook, and a
young servant boy. They come out every morning between
nine-thirty and ten and walk to the market to buy fresh vegetables."

"Let me ask you something," Collins interrupted. "Does the
old man ever accompany them, or leave the compound to visit
somebody?"

"Not to my knowledge. During the time I was there, he
never left. He follows the same routine every day. He leaves the
house at exactly eight-thirty and walks to the District
Headquarters. It's a good three to four hundred yards and with
his age, it takes him a while to get there. The guards at the
main gate make a game out of betting how long it will take him
to get to the bottom step.

"At noon he walks back to the house for lunch. He must
also take a nap because he doesn't return until three. Then
he's back home at six. He follows the same routine every day.
His following a strict schedule should work in our favor."

"What the hell good is that?" Collins spurted angrily as he threw his hands in the air. "If the old bastard never leaves the compound, how are we supposed to get him out?"

Walking over to the clay village, Collins put his hands on his hips. "Well," he sighed, "if he won't come to us, we'll have to go to him. If the only time he leaves is with an escort to Hanoi, you're going to have to get into the compound. Now I know why Headquarters left this part of the operation to us."

He rubbed his face nervously as he studied the layout. After a long period of silence, he spoke. "It looks to me like the only time you could get in there would be at night. You could scale the wall, throw a blanket over the embedded glass, and slide down the other side. It's going to be rough working in the dark, but the guard towers are far enough apart that you wouldn't be seen.

"Once inside, you would sedate Huy, wrap him up, and slide him back over the wall into the truck. It would be six or seven hours before anybody would know he was missing. You could put a lot of distance between you and Dien Ban in that time."

"It'll never work," Courage stated bluntly.

Collins and Thao looked at each other. "What the hell do you mean?" Collins shot back. "There's no other way of getting in there, unless you think you could drive right through the main gate and just snap him up."

Burt walked over to join Thao and Collins. "It won't work," he replied, "because we don't know enough about the place to go in there at night. We'd be stumbling all over each other." He paused. "But we're going to get him, all right. Just like you said, we're going to drive right through the main gate at high noon."

The other two looked at each other again, only this time their look shared the inference that Burt had been in the Black Jack too much. "Hang on a minute," Collins blurted, holding up his hands. "Are you trying to tell me that your plan is to drive up to the main gate, past the guards, and by the barracks to Huy's house, without arousing any suspicions, in the middle of the day? Burt, you're talking crazy."

Burt looked at Collins and winked. "John, the solution is right before your eyes. You just don't see it."

"You're right, I must be missing something," Collins chided sarcastically.

"Now," Burt continued. "From what Thao has shown us, there is a bunker next to Huy's house. Bunkers are made of sandbags." He then turned to Thao. "Have you seen many sandbags in Dien Ban?"

"There are many," Thao replied quickly. "They are sent south to repair bunkers along the trail. After the rainy season the bags have usually rotted and have to be replaced. There are pallets of them all over the area."

"Okay, so we can get all the sandbags we need. We've got a truck, and enough people to fill a few hundred of them."

"Where are we going with this?" Collins asked in an annoyed tone. "What have sandbags got to do with getting into the compound?"

"I'm getting to that. Now, when we reach Dien Ban, I hide out until Thao gets the truck, the casket, and the sandbags. We'll fill enough, say five or six rows on the back of the truck, to make it look like it's full. I'll be in front of the sandbags with the casket.

"Thao and his people will drive to the main gate. He, being the officer in charge, will have a work order to repair the old man's bunker. Nobody will be suspicious of a work party repairing bunkers. If the guards are as lax as Thao says, they'll probably just wave us right through.

"We'll drive up to the house, back in alongside it. We'll take out everybody but Huy, put him to sleep and put him over the sandbags in the front of the truck. We'll wait half an hour and then leave. If we get there at noon, we'll have better than a two-hour start before anybody knows he's gone."

Collins watched Thao's eyes for a reaction, but there wasn't one. "I don't know," Collins scowled. "I think any daylight attempt is too risky. You get caught in the day and you've got no way out. At least at night you could always slip away in the dark. I mean, what if he has people in for lunch? I still think over the wall at night is the best shot. What do you think, Thao?"

Thao had listened to both plans. He looked down at the overlay again. "Well," he said slowly, "there is good and bad in both ideas. But from what I have seen, I believe that Mr. Courage's plan has the best chance of succeeding. I also don't like stumbling around in the dark. We could easily get lost or run into somebody. The items needed are easy to get, and I could make up a work order. From what I have observed, no one goes to that house but Huy himself. All business is conducted at the District Headquarters. Yes, I like his idea."

Collins shrugged his shoulders. "Okay," he said reluctantly. "Looks like I've been overruled. You go in at noon."

"One more thing before we go any further on this," Burt interrupted. "I know Headquarters doesn't want the military in on any phase of the operation, except for the Special Forces camp. But if you could get the Air Force to drop a few bombs south of Dien Ban, it would make our story about repairing the bunker a lot more believable. Not too close though. We don't want to scare him off."

Collins' initial facial expression showed that it was out of the question, but after thinking it over, he nodded his head. "Yeah, I could arrange that. They're always looking for a spot to drop some ordnance. They can't land with it. I've got a few connections at MACV. I can get it done without arousing any suspicions.

"Now that we know how you're getting in," Collins continued, walking over to the wall, "let's discuss the route you'll be taking. I trust you went over the map I gave you yesterday?"

He pushed a button, to make the large map descend from the ceiling.

"Okay," he said, handing the pointer to Burt. "Let's see how you're going to get there."

Finding Danang on the map, Burt snapped the pointer against it. "It looks like we'll be dropped somewhere outside Danang. Probably between the Marines and some of the Viet Cong units in the area. Once out of the aircraft, we're going to have to stay put for the night. The entire area is sure to be loaded with booby traps and mines—no place to move around in the dark. Once we slip through the lines, we should be able to move on the trails. They don't mine the ones they use.

"From the map, plus my own experience, it looks like we'll be going through some of the toughest terrain in the country. With the exception of the mountains, it will be hot at night and even hotter during the day. Whatever you've got on the list for salt pills, you'd better double it.

"This is the toughest way in, but I figure it's the safest. We won't be running into any of the main infiltration routes used by the North Vietnamese. We may run into some of the local VC units, and maybe an NVA unit, but we expect that."

Burt studied the map before going on. "I figure," he said slowly, "that, going this way, we should make it in ten days. Once we get there, we'll hide out until it's time to move. That'll be Thao's decision."

He noticed the look of bewilderment on Collins' face. "Ah hah," Burt laughed. "You're asking yourself, where are we going to hide out? You just don't crawl under a bush and wait. True, but the area around Dien Ban is infested with caves. When the French were running the place, they thought there was silver in those mountains. I guess they did find a little, but not enough to make the work profitable. When I was in Special Forces, we had a wounded man who hid for weeks in one of those caves, before they got him out.

"After we snap up the old man and load him onto the back of the truck, we'll start down the Ho Chi Minh Trail. From Dien Ban to Quang Nhai, where we'll leave the truck, it's about seventy miles. You can make pretty good time if it hasn't been bombed, and if you don't run into too many convoys. By noon the next day, we should be there. If our Special Forces buddies are on the ball, we should make contact a few miles from where we leave the trail. And then it's homeward bound."

Two sharp rings came from the telephone at the far end of the room, and Collins held up his hand. "Hold on until I get back."

He returned in a few minutes. A look of excitement filled his eyes. "Well, guys, it's on for tomorrow night. The forecast is perfect around Danang. A light rain with no moon. You couldn't get anything better than that to start you off.

"Now, about your getup. The Chieus, your escorts, will be wearing NVA uniforms with the rank of Private and the insignia of the Twenty-sixth NVA Division. Their papers will show they are assigned to B Company 326, NCA Regiment, which is part of the Twenty-sixth. Intel reports I received this morning list the 326th in the Danang area.

"Thao will be wearing the uniform of a Lieutenant with the same insignia. They'll carry the regular issue AK-47 rifles and he will have a Russian pistol. It's some type of status symbol; if you have a pistol and leather holster, it means you are from a prominent Communist family. Ask Thao to explain it to you a little later. He knows more about it than I do.

"He'll also be carrying three NVA-issue canteens. One of them will be a dummy. Inside will be a small-caliber pistol with a silencer and enough needles and sedative to keep our guest quiet until you're picked up.

"While we're on the subject, you've got a meeting first thing tomorrow morning with a doctor who will show you how to administer the drug. Pay close attention. I'd hate to see you people go through all that work and then have him die from an overdose.

"Also, Thao will be wearing boots that have hollow heels. Inside one will be papers identifying you as Hans Kreuger, an East German journalist covering the war. You are a guest of the North Vietnamese government on your way to the front to take pictures of the glorious fighters defeating the American invaders. In the other heel there will be a beeper. It has a radius of about twenty miles. Once you leave the truck, you can turn it on. That'll make it easier to find you."

Collins cleared his throat and suggested they take a break. "I'm going to have a glass of spring water," he called out from the bar. "Burt, you want Black Jack on the rocks filled to the rim. How about you, Thao, can I get you something?"

"Yes, sir, the spring water will be fine."

Returning to the table, Collins handed each of them a glass. "Before I cut you two loose, there are a few more things I want to go over.

"In one of the Chieu's packs, beneath all of the other stuff he'll be carrying, there'll be a set of civilian clothes with East German labels, and an East German camera. I think with your brown hair and blue eyes, you won't have any problem convincing them you're a comrade."

"The only problem is that I don't speak any German."

"Don't worry about that, they don't either. But you do speak Vietnamese, and they think highly of people who talk to them in their own language. I don't think that's anything to worry about.

"Now, gentlemen, tomorrow morning the crates will be here with the uniforms and equipment. I want you two to go over every item you'll be wearing and taking along. One button out of place could blow the entire operation."

Collins stood, signifying that the day's conference was over. As they prepared to leave, Burt thought this would be a good opportunity to get to know the man he'd be walking into

North Vietnam with. "Hey Thao," he called out. "I've got a few bucks that I won't be needing for awhile. What do you say we meet at the Continental for dinner? Everything is on me."

Thao looked to Collins for his approval. He saw an immediate frown, but after some thought, Collins smiled. "What the hell, it's your last night in town. It's a big city and I don't believe you'd arouse any suspicions. Just be careful and don't pick up any of Courage's habits."

"Thank you, Mr. Collins," he replied with a bow. "That would be nice, Mr. Courage. At what time?"

"Let's say about six."

The Continental was one of the better known places in Saigon, located at the busiest intersection in the city. It stuck out like the last bastion of French defiance. The sidewalk tables, shadowed by the red and green awning, were a welcome rest to those who just wanted to sit and sip tea or coffee.

The inside dining area was also open, and gave a pretty good view of the heart of the city. The food wasn't the best, but it was French-owned, and they paid off the Viet Cong, so you could dine without worrying about somebody throwing a grenade in your lap. Because it was located across from the Carvavell Hotel, the fanciest place in town, there were always a lot of American journalists enjoying their meals in the main dining room.

Having selected a small table in the rear, Burt was on his second Jack Daniels when Thao walked through the door into the main dining room. He had to look around twice before spotting the figure in the dimly lit corner. As he moved towards the table, Burt watched him. He had to admit, Thao wasn't your average Vietnamese. He had that aristocratic walk and look about him—smooth olive skin, perfect white teeth, and not a hair out of place. He looked more like a diplomat than an Army deserter. But under it all, he was still born and raised in North Vietnam. This was the man the Agency would risk the outcome of the war on, Burt thought to himself. If he worked for the NVIS, it would be the end for everybody.

Burt looked up when Thao reached the table. "I would have ordered you something to drink, but I didn't know what you'd like."

"That's quite all right," Thao replied politely as he pulled up his chair. "I don't drink. When I first started working at the Duc, I had never seen liquor before. When they made me the bartender, I figured I had better know what it tasted like. I took one drink. It burned my throat and made me sick. So I learned to mix drinks from the bartender's guide. I haven't had very many complaints, so I figure they must be okay. But I do smoke. Do you mind?"

"No, go ahead. I'm going to have one myself."

Thao watched as the smoke drifted towards the ceiling fan. "I guess this is one vice I have. I love American cigarettes. But as of tomorrow night, there won't be any more of these. We'll have regular NVA-issue. They are made from tobacco grown in China. I can guarantee they aren't as good as these."

"That makes sense," Burt said. "I guess it wouldn't be too smart to walk around with American cigarettes, would it? I was looking for a way to quit anyway. But I think there could be a safer way than this." He then held up his glass. "There won't be any more of this stuff either. Geez, giving up two of my favorite pastimes at once. I hope my body can survive the shock."

An old man in a gray hotel uniform approached and handed them each a menu. When he finished taking their orders, Courage asked for another Jack Daniels.

As they ate their meal, Thao had an uneasy feeling. Something was wrong. He could tell by the glances he was receiving that Courage was worried. "Excuse me," he finally said. "Something seems to be bothering you. Is it me, the operation, or do you think it's none of my business?"

Jabbing his fork into his food, Burt took two more bites before looking up. "You're very observant," he replied tightly. "There is something bothering me. That's why I asked you here. We might as well get our differences aired out now. Once we get off that chopper, it's all business.

"As it now stands, we've got about a fifty-fifty chance of pulling this off. That's with a lot of luck on our side. The primary objective is to get the old man back alive. I'm aware of your feelings towards him. You hold him responsible for the deaths of members of your family, as well as another million or two people. I'm sure there isn't anything you'd rather do than put one right between his eyes. Maybe I'd feel the same way if I were in your shoes.

"We'll be going through some pretty rough times. I'm not going to have the time to be keeping one eye on the old man and the other on you. What I'm trying to say is, you keep your personal feelings on hold. If it ever comes down to a choice, I'd have to kill you."

Thao listened closely to what Courage was saying. When Burt was finished, Thao carefully wiped his mouth with the napkin, folded it, and placed it on the table. "Mr. Courage," he responded sharply, "I'm well aware of how important this operation is. Although it is true I'd like to see him dead for what he did to my people, I am also a realist. The future of my country is at stake. If getting him back alive will mean saving the South from falling into the hands of the Communists, I'd be willing to sacrifice my life. If you had ever lived under their regime like I did, you'd understand. Not everybody from North Vietnam is a Communist. There are those that hate Ho Chi Minh and all he stands for. But in your country, when you want to get rid of the opposition you vote them out of office. In my country they just liquidate those that disagree with them. When this is all over, you can just jump on a plane and go back to the States. This is where I must spend the rest of my life. This is my country, these are my people, and I am well aware of the importance of getting him back alive. I know the outcome of this war may rest on his return. But how about you, Mr. Courage; are you fully aware what is at stake here? If you have any doubts about my loyalty, I suggest you inform Mr. Collins, and he can find a replacement."

Courage was taken back by the verbal blast he was receiving. But he had to admit, this man had a lot of crust. He wasn't a regular Vietnamese "yes man." He said what was on his mind without pulling any punches. Nonetheless, Courage glared at him. Their eyes locked on each other, and neither one looked like he was going to give in.

Then Burt leaned back in his chair and started laughing. "Well, I guess I had that coming, didn't I?"

Thao was angry with himself for blurting out his words; this was no way to talk to somebody who was willing to risk his life. But he was always angered when someone questioned his loyalty.

"I want to apologize for what I said, Mr. Courage," he said somberly. "Sometimes I get angry, and should think before talking. But ever since I started working for the Americans, there has always been that feeling of mistrust.

"When I first started as a Kit Carson scout for the Marines, I did my best to prove myself. One time I saved an entire squad from walking into a Viet Cong ambush. When we arrived back at the base camp and the Lieutenant was told what had happened, I overheard him say, 'Well, he may have done all right today, but don't forget, he's still a slope-head from the North. You keep your eyes on him.'

"There I stood, outside, with two bullet holes in my stomach that they didn't know about. How do you think I felt? There may not be many of us, but odds don't mean much when you're fighting for something you believe in. Mr. Collins is the only one who ever let me prove myself, and I'm not going to let him down."

"Ah, don't worry about it," Burt replied, pushing it off. "What the hell, we're both a little edgy. And if there's something we both wanted to get off our chest, this was the time and place to do it. I gotta admit, you say what you mean, and that's one thing I admire.

"Now, to change the subject a little bit, I want to ask you about the Chieus. Collins went over it kind of fast. His opinion was that there was nothing to worry about. But he's not going to be there when they set foot back in the homeland. What are your feelings?"

Lighting another cigarette, Thao took a deep breath and leaned back in his chair. "I would agree with Mr. Collins' appraisal. The four I selected were just young farm boys caught up in a war they didn't want to fight. They know that even if they did say something, they would be shot anyway for deserting in the first place.

"If the operation is compromised, they know their families would be turned over to the National Police, and there would be no fifty thousand dollars. The money was promised to them by the Americans, not the South Vietnamese. They know the Americans will keep their part of the bargain.

"I have been working with them for the past month on every little detail—the unit they are assigned to, their Company Commander, the Division Commander, when they left the North, what different areas they were in.

"Unlike American soldiers, in this part of the world, discipline is very strict. A man can be shot for stealing somebody else's food on the orders of a squad leader. Privates in the NVA don't speak unless they are spoken to. I'll be doing all of the talking, so there shouldn't be any problems. And, finally, I told them I would personally kill all of them if there was one screw-up."

"Very good," Burt responded. "I guess that is one area that's pretty well covered."

Burt seemed more relaxed as he ordered another drink. "There is one more thing I want you to do for me."

"What is that?" Thao asked curiously.

"We're going to be living kind of close for the next few weeks. I'd like you to call me Burt. The only people who ever called me Mr. Courage were those I owed money to or who were trying to sell me something. And you don't fit either category."

Thao's eyes narrowed and there was a look of hurt on his face. "That is not our way," he replied. "It has been my training and culture that when you work for someone you call him 'Mister.' It would be disrespectful to call you by your first name." Thao thought for a few seconds and then a broad smile covered his face. "I have an idea. How would it be if I called you Mr. Burt?"

Finishing his drink, Courage slammed his glass on the table and returned the smile. "Mr. Burt," he repeated. "I like the sound of that. Okay, Mr. Burt it is."

It rained all the way from the Continental to the Duc; the air was fresh and crisp, and Courage took in all his lungs could hold. After the rain stopped, the old smell of Vietnam would be back.

                ☆         ☆         ☆         ☆         ☆

The following morning's appointment passed quickly. After finishing the course on how to administer the sedative, they were informed that Collins would be waiting in the conference room.

"Good morning," Collins called out cheerfully when they arrived. He came over and draped his arm around Courage's shoulder, then walked him over to the main table, which was covered with uniforms, weapons, boots, backpacks, helmets, and an assortment of smaller items, all placed in neat rows. "Now," he explained as they walked around the table, "this is all of the stuff you'll be taking. As you see, Thao is checking each and every item to make sure everything's perfect. Once he's satisfied, it will all be loaded into that crate over in the corner and sealed. It will leave tonight with you on the plane."

Thao was going over the uniforms like a surgeon preparing for an operation. Holding each one up, he scanned it from top to bottom, checking the rank and the unit insignia. When he was finished with the uniforms he started going over the rest of the equipment.

"Those," Collins said, pointing to the uniforms, "were flown down from Danang two days ago. They're from the Twenty-sixth NVA Division, so we know they're still in the area."

"This," he continued, as he picked up one of the canteens, "is the dummy. It looks just like the others, except it doesn't hold any water. When you push your two thumbs in the center like this, it snaps open."

Demonstrating, he placed the canteen gently on the table and showed them the contents. "Here are two needles and six vials of sodium pentothal. That's enough to keep him on ice for a couple of weeks. Here is the thirty-two with a silencer and six rounds. It all fits neatly in here."

As he snapped the canteen closed, Thao picked up a handful of watches from the table. "What are these for?"

"They're Russian watches for you and the men. If one of them breaks or gets lost, you'll at least have another to tell time with."

Thao shook his head. "Privates don't wear watches, only officers do. Anyone seeing them wearing these would become suspicious and start asking questions."

"Hmmm," Collins replied, rubbing his face. "It's a good thing you caught that. If you see anything else out of place, let me know."

Reaching the end of the table, they stopped. "There," Collins pointed, "is your clothing and uniforms. The civilian clothes all have East German labels. There is also an East German camera and your passport. All of this stuff will be at the bottom of one of the Chieu's packs."

Reaching down, he picked up a large sealed envelope. "This will be the last thing to be packed in the crate. It has your ID tags with the name Captain Wilbur Kinson, blood type B, Roman Catholic. That's your blood type and religion, just in case.

"Before I came up, I called for the latest weather report. Not only will it be rainy and moonless tonight, but it will be cloudy and overcast for the next three days. This should keep all of the planes grounded, so you won't have to worry about an air strike. By the time the skies clear, you should be far enough in country that there'll be plenty of cover."

Thao walked over and reported that he was finished. "Your people did a fine job. Everything checked out and is ready to be loaded."

"Before we go any further," Collins interrupted, "I want to brief you two on what will happen tonight."

"You have an Air America flight that will leave Tan Son Nhut at seven o'clock. This should put you in Danang at about eleven. I wanted to have all of you change before getting on the plane, but Air America put the kibosh on that. They said if something happened and the plane went down, they might have a hard time explaining five North Vietnamese on board. I guess they have to cover their asses too. So you'll change when you arrive in Danang.

"When the plane touches down it will taxi to the Air America hangar. There Mr. Andrews, or Mac as we call him, will be waiting. He'll have the choppers ready to go. Once you change, you'll load onto the choppers, and they'll take you to the drop zone. And then, gentlemen, the operation starts. Are there any questions?"

Thao and Courage looked at each other. After a long pause, they both shook their heads.

"I don't have any," Burt replied.

"Neither do I," Thao followed.

"Good. Thao, you pick up the Chieus at five o'clock and have them at the airport no later than six. Burt, you go back to the hotel, but don't check out. We've arranged to have your sheets pulled down every night. When you arrive at the main gate, drive to the Air America hangar. Blow your horn and they'll open the door. Then drive inside."

Collins then motioned for them to join him at the bar. After setting out three glasses, he proceeded to fill them with spring water. "Now I know this will be a shock to your liver, Burt, but you'll be sleeping out in the bush tonight. If somebody happened to come along and smell liquor on your breath, you may have a hard time explaining yourself."

"You got that right," he laughed, picking up the glass.

Collins took a long drink and then set the glass on the bar. "Gentlemen," he said slowly, "you're about to embark on an operation that will dictate the outcome of this war. If you're successful, not only will it prevent another offensive, but it will provide us with the name of every Commie in the government. They'll have to rebuild the entire infrastructure. By that time, the South Viets should be strong enough to defend themselves and we can get the hell out of here.

"From the time I worked with you, Thao, and in the short time I've known you, Burt, there's no doubt in my mind that you two are the best qualified and have the best chance of getting our man back. Now, before I start crying and slobbering all over myself, you two get the hell out of here. I'll see you at the hangar tonight."

When they turned to leave, Courage suddenly stopped. "One thing before I go. Jack Daniels is kind of hard to find over here. Make sure nobody drinks from that bottle you've got back there. I'll finish it when I get back."

Later, as Courage headed for the airport, it was raining so hard that the wipers couldn't clear the water fast enough, and he had to put his head out the side window to see the road. By the time he reached the main gate, he looked like he had been in a swimming pool. Reaching the hangar door, he gave two blasts on the horn, and the large doors opened.

As he drove inside he saw Collins talking to the pilot. In his dark raincoat and brimmed hat, Collins looked like something out of a Humphrey Bogart flick. Stepping from the jeep, Burt could tell by the look on Collins' face that he was amused at Burt's predicament.

"Here," Collins said, tossing Burt a towel. "Dry yourself off. What the hell did you do, drive with the top down?"

"Ah, it was those damned wipers," he replied in a disgusted tone. "I had to drive with my head out the window."

Collins waved for the man in the gray uniform to come over. "Burt, I want you to meet Jerry Kirkwood from Air America. He's the man who will be flying you people to Danang."

Burt shook with one hand and continued drying with the other. "Pleased to meet you, Jerry. Is there anything I should know before we leave?"

The pilot's craggy, worn face was proof that he had been flying for many years. He looked like an ex-fighter pilot put out to pasture by the Air Force and picked up by the Agency. "We should be able to leave on schedule," he said with a slight southern accent. "We've been cleared by the tower, and with the present weather conditions, we should arrive in Danang at eleven. Of course, we could run into a head or tail wind that could throw us off by ten or fifteen minutes."

He walked over and patted the plane. "This old Cessna ain't what she used to be. She's still a good old plane, but there's a lot of hours on her. With six passengers and two crates, we're going to be a bit overweight. I would appreciate it if you'd keep your people in their seats and tell them not to move around. If you have any questions during the flight, feel free to come up to the cockpit. I've got a few more things to check on before we start loading. Do you have any questions?"

Burt thought for a few seconds and then shrugged his shoulders. "I can't think of anything right now. How about you, John?" Collins shook his head.

Looking up, Burt spotted Thao over in the corner. The four squatted figures in front of him had to be the Chieus. They were taking in every word Thao said while he paced back and forth.

In a few minutes, Kirkwood called out that he was set to go, and they could start loading the crates. When everything was loaded, they walked to the bottom of the stairs. The engines were started, and a loud, screeching noise filled the hangar. Collins had to cup his hands over his mouth to be heard. "Burt," he hollered. "From the Director, the Ambassador, myself, and I guess we should throw in the American people, you'll be in our prayers. And I'll be right here when you get back."

As Courage grasped Collins' hand, he noticed a little moisture in the older man's eyes. Could that be what he thought it was? If so, Collins was the first Agency person to ever show any emotion. "Don't worry," Burt shouted over the noise. "I'll be back. I was once told by a palm reader that I could only die in August. Hell, I've got nine months."

He started up the stairs into the plane, then stopped and turned around. "One more thing, John. If you're going to be right here when I get back, bring along that flask you've got inside your raincoat."

Walking outside, Collins pulled up his collar and turned down the brim of his hat to keep out the rain. As he watched the plane roar down the runway and lift off into the darkness, he reached into his pocket, pulled out the flask, and took a long gulp.

"How the hell did he know I was carrying this?" he thought to himself. "That guy's got talents we don't even know about."

# FIVE

As the plane climbed to reach its altitude, Burt could tell by the way the engines were laboring that the pilot was right. There was too much weight. Glancing over his left shoulder, he took one last look at the lights of Saigon. How peaceful they looked from up here.

As the plane leveled off, the pilot throttled back, and now there was just a hum and the darkness outside. Burt dropped his head back and closed his eyes. Rest would be a rare commodity for the next few weeks.

Burt had fallen into a deep sleep when there was a sudden loss of altitude and his head hit the ceiling. It was just some turbulence, but it was enough to wake him up.

He raised his wrist close to his face to check the time. Then he remembered that he didn't have a watch. Peering through the darkness he could see the outlines of Thao and the Chieus. "Thao, Thao," he called in a loud whisper. "Come back here for a minute. But walk real slow."

When Thao arrived at the seat, Courage looked up. "What time is it?" he yawned.

Thao held the watch close to his face to see the dials in the darkness. "Just about ten-thirty. We should be landing in a half-hour."

"Damn," Burt commented through another yawn. "I didn't think I'd slept that long. Well, I probably needed it. While you're here, I want to go over some last minute details. What do you say we have a cigarette?"

Reaching into his shirt pocket, Thao took one from the pack and put it between Courage's lips. He flicked his lighter, and bent to give Burt a light. One drag was all it took to get him coughing and gasping.

"What the hell are these made out of?" Burt managed between coughs. "They taste like sawdust rolled in kerosene!" After another drag he was coughing even more. "Christ, they're worse the second time!" He looked at the cigarette in the darkness, contemplating whether it was worth another try. "Nah, these things will kill you," he said as he crushed it out in the ashtray.

Burt could see by the outline of Thao's face and his white teeth that his companion was having a good laugh. "I don't know what they are made of," Thao remarked, "but I suggest that if you want to smoke, you get used to them. That's all we'll find where we are going."

The smell hung in the air and Courage moved his hand in a fanning motion to dissipate the remaining smoke. "Okay," he resumed. "Once we get off the plane, we've got a half-hour to change and get loaded onto the choppers. The first thing I want you to do is strip each of the Chieus down to their bare asses. You check over every inch of their bodies to make sure there aren't any American bandages, marks, or anything visible that would show they were in American hands. When we get ready to load the choppers—"

Suddenly the intercom light came on with a green flash. "Mr. Courage," the voice echoed, "would you kindly come to the cockpit?"

When Burt arrived, Kirkwood looked up and pulled off his headset. "We're going to have a bit of a delay. 'Charlie' just rocketed the airport. It sounds like five or six rounds landed. Let's hope none of them hit the airstrip. They're checking it now."

"That's great," Burt replied with a sigh. "What happens if we can't land?"

"Well, let me see here," Kirkwood said as he thumbed through a map. "The nearest place would be Hue, but that wouldn't do you fellas any good."

He was still studying the map when the radio started to crackle. Kirkwood held the headset to his ears. Burt could make out a few aeronautical terms, but he did not understand them. Then the pilot looked up, relieved. "This must be your lucky day. The tower says there was a little damage, but not enough to prevent us from landing. We should be on the ground in a few minutes."

When the plane came to a stop in the Air America hangar, Kirkwood stepped out of the cockpit and wiped his brow. "I'm getting too old for this," he said with a nervous smile. "From now on, I'm flying strictly days. Let them young bucks fly these suicide missions."

"Okay, Thao," Courage called out. "Let's get the crates unloaded." It didn't take long, with the Chieus working at it. When they were done, Burt was the last one down the stairs.

"Welcome to Danang," a voice called out.

At the foot of the stairs was a stocky, round-faced man in a raincoat. This, Burt figured, had to be Mac Andrews.

"That was some reception," Burt joked as he grasped Andrews' hand. "You sure know how to make someone welcome."

"You sort of get used to that up here," Andrews' replied. "It's usually a nightly affair. They fire their 122s at the base. Sometimes they get lucky and damage a few planes or chew up one of the runways. The Marines try to keep them on the run, but with a range of ten miles there are thousands of places that can't be covered."

Thao had the crates open and walked over to hand Burt his uniform.

"As you probably guessed," Andrews continued, "I'm Mac, the Province Officer in Charge, or POIC, as most people call it."

As Andrews talked, Courage started removing his clothes. "You'll have to excuse me," Burt said. "But we don't have much time, and I've got to get changed."

"Go right ahead," Andrews replied. "Pay no attention to me. I'll brief you in the meantime."

At a quick glance, Mac reminded Burt of someone who would make a perfect Santa Claus at Christmas. Short and stocky, he had a round, red face and a receding hairline. His deep-set green eyes sparkled with the look of having joked and laughed with the best. But this man was also with the Agency. And when it came down to business, he was the type that would get the job done.

"Outside of the hangar," Mac began, "are three choppers. Two of them are armed and will fly ahead of the one you and your people will be in. The two lead choppers have large spotlights attached to the front. When they reach the area we've picked out, they'll swoop down and turn on those spotlights. If there are any enemy in the area, the chopper will draw their fire. Then they'll quickly douse the lights, pull up, and go to another area. It's kind of a cat-and-mouse game, and a very dangerous one at that.

"They'll continue this way until they light up an area and don't receive any hostile fire. The area will then be checked by a Starlite scope to make sure it's clean. If everything checks out, they'll radio back to your craft. You'll come in from about six feet, you'll jump to the ground. It's wet and soggy from all of the rain we've been getting, so the ground should be soft.

"The area is about ten miles from here. We've got all the friendly units pinpointed, but the local VC units move around. That's why we're using this method. Now, just because there's no hostile fire, that doesn't mean there are no Viet Cong in the area. So once you've dropped, I suggest you limit your movements. Moving at night could be dangerous."

When he was finished changing, Burt stepped back for Mac's assessment. "How do I look?"

Mac rubbed his face as he looked Burt over from top to bottom. "I guess you look grubby enough to have been in the bush for a while," he commented. "I imagine you'll get plenty of mud on that uniform tonight when you start crawling around in the dark. How about your ID tags and other identification?"

"I've got them right here," he replied, patting his shirt pocket. "Let's see how Thao and the Chieus are doing."

As they walked around the plane Burt suddenly stopped, his eyes frozen on the NVA uniforms. They brought back bitter memories.

"Is anything wrong?" Mac asked.

"No," he replied quickly, shrugging it off. "I just haven't seen one of those uniforms up close lately. But I'll get used to them."

Thao was walking around checking each of the Chieus. His uniform was a perfect fit. With his lanky build and professional mannerisms, he would have no problem passing as an officer. "Are you about ready to move?"

Finishing the job of adjusting a strap on one of the packs, Thao looked up. "Ready, Mr. Burt."

"Okay," Burt said in Vietnamese. "When we load onto the choppers, I'll go in last because I'm going to be the first one out. Thao will load just ahead of me. Once we leave the chopper, we don't move until everyone is accounted for. And when we do move, it will be on the ground, crawling on our bellies. You'll take your right hand and put it on the right heel of the man in front of you. That way no one gets lost. And finally, there will be no talking. Everything will be done with hand signals. Are there any questions?" He waited for a few seconds. "All right, if there are no questions, let's get loaded."

Mac stood next to the chopper and nodded to each of the Chieus and to Thao as they loaded. When Courage wedged into the cramped quarters, Mac reached over and put his hand around his shoulders. "It's too bad you couldn't stay longer, but I'll show you around the place when you get back. Have a nice trip."

As the engines reached full power, Mac stepped back and gave a last wave. Fifteen seconds after the first two choppers lifted off, theirs followed into the darkness.

"Good evening, sir," a voice called out next to his ear. "I'm the crew chief. I've been advised that you have already been briefed. Is that correct?" Looking up, it was too dark to see the face inside the helmet, and it was too noisy to answer. Burt responded by nodding his head.

"Very good. Once they've found a secure area for the drop, we'll descend to just a few feet from the ground. You be ready for the tap on your shoulder. That will be the signal to jump. Exit as fast as you can. With no firepower, we're vulnerable that close to the ground." Again Burt nodded his head to show that the message was understood.

As the chief moved back to his seat, Courage looked out the open door into the darkness. The faintly blinking lights on the lead choppers splintered the black night. He leaned back and closed his eyes. The soft rain and cool breeze felt good against his face.

How ironic, he found himself thinking. It was so calm and peaceful up here, yet five hundred feet below, men were waiting for the sun to come up so they could kill each other.

It seemed about fifteen minutes later when he felt a tap on his shoulder. "This should be it," the chief called out. "The lead choppers should be turning on their lights any time now."

Burt could see the two blinking lights below. Suddenly they stopped, and the ground was lit up by the spotlights. Within seconds, the sound of automatic weapons broke the silence and red tracers filled the air. He could tell by the familiar bark that they were taking fire from AK-47s. The lights were quickly doused and the choppers made a hasty retreat.

The second area they tried was as hot as the first. In the next place they took fire from only one AK, but that was one too many. They decided the area had too many enemy troops and that they should try going a little further north.

Upon reaching the next area, the lights went on again. This time there were no red tracers. Either the area was clean, or "Charlie" was waiting to get a better shot. They inched down closer to the ground, and still there was no hostile fire.

"It looks like they've found you a spot," the chief yelled in his ear. "As soon as they Starlite scope it and give us the okay, we'll be going in. Get your men ready."

Burt looked at Thao and gave him a signal. Thao nodded that he understood.

"Here we go," the chief called out. "It looks like it's clean." Burt moved up and positioned himself next to the door.

The descent stopped; the chopper was hovering. He could feel the backlash from the blades pushing air against the ground. Feeling the tap on his shoulder, he pushed himself out into the darkness.

What was supposed to be five or six feet turned out to be at least ten. Burt landed face first. It was fortunate the ground was soft, or he could have been hurt. Although stunned, Burt rolled over quickly, knowing that there would be five behind him with full loads of equipment.

By the time he looked up, the chopper was gone, and there was just a faint blinking light getting smaller and smaller.

Groping through the dark, Courage made contact with ten hands before making any plans to move. It was pitch black; he couldn't see his hand in front of his face from six inches away. From feeling the ground, he could tell there was mud and grass. He guessed they could be on the edge of a rice paddy. Looking up, he saw a silhouette of trees to the west.

To find Thao, he had to feel the men's collars. Thao's would be the one with the metal insignia. When Burt found him, he whispered to him to crawl towards the tree line. As Thao started to crawl, Burt grabbed onto his right heel and followed. The Chieu then grabbed Burt's right heel as planned.

Snaking their way across the soft ground, they had gone about twenty yards when Thao slipped from Burt's grip. Feeling with his hand, it seemed Thao had gone into some type of ditch.

Thao backed out and after feeling Burt's hand on the back of his boot, he started back down. It was about four feet to the bottom. The grass was thick. As they moved forward, it seemed they were in a ravine. There was some noise as they brushed the grass, but it was drowned out by the chirping of the crickets.

Suddenly Thao stopped and signaled that they would stay there for the rest of the night. As the Chieus unrolled their blankets and mosquito netting, Thao came over to where Burt was lying. After tying Burt's hands behind his back, Thao stood him up and placed him against the embankment, then tied his feet. If someone happened to walk in on them, it would be difficult to explain an American prisoner who was not tied up.

When he was finished, Burt felt Thao's hand rub his face in a gesture that meant, "have a good night." Then he disappeared.

It started to rain harder now, and as Thao and the Chieus wrapped up in their rain gear to keep dry, Burt stared at the sky. "Damn," he mumbled to himself as the water ran down into his eyes. "And I thought Saturday nights in Scranton were long and boring."

He soon discovered that it wasn't just the rain that was going to make it a long night. He could feel insects crawling down his back and up his arms. He tried rolling back and forth to crush them, but that made it worse. They were now on his neck. If only he had his hands free for just one minute—just enough time to brush them off and scratch.

He wanted to call out to Thao to come over and untie his hands, but he quickly pushed that from his mind. If there was anyone close by, yelling to Thao would give away their position.

It now felt like something was either crawling or biting all over his body. He had to think about something else or he'd never make it. He started to reminisce about some of the funniest things that had ever happened to him. That made it a little more bearable, but it felt like an eternity before there were no more bites and he fell asleep.

At first light, Thao awakened and looked around. They were in a ravine. It was about fifty feet long, ending where the tree line started. Reaching down, he touched each of the Chieus and circled his finger for them to get ready to move.

When he reached Courage, he smiled. The rain-soaked body had slid down to a sitting position. Noticing a nasty leech on Burt's neck, Thao thought he'd try to remove it without waking him up. Using his knife slowly and cautiously, he had managed to pull it halfway off when Burt's eyes opened suddenly and he tried to move away.

"Shh," Thao whispered. "Stay still while I pick this slimy creature from your neck. What are you afraid of?"

"Well, to tell you the truth," Burt whispered softly, "I'm not used to waking up in the morning with an NVA Lieutenant holding a knife at my throat."

With one swift movement, Thao flicked the leech off and tossed it into the grass. "Now," he said in a low voice, "while the men are rolling their packs, I'm going to have a look around. I thought I saw some smoke a little west of here. I should be back in a few minutes."

As he disappeared into the grass, Courage looked at the sky. "Looks like another cloudy day," he said to himself. "There shouldn't be any danger of being seen from the air."

Everything was packed when Thao returned. "We'll walk in single file, two in front of the prisoner and two behind. I'll take the lead."

The ravine snaked its way to the tree line, where it came to an end. As they walked up the embankment, they found the tree line they had seen the night before. On the other side was a dry rice paddy.

Thao pointed to a wooded area across the paddy. "While I was checking out the area, I noticed smoke coming from those trees. Now, it's been my experience that regular North Vietnamese units would never be allowed to build fires this close to enemy lines. It's my guess that it's a local guerrilla unit, but we'll find out shortly."

Courage hesitated, then questioned Thao's decision. "I thought we were going to try to avoid any contact."

"Normally that would be the case, but there is no other way to go. Besides, being a local unit, they'll know where everybody is located. Once we learn that, we'll just head the other way."

Burt looked at Thao, showing his disapproval. "Okay, but if it's a South Vietnamese unit, you and your people can kiss it good-bye."

The paddy was about two hundred yards across, and the wind was blowing the smoke into their faces. Thao took a whiff. "They're making breakfast; those are cooking fires."

They were halfway across the paddy when Thao stopped and pretended to check the ropes on Burt's hands. "If you'll take a look at the ground," he whispered, "you'll notice the footprints we are following are made from what your people call the 'Ho Chi Minh slipper.' They are made from old tires. The South Vietnamese wear American boots. We're heading into a Viet Cong camp."

Following the tracks to a small trail leading into the woods, Thao held up his hand for everybody to stop. After looking cautiously both ways, he motioned that they follow him. They hadn't gone more than ten feet when there was a noise in a bush, and before anybody could see where he had come from, there was a young, dirty-faced Vietnamese clad in black pajamas pointing a rifle at them. The Chieus, quick to react, shouldered their AKs at him, waiting for the command to shoot.

He looked no more than sixteen, and kept his rifle pointed at Courage. He didn't seem worried about the ones pointed at him. Thao could sense by the scared look on the boy's face and the way he nervously fingered the trigger that he would have to be careful.

"You are very alert," Thao called out, as he signaled the Chieus to lower their weapons. "I hope all guards are as watchful as you. I will bring this to the attention of your commander. As for that American, you don't have to worry. He'll bring no more harm to our people."

For the first time, the young soldier took his eyes off the American and looked at Thao. Then a smile crossed his face and he lowered his rifle and saluted.

"Is your unit down this trail?" Thao asked.

The youth seemed intimidated by the tall officer from the North; he was afraid to talk. Nodding his head, he pointed his rifle down the trail.

"Thank you," Thao replied. "You may go back to your position and stay alert. There are enemy forces close by."

With a quick smile and a final salute, the boy disappeared.

The trail grew wider as they went deeper into the woods. The smoke was now visible, filtering through the trees and hovering close to the ground. Close enough now to smell what was being cooked, Courage held his breath to avoid the pungent smell. He didn't know what it was, but there was no way he could eat anything that smelled that bad. He hoped they wouldn't be invited for breakfast.

They weren't even noticed as they entered the main camp. It appeared to be a unit of twenty-five or thirty men. There was a small group of five or six men laying on mats, who looked either sick or wounded. Scattered between the trees were three fires with large cooking pots hanging over them. Each of the fires had five or six men waiting for whatever was cooking to be ready. No wonder they hadn't been noticed; everybody was more interested in eating.

Thao was right; it was a local unit. No two uniforms were alike, and they all looked to be in their teens. Some had their weapons slung on their shoulders, others were leaning against trees, and there were a number sitting on the ground.

When he had finished surveying the situation, Thao brushed off his uniform, straightened his helmet, and walked briskly towards the closest fire. "Who the hell is in charge here?" he screamed. "Who's in charge of this mob?" He kicked the bamboo tripod holding the pot, spilling the morning meal onto the ground. "I want the man in charge of this unit," he screamed louder. "I want him right now!"

After kicking the rest of the tripods over, he knocked over the weapons leaning against the trees. When he finished kicking over everything that was standing, he started kicking the men on the mats. "Get on your feet, you cowards," he ordered. If they were wounded, that was secondary now. They were more afraid of the big officer from the North who was trying to dislocate their ribs. Quickly, they jumped to their feet and snapped to attention.

When he had them all at attention, Thao walked to the center and turned around. "I want the commander of this unit to step forward right now," he yelled again. There was total silence. Only the crackling of the fire could be heard. Thao scanned each of the faces, and when his eyes met theirs, they looked to the ground.

He had just about finished scrutinizing the entire group when a small man wearing a dirty khaki shirt down to his knees and a mud-caked black pajama bottom stepped out and walked towards him. The stock of the man's rifle almost touched the ground.

"I am Sergeant Pao," he said sheepishly, looking at the ground as he stopped in front of Thao. If he had any more to say, he didn't get a chance. Thao's hand caught him across the side of his face with such force that it sent him backwards, falling to the ground. The sound was loud enough that

Courage and the Chieus could hear it from where they were standing.

As the startled Pao struggled to get to his feet, Thao's boot dug deep into his side, and he let out a groan, falling to the ground again. Reaching down, Thao grabbed him by the front of his shirt, picked him up, and slammed him against a tree. They were eye to eye, but Pao's feet dangled in the air.

"You dare tell me," he screamed in his face, "that you are the leader of this bunch of rabble? You call these men soldiers? They're nothing but an unorganized mob. You have one man on duty who doesn't even know how to salute. You build fires when there are enemy forces within a few miles. I look around and see undisciplined soldiers and filthy weapons. If you were in my unit, I would have you shot. Do you understand me? Shot!"

When Thao finished shaking the terrified Pao, he pulled his hands away and let him fall to the ground. Turning quickly, with anger in his face and voice, he pointed at two men standing close by. "You two," he called out. "Get your weapons and head down that trail. Find the guard and set up a defensive perimeter. You over there, start putting out these fires. And the rest of you, start cleaning your weapons."

They were falling over each other to carry out the orders. If Thao had intended to get their attention, he had succeeded.

As the soldiers scrambled about, Pao mustered enough courage to speak. "I'm sorry, Lieutenant," he said apologetically, still looking at the ground. "You were right in disciplining me. We don't look like much of a fighting force, and as the commander, I must take the blame. But as you can see, most of them are young boys and we have been fighting a long time. They are very tired of war."

"Where are your officers?" Thao asked.

"Dead," he replied, shaking his head. "All dead. They were killed during the Tet Offensive. At one time there were over one hundred and fifty men and five officers. But we were guerrillas, trained to fight in the jungle, not in the cities. During the offensive we were ordered into Danang. Many had never seen a city before. They became confused and got lost. By the time we were ordered out, there were only forty of us left.

"All of the officers were killed, and with me being the ranking man, I was placed in charge. I am just a poor farmer. I have had no leadership training. As you can see, these men need training and discipline."

"Look at me, Sergeant," Thao ordered.

The sergeant slowly raised his head, anticipating another blow. But Thao had calmed down, and there was a smile on his face. He put his arm around the Sergeant's shoulder and called for the soldiers to gather round.

"Your commander tells me that you fought bravely in our latest victory against the Americans and the South Vietnamese puppets. Your sacrifices were many, with the loss of all of your officers and many comrades. But all of these losses will be for nothing if final victory is not achieved. The struggle must go on."

Taking his arm from around Pao, he walked among the men. "Your commander tells me that you are tired. I also am tired. It has been over two years since I left my homeland to help my brothers in the South. I was one of many who heard your cries for liberation, and I am willing to give my life for the fatherland. It has been a long and bloody struggle, as you have all seen.

"But victory is at hand. The Americans grow tired, and without their support, the Thieu puppet forces will crumble like a rice cake. But now is not the time to sit around the fires feeling sorry for ourselves and saying how tired we are. There will be plenty of time for sleeping when the Thieu regime is smashed and the Americans are driven into the sea."

Burt and the Chieus were still behind the tree. Burt couldn't hear everything that was being said, but with the outbursts of cheers every few minutes he could tell that whatever it was, it was rallying the troops.

When his propaganda talk was done, Thao came over to where they were standing. Grabbing the rope around Burt's neck, he jerked with such force that Burt almost fell to the ground. This was the first time they had seen the American, and as he was paraded in front of them their eyes widened. For many, it was the first American they had ever seen this close.

"This," Thao boasted, "is our enemy. He was captured by liberation forces not far from here while poisoning a village well. Many of our brothers and sisters died from the chemicals spread on our water and food supplies by this aggressor. But he will not escape our vengeance.

"For his actions, he has been judged as a war criminal. He is on his way to Hanoi to answer for his crimes. Although I have not seen my home for many months, this American pig will never see his again. He will pay the price for invading our land."

He then turned to Pao, who was close behind. "Sergeant, you're familiar with this area. It is important that this prisoner be delivered to the nearest NVA unit. They will then make arrangements to transport him north. How far away are we from a major unit?"

Pao thought for a minute before answering. "There is a battalion about ten kilometers west of here. One of my men just returned yesterday from their hospital. He didn't remember what unit it was, but they wore new uniforms. I'm sure they could take the prisoner off your hands."

"I hope so. The sooner we can get rid of him and get back to our unit, the happier we'll be. But I was told when we left that all of the major units were northwest of here."

"No, no," Pao replied, vigorously shaking his head. "There are no units in that area. Everything is west of here. There is better cover from air strikes. There are also rumors that all units are being resupplied for another attack. I have not received any word, and I don't know where or when this will take place. I don't have enough men for another attack, but if I'm ordered to attack, I will follow orders."

Thao then glanced down at his watch. "Well, if we must travel that distance, we must be leaving. Do you have somebody who could show us the way?"

Pao snapped to attention and threw out his chest. "I will take you to where you will find the trail leading west," he declared proudly. "It will be my honor." As they prepared to leave, Pao called out that by the time of his return, all weapons must be cleaned and ready for inspection.

It was a good thing that Pao volunteered to show them the way. They never would have found it themselves. With the thick vegetation it appeared that there was no trail, but Pao, knowing the area by heart, picked his way through.

They followed him through a maze of winding paths and dense undergrowth. He moved so fast that they had to jog at times to keep up with him. Between stepping over decaying palm logs and getting hit in the face with banana leaves, Courage was starting to feel the heat. But he knew this was nothing. It would get a lot worse.

It was just before noon when Pao stopped near a narrow bamboo bridge that zigzagged across a wide stream and disappeared into another wooded area. "There is the trail, Lieutenant," he called out, pointing to the other side. "Just take this footbridge to the other side. When you get there, you'll find the trail between two large trees. It is much larger than the one we just took. Stay straight on it for about ten kilometers and you should reach your destination."

Thao walked over and grasped his hand. "I want to thank you for your help, Sergeant Pao. Before I leave, I want you and your men to remember that what we are fighting for today brings us a united Vietnam tomorrow."

"I will remember that, sir." Pao stepped back and saluted.

Halfway across the bridge, Thao looked back and gave a final wave. He then looked at Courage and winked. "Well, so far, so good."

☆        ☆        ☆        ☆        ☆

Pao's information was accurate. The trail between the trees was wide enough to walk four abreast, but they stayed in single file, with Thao in the lead. Checking his compass, he saw they were heading directly west. They didn't want to go too far in that direction—that NVA unit wasn't far away. They passed two trails that led south, but that was the wrong direction.

Not wanting to move too much further west, Thao was contemplating taking his machete and cutting a trail when he saw trampled grass and a small winding path. It wasn't as wide as the one they were on, but at least it was heading north.

They had to walk single file, and as they journeyed they saw signs on the trees every few hundred yards pointing to where a bunker could be found in case of an air strike. They had been moving for about two hours when they broke into a clearing. Straight ahead was what looked like an abandoned hamlet. At least it appeared that way until they started walking through. Thao caught movement out of the corner of his eye and called out for everybody to be on the alert. Suddenly a Viet Cong soldier dressed in a tattered uniform stepped out from behind one of the huts. He had his rifle slung over his shoulder, and he waved at Thao.

As Thao acknowledged his presence, two more soldiers walked out of another doorway, followed by three more. The men were followed by women carrying babies. Soon there were over twenty of them.

The women, with drawn faces and glazed looks, shook their fists at the American. To the men, he was the enemy, and they were curious. But, to the women, he was the one that brought death from the sky. He was the reason there was no food to give the children and why they had to hide in the caves. It was his fault the children's bellies were swollen, and they cried for something to eat. And when the crying stopped, they had to dig the grave with their bare hands. He was the one responsible for all of the misery they had suffered.

Not knowing what their intentions were, Thao called out for the Chieus to take Courage and move out. He would catch up with them later. Figuring the soldiers were close enough, Thao stopped and turned quickly. He never said a word; he just looked at them, and they froze.

As they passed by without incident, Courage remembered something he had read about the Vietnamese people. Although the North Vietnamese and the Viet Cong were on the same side, the people from the North always considered themselves the elite. They believed that the southerners were peasants, and were only good for growing rice—something they couldn't produce enough of. That's why they needed the South.

There must have been some truth to it. When they looked up at the officer from the North, they knew who was in charge. One of the soldiers, who must have been in charge, gave Thao a half salute. Then Thao started yelling for everybody to get back to whatever they were doing. When they didn't disperse fast enough, he pulled his pistol from the holster and fired three quick shots into the air. Thao's firing quickly got their attention and after some mumbling among themselves, they slowly withdrew back from where they had come. When they had all disappeared, Thao joined Burt and the Chieus, who were waiting a few hundred yards ahead.

The sun was just ready to disappear when they came upon another hamlet. This one was deserted. The grass had grown as high as the roofs. It looked like it hadn't been lived in for years. Only one of the huts still had a roof, and they had to cut their way to the entrance.

"This should do for the night," Thao said, breathing heavily as the last swipe of his machete cleared an opening.

Stepping inside, he looked around. "I'm sure you've seen better, Mr. Burt, but it'll be dry for the night."

"Anything is better than what I had last night. This place looks like a palace."

He had the Chieus stack their packs in the corner, and then handed each of them a piece of string. "Each of you will take one of these and go out in four different directions. They're each about fifty yards long. If you hear or see anything, pull on the string. It will be tied to a can next to me. I don't want any shooting unless it's absolutely necessary."

After Thao gave each of them their rations, the Chieus disappeared. When all four strings were tight, he tied them to the cans. "That should keep us secure for the night," he said cheerfully as he walked over and untied the ropes from Burt's neck and hands. "We'll keep the ropes close by, just in case."

"Boy, that feels good," Burt sighed, slumping to the floor and leaning against the wall. "I've never felt so helpless in my life, being tied up like that. I hope we don't have to go through that again."

Thao got a fire going under a pot in the small earth stove in the corner. In a few minutes he poured the contents from the pot into two bowls, and, sitting next to Courage, he handed one to him. "Here, it's been a long time since you ate anything."

Burt held the bowl to his nose and took a whiff, and then a longer one. "Doesn't smell too bad," he commented. Putting a spoonful into his mouth, he started gagging. "What the hell is this stuff?" he yelled, spitting it out. "It tastes like wallpaper paste."

Thao looked over and held up his bowl. "That, Mr. Burt," he responded softly, "is what the regular soldiers eat every day. It is only water and rice that has been dried. When you add the water again, you have this filling meal. Just like your instant foods in America."

Holding up a spoonful in a mock toast, Thao shoved some into his mouth. "You say you don't like it now, but in a few days, you'll be asking for seconds. You know yourself, if you don't eat, you'll never last two days in this climate."

With a scowl on his face, Burt took another mouthful. Thao, seeing he was having a hard time swallowing, handed him a cup of tea. "Here, you can wash it down with this."

"That ain't too bad," Burt replied, sipping the tea. "At least it takes the taste out of my mouth." By using the tea as a wash, he finally managed to finish his food.

When they were finished, Thao pulled out a map, and using a small pen light, they traced their path from where they were dropped off.

"Okay," Burt said. "It looks like we're right about here. If we keep going in the same direction, we should be able to reach the Ho Chi Minh Trail in about four days. Once we get there, I think we should cross over and move parallel to the trail. It's going to be a little rougher traveling, but it's the only way to go if we want to avoid contact."

Thao studied the map and nodded his approval. "I agree there's too much traffic, and someone might start asking questions."

When they had finished their tea, Thao threw Burt a blanket and some mosquito netting. "This should make up for last night." They settled in for some sleep.

It was still dark out when Burt heard Thao stirring. "What's the problem?" he whispered.

"Nothing," came the soft reply. "It'll be light in about an hour. I'm going out to bring the men in. I'll be back in a little while."

They began the day's journey. The further inland they went, the bigger and better the trails. What started as two feet wide became ten feet wide, and many of these trails had bamboo mats across them that came in handy during the rainy season.

The high trees provided a canopy for the trail which prevented seeing it from the air. They also blocked the rays of the sun, but not the heat. They could count on a daily afternoon downpour, which would bring some relief. But when it was over, they would see the vapors rise, turning the jungle into an outdoor steam bath.

Everybody was feeling the effects of the humidity. They stopped every half-hour to take salt pills, but the heat was sapping their strength. There was still about an hour of light left when Burt called a halt. "Damn," he said wiping his face, "this is like walking through an oven."

Looking at the Chieus, he saw that their uniforms were drenched. They'd go as long as Thao told them, but from their looks, that wouldn't be much longer. Burt looked over at Thao. He didn't look much better. "I think we should call it a day," Burt suggested. "We all look like good candidates for a heat stroke. There's no sense in killing ourselves getting there."

Thao nodded his approval. "I agree," he gasped. "We can make up the time when we reach the mountains."

Moving off the trail a few hundred yards, they found a place to camp near a small stream. After sending out the Chieus, Thao started a small fire. When the meal was ready, he walked over to where Burt was slumped against a tree. There wouldn't be any complaints about Thao's cooking tonight; Burt was fast asleep.

# SIX

The next day seemed hotter than the one before. During a break they discussed why there weren't signs of more people. Courage contended that the area was too hot, and was only used during the rainy season, when it was cooler.

After three days, the vegetation was getting thinner and the terrain was getting steeper. They were finally getting into the mountains.

There were also signs of recent movement. Thao bent down and inspected footprints and matted grass. "It looks like about a hundred men, maybe from yesterday. They came down the same way we're heading. I'd better put one of the Chieus out on point."

They had been moving less than an hour when the man on point came running over the top of the hill, waving his arms. Thao went up to meet him. After a short discussion he returned to where the rest were standing.

He checked the ropes on Burt's wrists and neck. "There's a company of NVA just over the hill. The Chieu said it looks like they've been there for a couple of days and are just waiting for orders to move. There's no way around, so we'll just walk slowly right on through."

"Don't look so serious. The way you handled Pao, this should be a piece of cake."

"These aren't farm boys, Mr. Burt," he replied sharply, "they're professionals. There may be some questions, but with the papers from General Minh, we shouldn't have any problems."

Reaching the crest of the hill, they saw groups of five to ten soldiers gathered around numerous fires on both sides of the trail having their noon meal. It looked like there were about two hundred men dressed in brown uniforms and pith helmets.

It was quiet until someone caught a glimpse of Courage and started shouting that there was an American prisoner in the area. The soldiers scampered from everywhere to see the helpless enemy with his hands tied behind his back; there was instant cheering and waving of hands.

As they shook clenched fists at him and screamed obscenities, Burt felt like an animal in the zoo. When they started to get too close, Thao stepped in and pushed them back. "You'll be seeing your share of Americans soon enough. Now go back to what you were doing," he shouted.

Since discipline was strict in the NVA, they moved back on Thao's orders. Slowly drifting back, they continued to laugh and make gestures at the grubby American. Thao held up his hand for them to halt across from a bunker built into a hill. With a flag flying on top, he figured this would be the Company Headquarters.

With all the commotion about the prisoner, Thao felt it was wise to go in and talk to the Commander. Across from the bunker were three Russian trucks parked beneath a bunch of palm trees.

"Go over and sit next to the trucks," he said softly. "It'll get you out of the sun. I should be back in a little while."

Courage and the Chieus moved to where the trucks were parked in a semicircle. As Burt eased himself down against one of the front tires, he noticed that they appeared to be new. There were only a few scratches and dents. They had to be less than a day's journey from the Ho Chi Minh Trail.

As they waited for Thao, a few men came over to get a glance at the American, but for the most part the novelty had worn off already, and everybody was back doing the same things as when they had arrived.

When Thao returned in about an hour, he was carrying a pot. Placing it at Burt's feet, he untied his hands. "Here," he said, loud enough for those close by to hear, "is some meat and vegetables. The Commander wants to show you how humane the Vietnamese people can be. He wants you to be healthy on your journey to Hanoi. And this is his contribution." He then turned to a group of soldiers nearby and pointed at the American. They got his meaning and started to laugh.

Burt didn't waste any time scooping it out with three fingers and shoving it into his mouth. It was the best thing he had eaten since leaving Saigon. The Commander hadn't shown that much humanity—there were only a few mouthfuls in there.

"Let's go," Thao ordered, as he kicked the bottom of Burt's feet. "We've got a long journey." After retying his hands, they headed north.

When they were out of sight, Burt asked Thao, "What did your comrade have to say?"

"Nothing much. He wanted to know why you were so special and separated from the rest of the Americans. I had to explain the entire story about you being a war criminal, with all of the details. He then wanted to know how things were going at the front. Before I left, he told me that the reason they are just laying around is that they are awaiting orders for another offensive. The rumors going around are that it will be in about ten days. If that's true, we don't have much time."

They passed another company moving south. There were the usual stares, but they were on the move and kept walking. When they had passed, Thao and Courage looked at each other. "I think, Mr. Burt, that the worst part is over until we get to Dien Ban. No one has suspected a thing."

After breaking for camp, a check of the map showed that if their calculations were correct, they would be hitting the main trail within a day. Burt, Thao, and the Chieus settled in for another night. It was cool enough in the evenings that they used blankets to keep warm.

The next morning they got started early. Walking through two more downpours, Burt wondered if they'd ever see a day when it wouldn't rain. Thao was busy looking at the map, bewildered as to why they hadn't found the trail.

Courage was the first to see the five figures moving towards them from the left, through the trees. "Heads up," he whispered. "We've got company."

Thao folded the map and stuck it in his shirt. As they came closer, he could make out a Sergeant and four Privates carrying machetes. The Sergeant held up his hand for the others to stop as he walked up to Thao, snapped to attention and introduced himself. "Good afternoon, Lieutenant. I am Sergeant Than of the Forty-first People's Army. My men and I are out gathering wood for our unit which is camped just over the hill."

As he talked, he kept looking around Thao, apparently more interested in the enemy standing behind him. "Ah, that must be the American we have heard about?" he asked inquisitively.

"What do you mean the American you have heard about?" Thao replied sharply.

The Sergeant looked at Thao and shrugged his shoulders. "There were rumors going around our camp that a very important prisoner would be coming this way. He would be escorted by four soldiers and an officer. I think maybe this is him."

The Sergeant walked around Thao, and stopped in front of Courage. Smiling, with his hands clasped behind his back, he started walking around the lanky prisoner. "I see that he is an officer. This is the first American I've seen since last year in Hanoi, when the bandit pilots were paraded through the streets. They didn't look very good, and neither does he. By the way, how was he captured?"

Figuring he had heard enough, Thao reached over, grabbed the pudgy Sergeant by the back of his collar, and jerked him with such force that his helmet flew through the air and rolled to the ground, quickly followed by Than himself. "How long have you been in the Army?" he screamed.

"Al—almost ten years," Than stuttered, his eyes glazed with fright, as he looked up at the angry Lieutenant standing over him.

"Ten years," Thao screamed at him. "I suppose you're in the intelligence field?"

"No, sir," he replied meekly. "I'm a cook."

"A cook," Thao mocked. "Do you know what the General's staff would do to you if they found out this prisoner was inter- rogated by a cook? They'd cut your tongue off and stick it in your ear. Now, you get up and take your woodcutters and get out of here."

The frightened Than cowered close to the ground. "Please, Lieutenant," he pleaded. "I have a family at home. I don't want any trouble from the secret police. You are right, it's none of my business. Please forgive me."

After taking a moment to think over his request, Thao reached down and helped the shaky Than to his feet. Walking over, he picked up the helmet. "Okay," he replied, placing it on his head, "we'll forget this ever happened. But in the future, you be very careful. That way you'll live to have twenty years in the Army."

"Yes, sir," Than replied proudly. "I'm glad the Lieutenant will not say anything about this. If there is anything I can do for you, just ask."

Thao looked around. The sun would be going down in less than an hour. "Well, we're going to need a place to camp in a little while. Do you know of a place where we could stay dry?"

"Ah, Lieutenant," Than boasted, "this is perfect. Our regi- ment is less than a mile away. It would be an honor if you would stay with us. We have huts with wooden floors, fresh bedding, and the best of food. You and your men could get a good night's rest, and fill your stomachs. I'm sure that the

Regimental Commander would like some fresh news from the front. Sometimes it takes months to find out what is going on."

Thao pondered the invitation. There hadn't been any problems so far, and if they walked by without checking in, especially when there were rumors flying around, it could arouse suspicions. "Thank you, Sergeant," he replied. "Perhaps you are right. It's been a long journey, and a good night's sleep and some good food are just what we need. Lead the way."

As they departed, the woodcutters fell in behind with the Chieus and started asking questions. It was only small talk, but one wrong word could bring disaster. Courage made eye contact with Thao and nodded at the Chieus and the other soldiers. Thao got the message fast. Turning, he held up his hand for everybody to halt. "You four woodcutters," he called out, "you move up front with the Sergeant. You other four stay where you are. I don't want any more talking."

When they had walked by him, he called out for Than to join him. As he walked towards the tall Lieutenant, he was puzzled as to why he didn't want the soldiers talking to each other.

Thao put his arm around him and led him to where they couldn't be heard. "We have just returned from the front, fighting the Americans and their puppets for over a year now. There have been many of our comrades killed, but it has been worth all of the sacrifices. We are winning the war.

"I can tell by looking at your men that they have not yet tasted battle. I'm sure when the time comes they will be brave, but they must have clear heads when meeting the enemy. Many times, soldiers returning from the front tell what are called 'war stories.' They tell tales about American firepower that are not true. The soldier who hears these stories tells them to others. After five or six times, you'd think the enemy was ten feet tall with three heads.

"These so-called 'war stories' can create a morale problem. They can cause men to desert or become afraid. A soldier is no good if he is afraid of his enemy. There are a lot of the enemy where you are going. Do you know what a few wild stories could do?"

"You are right, Lieutenant," Than responded. "I have heard of this. It is good you stepped in. I will make sure it does not happen again." As he ran to rejoin his men, he told them that if there was any more talking, they would receive the toe of his boot.

Than knew a shortcut through the woods. When they came out, it wasn't long before they reached a green valley nestled between two mountains. The hundred-foot trees on each side provided a canopy, hiding the valley from air observation.

As they passed the main entrance, the guards jumped to attention and gave Thao a sharp salute. These are your real soldiers, Courage thought to himself. Hard-core and well disciplined. There were bamboo platform huts scattered among the trees as far as he could see. There had to be hundreds of them. They were about four feet off the ground with a ramp as an entrance. They reminded him of chicken coops. Some looked large enough to hold twenty-five or thirty men. This had to be a staging area.

Burt drew the usual stares, but he was getting used to that. As they passed a group sitting in a circle, cleaning their weapons, he noticed that their uniforms were fresh, and they had white UNICEF bags dangling from their belts. They were new arrivals.

On his previous encounters with the NVA, he could always tell how long they had been in country by the condition of their uniforms. Whoever made the uniforms must never have heard of humidity. Sewn together with a cloth thread, it would take only two or three months before the stitching would start to rot. Then, piece by piece, it would start falling apart. After six months, they either scrounged up uniforms from dead comrades or wore the local Viet Cong garb, depending on what area they were in.

Burt also remembered a story about the UNICEF bags, or "ditty bags" as they were called in the Special Forces. Before each soldier was sent south, he was given one of these bags which had a picture of an American flag and two hands joined together in friendship. They contained only a few days' supply of soap, aspirin, bandages, iodine, and toothpaste—the toothpaste was used to clean the soldiers' weapons, since they never brushed their teeth.

The camp he'd been in was close to an area that was known as a major infiltration route, and was a prime target for B-52 strikes. After each strike they had to go in and do a body count. If a large unit happened to be caught in one of the strikes there would be pieces of bodies strewn everywhere, making it difficult to get an accurate figure. Then somebody came up with the idea that it would be a lot easier to count the UNICEF bags hanging from the trees or scattered on the ground than to try piecing the bodies back together.

As they wandered past a long, narrow building, the sound of a generator could be heard. There were lights and fans inside, and men lying in beds surrounded with mosquito netting. This had to be the regimental hospital.

After passing two more open-sided huts with stacks of munitions, Than stopped at a small building. Holding up his hand, he told Thao he would be right back. Scurrying up the stairs, he disappeared through the door.

He returned in a few minutes accompanied by a Captain. After he and Thao exchanged salutes, the Captain pointed to where the Chieus could set up for the night. "Colonel Bon, the Regimental Commander, is dining at this time," he said politely. "But when informed that there was a prisoner along, he insisted you both join him." He then bowed and pointed towards the door. "He will receive you now."

The smell of kerosene filled the air as they entered. There were four kerosene lanterns in different parts of the room to provide light. There was an American cot in the corner, a small cookstove, and a Viet Cong flag hanging on the wall.

Seated in the middle of the room, behind a wooden desk, was an overweight Colonel stuffing his face. Thao walked smartly to the front of the desk and snapped to attention. "Lieutenant Nguyen Van Thao, B Company, 326th Regiment, 26th Division," he called out.

"Yes, yes, Lieutenant, I know who you are," he grumbled, and returned the salute by holding up two chopsticks in his right hand. "I have been advised by my Adjutant that you have an American prisoner and four soldiers with you. Is that correct?" he asked, shoveling more food into his mouth.

"Yes, sir," Thao replied promptly.

Lowering the bowl from his face, Bon looked around Thao to where Courage was standing. "Bring him over here," he ordered. "Let's see what he looks like."

After giving a sharp bow, Thao grabbed the rope and led him to the front of the desk.

As Courage stood in silence, looking straight ahead, he could feel Bon's hatred. "Look at me," Bon shouted. "I want you to look at me."

As he lowered his eyes, to meet the sitting Colonel's, Burt expected more of the same hatred. But when their eyes met, Bon started laughing. "I just want to welcome you to my humble quarters," he said sarcastically. "I know it's not what you're used to, but under the circumstances, it's the best I can do." He then looked at Thao and started laughing louder. "What am I doing, the man doesn't understand a word I'm saying!"

Courage watched as Bon laughed so hard that he had to lean back in his chair and hold his stomach. And that was a lot to hold. Even though he was seated, he looked as round as he was tall. He had a full-moon face covered with pockmarks. It appeared that he had smallpox at some time in his life and the scars had never healed. His hair stopped halfway down his head and was combed straight back. A flat nose and deep-set eyes were signals that this was a tough son of a bitch who had been around a long time. He had a neck size of perhaps twenty-two inches, and his Army collar looked closer to sixteen. He'd never be able to button it.

When he finished laughing, Bon picked up his bowl and started eating again, pointing to the chair in front of his desk. "Sit with me and have something to eat."

Filling a bowl, he handed it across the table to Thao. "You know, Lieutenant, the Generals running this war amaze me. They continuously cry about the shortage of men. Everyone is under strength, especially after the last offensive. They're drafting them so fast that I've got fifteen-year-old boys out there. They can barely carry a rifle, let alone fire one.

"I have been told many times that there will be no replacements, that I will have to accomplish my objectives with the men I have, and I believe this. Now I see that the Twenty-sixth Division can take an officer and four men from the front line and use them to escort one prisoner. They must have an abundance of people."

"No, Colonel, we are also short of troops," Thao replied. "But this prisoner could turn the war in our favor, and we were selected by the General's staff to escort him to Hanoi."

"I don't believe any one American could be that important," he interrupted angrily. "He could have been kept in one of our camps in the liberated areas. Five men to escort one man is crazy. But what is done is done.

"Tonight you can brief me on the Danang area. That is the area we are headed for. Tomorrow you and your men can start back to the Twenty-sixth. I'll take charge of the American and will provide transportation north."

Burt had to pretend he didn't know what was being said, but he could feel the sweat starting to run down the sides of his face. He was hoping the Colonel didn't see it. Shit, he thought, that's all I need is to have Porky Pig throw me in the back of a truck heading north. Why the hell did we accept Than's invitation?

Thao remained silent. He finished his bowl of food and placed it gently on the table. Then, picking up his tea, he took a long sip and looked across the table at Bon. "I'm afraid that's not possible, Colonel. I have written orders from the Division Commander that this prisoner will remain in my custody until his arrival in Hanoi. Until those orders are changed, we will proceed tomorrow morning for our destination."

Bon looked at the young Lieutenant, disbelieving what was being said. He stopped eating and leaned back in the chair. He stared at Thao, with anger building up in his face. "Do you see this?" he yelled, pointing to the rank on his collar. "That is the rank of a full Colonel. The rank on your collar is that of a Lieutenant. That means, my insubordinate friend, that I give orders and you obey them, without question. I am now giving you an order. I will take charge of the American, and you and your men will return to your unit. We will discuss this matter no further. Now, have some more to eat."

Thao did not move, nor did he take his eyes off the Colonel. "I'm sorry, sir," he replied sternly, reaching into his pocket and pulling out a folded paper, "but I have a signed order from General Minh, and you have no authority to change it. Here, read it for yourself."

As he was unfolding the order to pass it across the table, Bon angrily knocked it from his hand. "How dare you question my authority?" he screamed in Thao's face. "I could have every one of you shot right here and now. All I have to do is give the order."

Bon eased the pistol from his holster, chambered a round, and put the barrel between Burt's eyes. "We could resolve this problem very easily, Lieutenant. All I have to do is squeeze this trigger and we'll have no more problems." Burt could feel the barrel pushing against his forehead, and closed his eyes.

"That's not going to change things," Thao countered. "Two weeks ago the General had two men shot for sleeping on guard duty and another one shot for stealing food. What do you think he would do to someone who disobeyed one of his written orders? If I give up that prisoner, I'm dead anyway, so it might as well happen here."

After a long silence, Bon sat back in his chair, eased the hammer on the pistol, and placed it back in the holster. "You are a good soldier, Lieutenant. You would risk your life rather than disobey an order. That is a good quality. I wish there were more men like you in my command.

"I have known Minh a long time. He was my commander when we fought the French. I do remember that he was a disciplinarian." He laughed. "It's a good thing you talked me out of killing that American."

Reaching under the desk, Bon pulled out a bottle of rice wine. After he poured two glasses they toasted an end to the war and a reunification of the homeland. As they were sipping the wine, Thao noticed that there were a few scraps left in the pot. "Excuse me, sir," he said. "I notice there is a little food left. Our American friend has not eaten much since his capture. As you can see, the journey has taken its toll. Would it be all right if I gave him our leftovers?"

Bon leaned back in his chair and rubbed his face as he pondered Thao's request. Thao could sense that the few scraps would come at a price. "All right, Lieutenant, he can have the food under one condition. The propaganda officer will be lecturing the troops tonight. As you've seen on your way in, these men are green and have never seen an enemy soldier, especially an American. Maybe if you drag that helpless creature around in front of them, it could be a boost to morale."

"That's fair enough," Thao replied, picking up the bowl. After removing the ropes from Burt's hands and neck, Thao waved for him to move over to the corner and sit down. He then dropped the bowl in his lap.

As Burt scooped the contents out with his fingers, Bon watched closely, enjoying the plight of this starving piece of humanity shoving food into his mouth with both hands. "By the way he eats, he must like our food," Bon said, still mesmerized by the American. "I guess he had better get used to it. He's going to be eating it for a long time."

Burt felt like an animal in a cage at feeding time. The Colonel continued to laugh and joke with Thao agreeing and laughing along. When he was finished eating, the ropes were retied.

Over more wine, Thao swore Bon to secrecy, and then proceeded to tell the story of how this American Captain was captured in the act of poisoning water supplies and spreading germ warfare. "That is why he is so special. He has been declared a war criminal. Once he admits this before the Vietnamese people, the world will know we were telling the truth about the Americans. They will be condemned by all other nations as the aggressors and the killers of babies and old people. Then we will drive them into the sea."

As Bon listened, he didn't seem as enthusiastic as Thao. "I don't know," he replied, with skepticism in his voice. "They have tried to get many of the American flyers who were shot down to sign a confession that they were using chemicals, but they've had no success. He's an officer; even if he is tortured, he may not sign."

"The American flyers were doing their job, bombing our cities. This happens in all wars. But the acts he was committing are against all rules of war. Chemical warfare has not been used since World War I. If we can't get him to talk, I'm sure some of our comrades from the KGB could help. They've broken men a lot stronger than he is. I have seen their work. We will get our confession."

"The KGB," Bon scoffed. "I don't trust them any more than the Americans. Don't ever forget that they are also Caucasians.

The problem with the Russians is that once they get in, it's impossible to get them out. Always keep that in mind."

After more wine and a few cigarettes, Bon glanced down at his watch. "It's just about time for the evening lecture. Get your prisoner and follow me."

Grabbing a lantern off the desk, Bon led the way out into the darkness. They had walked for a few minutes when Thao saw an area lit up with what looked like huge fires. As they drew closer, he saw that they weren't fires, but torches held by hundreds of soldiers gathered around a stage. It looked about four feet off the ground and similar to a boxing ring, but without the ropes.

It was surrounded on all four sides by soldiers ten deep, sitting cross-legged and listening to the propaganda officer. Bon had to push his way through. Reaching the stage, he jumped up and helped Thao lift the American. He walked over and took the megaphone from the other officer.

"Soldiers of the Liberation Army," his voice echoed. "I have a special treat for you tonight. As you can see, we have an American prisoner. This is the swine that has invaded our land. He and his people are responsible for bombing our cities, killing our women and children and forcing our young girls into prostitution. This is the enemy who has used his money to enslave our brothers in the South. This is the enemy who has used germ warfare against our people. And this is the enemy we must defeat."

Walking over to Burt, Bon grabbed the rope around his neck and forced him to kneel. Then, kicking him in the side, he knocked Burt onto his back. Putting his foot against Burt's neck, he held his hand high for everyone to see. "You see how weak these Americans are," he boasted. "All of his capitalistic money cannot save him now. He will answer for his crimes. He will find out just like the French, the Japanese, the Chinese, and all other invaders, that the Vietnamese people will never be conquered."

Pulling his boot from Burt's neck, he started to walk around the stage, making sure everybody heard what was being said. When he was finished, he called the propaganda officer over and returned his megaphone. He picked up where Bon had left off, only he had pictures. Walking over to a small stand in the corner, he picked up a copy of the *Washington Post* and held it high enough for everyone to see.

"Comrades," he called out, "this is an American newspaper." He then walked slowly around, pointing to the picture on the front page. "Here are students in the high schools and universities rioting and protesting their government's involvement in this unjust war. Look closely and you'll see pictures of many students waving our flag in support of the Vietnamese people. These people know it's the military and the capitalist warmongers who want this war. They get rich while these young people get slaughtered."

The officer threw the copies to the crowd, walked back to the stand, and returned with the *New York Times*. "Here are more pictures of Americans burning their own flag in protest. At this very moment they are marching by the thousands against the Pentagon to stop this war that cannot be won. They have vowed to take over the government and destroy those who have sent soldiers to our land."

More copies floated through the air into the waiting hands. Then more newspapers and magazines showing protests and flag burnings were thrown to the young soldiers. They couldn't read the captions, but the pictures said it all. Their faces glowed with pride as they gathered around, pointing at the pictures. Even the American people supported their cause. Surely these pictures could not be lies.

Many shook their heads in disbelief as they talked amongst themselves. It was hard for them to understand. If someone walked down the streets of Hanoi carrying an American flag, or publicly burned one of their own, they would promptly be picked up and shot. These Americans were strange people.

As Burt looked at the young faces, they reminded him of the ones on the plane he'd seen when he was landing in Saigon. These were young and anxious, too. With the exception of the difference in eye shape and skin texture, you could throw both groups into a bag, shake it up, and they'd all look the same. Just a bunch of kids from different parts of the world whose only job now was to kill each other.

From his position, the ones Burt could see looked no older than seventeen, and a few were younger than that. Even in the precarious situation he was in, at least a hundred miles from friendly lines and trussed up like a hog ready for market, he felt sorry for them. They didn't want to be here any more than those baby faces on the plane. But that was politics, and he had no control over that.

As more copies of the newspapers were tossed to the hundreds of waving hands, Burt wondered if this would be the last time these kids would have something to be happy about. He was well aware of the plight of the average North Vietnamese soldier, who was taken from his rice paddy, given a few weeks of military training, and then, after receiving a five pound bag of rice, an old Russian AK-47 and a uniform that would rot in the humid weather, was told to head into South Vietnam to save the homeland. The trip would take eight to ten months through mountains, swamps, jungle, and vegetation so thick that it had to be cut with a machete. Half of the people would never make it. If they weren't killed by American air strikes, they would die from malaria, dysentery, snake bites, or from hunger or heat exhaustion. Those that did make it would likely be killed on some battlefield. Very few would ever see home again.

As one of the papers floated down next to him, he looked at the picture of the young American student who was carrying a Viet Cong flag, with his fist clinched and his mouth open. Burt shook his head. If only those students and protesters knew how much they were helping the enemy, that the North

Vietnamese were using the photos for propaganda, to boost morale, and that they were helping to kill Americans and South Vietnamese. But he doubted they even knew. To them, this was the way to stop the war and save American lives.

Burt was brought back to reality when the propaganda officer put the megaphone next to his ear and screamed an obscenity, then introduced Thao and handed him the megaphone.

"What you have heard here tonight," Thao's voice crackled, "is true. I know this because, having just returned from the front, I have seen firsthand how we are defeating the Americans and their puppet Army. I have fought shoulder to shoulder with my brothers from the South for the liberation of our land. The Americans are growing tired of this war. They are killing their officers, and many have defected and joined our cause. Victory," he screamed, "is close at hand."

Reaching down, he grabbed Courage by the hair and pulled him up to a kneeling position. Taking the pistol from his holster, he put it to Burt's head. "I would like to kill this one right now. But death would be too good for this killer of women and children." Thao raised his hand and called out. "When he is judged by the Vietnamese people, what will their verdict be?"

"Death! Death!" the soldiers chanted in unison. "Death to all Americans!"

As Thao led Courage around the platform, the chanting got louder and louder. They were all on their feet, shaking their fists at the hated enemy. When he figured they had reached a high point, Thao stopped and fired a shot into the air, which brought immediate silence. "Thank you, comrades," he called out, "but save some of that energy for the Americans. I must leave now, but I will be with you in spirit. When my mission of delivering this prisoner is over, I will be rejoining you in more glorious victories."

As they stepped from the platform, Bon was waiting. By the glow on his face, it was clear he was pleased. "Lieutenant," he said, cheerfully grasping his hand, "you did a fine job. I have never seen my men so anxious to do battle. You are a fine talker. When I meet General Minh, I will tell him he couldn't have picked a better officer. Now, if there is anything you need before you leave, you let me know. I will personally see to it."

"Thank you, Colonel," Thao replied, "but the thing I need right now more than anything else is a good night's sleep. It's been a long journey and my men and I are worn out, and it's not over yet."

"Of course, Lieutenant," Bon answered in an apologetic tone. "I have been here waiting so long, I sometimes forget how the weather and jungle can sap your strength. You are free to go. But remember, if you need anything, let me know."

# SEVEN

At first light they broke camp and headed west. In less than two hours they reached the Ho Chi Minh Trail. Crossing over, they pushed another half mile and then set their course north. It would be rougher breaking a new trail, but they couldn't take any chances since Bon might check out their story.

The terrain was different than what the map showed. The hills were much higher and steeper. It was up one and down the other. They were walking five miles up and down to advance a single mile north. On one of their breaks, Thao suggested that it was taking too long and that maybe they should move closer to the main trail where the going would be easier, but the sounds of moving trucks and laughing soldiers put an end to that idea.

Camping in a ravine that night, Thao made his usual wallpaper paste and tea after positioning the Chieus. He hadn't even started to eat when Courage handed him his empty bowl for more food. He knew what Thao was going to say, so he jumped in first. "I'll tell you one thing about this trip. It's made you a much better cook. Just a few nights ago this stuff tasted terrible; now it's delicious. See what practice can do?"

Thao laughed, handing the refilled bowl to Courage. It was the first time Burt had ever seen him laugh. He had seen him smile on a few occasions, but this was a first. "My humor must be rubbing off," he commented. "That's the first sound of laughter I've ever heard from you. And don't tell me it's not part of your culture. I've seen pictures of some of the North Vietnamese, and they were always smiling."

Thao refilled his tea cup, leaned back against a tree, and made himself comfortable. He thought for a while before answering. "You're right, Mr. Burt," he responded slowly. "It's been a long time. My country has been at war all of my life. I have lost most of my family and all of my homeland. I see death and misery on a daily basis. Somehow I can't find anything amusing about that. You've been here a long time, you've seen my people. How many have you ever seen with smiles on their faces?"

Thao turned to look directly at Burt. "You, on the other hand, can find something amusing about anything. I know we were raised in different cultures, and that humor is part of the American way, but with all you've gone through, the way you can make light of life-and-death situations is confusing to me. Maybe I don't understand Americans as well as I thought."

Finishing his rice, Burt tossed the bowl onto the ground, picked up a stick, and prodded the fire. When the flames reappeared, he tossed it away. He looked over at Thao. "I'm going to tell you something," he finally replied, "that's between you, me, and the jungle. I've never told anybody this, so keep it under your helmet.

"On my first tour over here six or seven years ago, I was at a Special Forces camp close to the Cambodian border. A real hellhole. You didn't measure time in hours, days, or weeks. There was only darkness and light. I used to wake up in the morning and marvel at the sunrise, not knowing if I'd live to see another one.

"You never wanted to get close to anybody, because you'd never know how long they'd be around. If they weren't killed or wounded, they'd go out on some long-range patrol and just not come back. I knew that in order to survive, the first thing I'd have to do is keep my sanity. I was more afraid of losing my mind than my life.

"One day we were out on an operation and all hell broke loose. We ran into an NVA battalion of about twelve hundred.

There was one other American besides myself, and we had about a hundred strike force. I thought for sure it was 'good morning, Jesus' for all of us. They had us pretty well pinned down. I knew that if any of us wanted to get out of there alive, somebody had to do something in a hurry.

"For some reason I started yelling and telling funny stories in Vietnamese. The strikers looked at me like I was crazy, but then a couple of them started laughing. Then they all started. They were firing and laughing like hell. 'Charlie' must have thought we were on drugs. A few minutes later, they broke contact and faded back into the bush.

"I guess if I couldn't laugh once in a while, this place would have gotten to me a long time ago. Does that make any sense to you?"

Thao, who was preparing his sleeping blanket, looked up. "None whatsoever," he replied.

"That's what I thought, but what the hell, I figured I'd tell you anyway."

As they made their way north, the hills leveled out, and they only had to use the machete a few times a day. On the morning of the third day they found an old footpath leading north. They decided they'd follow it as long as it went in that direction.

They hadn't seen anybody since leaving Bon, and for the past two days there had been no vehicle noise. Thao checked the compass and map. He figured they were a little off-course, but still within a mile or two of the trail.

It was still two or three hours before sundown when they came upon what looked like an old pagoda. It looked like it hadn't been used for a number of years. Thao ordered everybody to halt. He walked slowly up the stone stairs and disappeared through the door.

He returned in a few minutes. "It looks like somebody has stayed in there recently," he said. "There's straw on the floor and an earth stove in the corner. It would make a nice soft bed tonight, and we wouldn't have to worry about the rain. What do you think, Mr. Burt?"

Courage looked around. He saw ashes from a fire and trampled grass. Someone had been here, all right. He figured it had been a week to ten days ago. For some reason he had a bad feeling about the place, but the thought of sleeping on something besides the hard ground and not being awakened in the middle of the night by a downpour was tempting.

Thao could sense that he didn't like the idea. "We can move on if you want to. We could make five or six miles before dark."

"How far are we from Dien Ban?"

"I figure maybe one day. We should be able to see it by tomorrow afternoon."

"Well," Burt replied after another minute of thought, "I think we've earned ourselves a good night's rest. We're right on schedule."

As Thao gathered the Chieus to put them out on post, Burt walked over to them. "I don't think we have to put out any guards tonight. There haven't been any signs lately, and if we'll be hitting Dien Ban tomorrow, we'll all need a good night's rest."

Courage piled three feet of straw in the corner and threw his blanket on top. He hurried through supper, anxious to ease himself into his first soft bed since leaving Saigon. Collapsing onto the straw, he didn't have a chance to feel how comfortable it was. He went to sleep too fast.

Burt was having a strange dream. There was the sound of firecrackers, and he felt like he was being hit with small pieces of wood. Suddenly he opened his eyes. The firecrackers he was dreaming about were AK-47s, and he was being hit with bamboo and straw flying from all directions.

Rolling off the bed, he started crawling towards the front door on his stomach. Shooting was coming from all sides, splintering the bamboo windows and ricocheting off the walls. He and Thao made it to the door at the same time.

"Cease fire," Thao called out. "Who are you and why are you shooting at us?"

Another volley sent more rounds bouncing off the stone floor, and walls and pieces of straw drifted like confetti through the air. Everybody was on the floor with their hands covering their heads.

Then somebody yelled out an order, and the firing stopped. When they felt it was safe, Courage and Thao peered around the door. It was light enough that they could see somebody standing in the clearing about a hundred yards away, with his hands waving to the men behind him, signaling to them to come closer. They could see movement in the tall grass on both the left and right. The Chieus, who had taken positions at each of the windows, signaled that there were also men behind the trees with weapons.

"Well that's just great," Courage said disgustedly. "The one night we don't put out guards, and look what happens."

Thao, who was studying the man in the clearing, looked over. "It's a good thing I took your advice. If they had been out there, they'd have their throats cut by now."

When it appeared that all of his men were in position, the leader started walking towards them. When he was fifty yards from the door, he stopped and put his hands on his hips.

"We know that you are in there," he called out. "As already demonstrated by my firepower, the entire area is surrounded. There is no chance of escape. Throw out your weapons and come out slowly with your hands behind your head."

Courage looked at the man's uniform. It was neither North Vietnamese nor Viet Cong issue. It was light tan, almost white, and the leader wore a red hat. As he talked, Burt could make out a few Vietnamese words, but then there were some words he could not understand. "Who the hell are these people?" he whispered.

Thao, who had seen enough, moved back from the door and sat against the wall. "Son of a bitch," he cursed between his teeth. "Of all the rotten luck."

"Who are they?" Burt asked.

Thao grabbed a handful of straw, and threw it angrily against the wall. "They are Pathet Lao."

"Pathet Lao—what the hell are they doing in Vietnam?" Burt whispered.

"The border is very close, Mr. Burt. Maybe we are in Vietnam, or maybe we wandered into Laos. The trail is close to the border, and there are no markers. It really doesn't matter which country we're in; he's got us surrounded and out-gunned."

When the leader started calling out again, they moved back to the door. "I will give you one minute to throw out your weapons," he demanded. "If my orders are not followed, I'll have my men destroy the building and everything in it. You have one minute."

He was close enough that they could see he was short, with dark skin. When he opened his mouth it looked like a jewelry store with his gold and silver teeth.

"I thought the Pathet Lao were your comrades in arms," he whispered, "united to defeat the Yankee imperialist. That guy looks like he'd shoot Ho Chi Minh if he got a chance."

"That's what your people say," Thao replied. "They claim to be Communists to get a handout from the Russians and Chinese. But for the most part, they are just a bunch of bandits who prey along the trail. They rob and kill stragglers and deserters and strip abandoned vehicles. They even dig up the graves of dead soldiers and pick them clean. The Vietnamese hate them, but with the war in the South, they don't have the time or the men to clean them out of these mountains."

"You have twenty seconds," the voice called out again.

Thao stood up and cupped his hands around his mouth. "I am Lieutenant Nguyen Van Thao of the Twenty-sixth NVA

Division. I have four men and an American prisoner who is being escorted to Hanoi. What is it you want?"

Short Round, as Burt had already named him, smiled and bowed towards the door. "Ah, Comrade Lieutenant. It is good to know that you are friends, but what are you doing in my country?"

"We were looking for a place to camp last night and got lost. When we found this place, we decided to stay until morning. If we have crossed the border, then I am sorry. We will pack our equipment and be on our way."

Short Round must have been amused by the answer. He called out in Laotian to his men what was said, and then started laughing. "Comrade Lieutenant," he called out, "I have already told you the area is surrounded. It is I who will decide when you can leave. Please, don't try my patience. Throw out your weapons and come out slowly. And warn your people not to try anything foolish."

Thao looked at Courage. "What do you think?" Thao asked quietly.

"Well, we don't have much time to decide. But that little bastard wouldn't be standing out there in the middle of the clearing if he didn't know we were at his mercy. Go ahead and tie my hands and tell him we're coming out." He then looked at Thao and winked. "You're a pretty good talker. See what you can do with this country comrade."

When the last of the weapons and equipment had been tossed through the door, they walked out in single file with their hands raised. As they reached the bottom of the steps, Thao held up his hand for them to stop. Alone, he walked towards the leader.

Courage watched from the corner of his eye as the men hidden in the trees and bushes made their appearance. As they circled Thao and their leader, they reminded him of a group of people he'd once seen in a *National Geographic* magazine.

They looked like pygmies. There were none over five feet, and some were smaller, as if their growth had been stunted.

Long, black, bushy hair covered half their faces. Many had sores on their bodies that had never been treated and were festering. They wore an array of clothing, from oversized NVA shirts to loincloths. One was wearing an American flight jacket.

When they were all out in the open, it looked like there were at least fifty of them. Most of them had AK-47s. There were a couple who had old Chinese bolt-action guns, and a few who were wearing loincloths were carrying crossbows. As they mumbled amongst themselves they kept looking at the tall American, but all of their weapons were pointed at Thao.

Thao had walked briskly up to the Lao leader. "I've already introduced myself," he said sharply, looking down at the leader, who was over a foot shorter than he. "Now I would like to know who you are."

"I am also a Lieutenant," Short Round replied proudly with another bow. "I am Hoi Muong of the Nineteenth Loyal Pathet Lao Army. We are from these mountains, but I'm the only one who speaks your language. As you can see, I am the only one with an official Army uniform." He stepped back and straightened his jacket for Thao to see.

Burt watched as the two sized each other up. That was something interesting about Orientals; if there were two people of the same rank, one would have to dominate. They looked at each other like pit bulls, each waiting for the other to make the first move. Thao was an expert in this field, and he could tell by Muong's facial expressions that he was uncomfortable having to look up at the towering Vietnamese in his fancy uniform.

Seeing the bulge in Thao's shirt pocket, Muong figured a cigarette would break the ice. As he reached his small fingers into the larger man's pocket, Thao brought up his hand and hit him with a loud smack that sent him sprawling backwards onto the ground.

Burt froze as the metallic clicking of rounds being chambered filled the air. He waited for the rounds to tear into his body as a dozen rifles quickly pointed at him, just awaiting the order to fire.

The startled Muong quickly jumped to his feet. "Hold your fire, do not shoot, do not shoot," he shouted. "These people are our friends." He picked up his hat, which had been knocked from his head, brushed it off, and walked over to Thao. "That was a very foolish thing to do, Lieutenant," he shouted. "I could have all of you killed. All I have to do is give the word. All of your lives are in my hands. Remember that."

Thao never flinched or changed his expression. "If you want a cigarette, why don't you try asking? If they were in your pocket, I would have asked."

Muong signaled to one of his men. When he arrived, Muong took a small towel from him and wiped a small trickle of blood from the side of his mouth. "You know, Lieutenant," he said coldly, "you have made me lose face in front of my men. That is dangerous, when a leader loses the respect of his men. Don't you agree?"

"Very well put," Thao replied. "But if I had allowed you to take something from me, I would have lost face in front of my men. You have only a small band here, but there are many thousands in our Army. I would have to answer to my superiors. You have no one to answer to."

Reaching into his pocket, he pulled out the cigarettes. "Now, we'll have one together," Thao said, smiling. Muong maintained his defiant look until the cigarettes were offered. Taking the pack from Thao, he emptied half of them into his shirt pocket before handing it back.

"You know, Lieutenant," Thao said slowly as he leaned over and gave Muong a light, "the last time I was in Hanoi, there were grumblings by some of the General's officers that some of our comrades living in these mountains were murdering our soldiers and desecrating their graves. There were some who wanted to take a division of troops and clean out these murderers, kill every man, woman, and child, and then destroy all of the animals and rice paddies so that no one could live here for at least twenty years." He turned and looked at the mountains. "It would be a pity to destroy such beautiful land as this."

Pulling the cigarette quickly from his mouth, Muong showed Thao a look of disbelief. "Surely, Lieutenant, you don't believe that we would ever do a cowardly act like that to our allies?" he replied. "We are brothers in the same struggle. If there are cutthroats doing these things you say, it must be south of here. You can tell that my soldiers and I are honorable men."

The tension had eased by now, and there were no more rifles pointing at them. Thao walked over and put his arm around Muong's shoulder. "I'm sure you're right. In fact, when I get to Hanoi and tell them that we got lost in the mountains and that it was a Laotian Lieutenant who helped us, it will put an end to the rumors that the marauders are from this area."

He could tell by the gleam in Muong's eye that he had hit the mark. "Of course," he shouted. "You tell your people that it was Lieutenant Muong who found you, that it was I who showed you the way back to your country. That would make me very happy."

Seeing Courage still standing there, Muong walked up to him, with Thao close behind. Looking at the rank on Burt's collar, he turned to Thao and pointed to the rank on Thao's collar. "You and I are both Lieutenants, but this man is a Captain. He is the ranking officer here. We should put him in charge." He then stepped back and gave a salute.

"We await your order sir," he mocked. "You give a command, we will obey." He turned to Thao and started laughing. As he turned around, all of his men joined in. Thao and the

Chieus followed suit. They were all laughing as he gave anoth-er salute. "American Captain," he shouted, "where are your air-planes and armies now? Why aren't they trying to rescue you? Maybe they have forgotten all about you!" He doubled over with laughter.

Courage looked on. He couldn't understand what was being said, but he didn't have to. He was the main attraction, and as long as Muong laughed, everybody laughed. Shit, he thought, here I am in the middle of some Godforsaken place with the Don Rickles of Laos.

When Muong felt there had been enough laughter, he held up his hand. "It's been a long time since I've seen an American," he sighed. "A few years ago I helped carry an American flyer who was shot down not too far from here. He had a broken leg and many other injuries. I doubt he is still alive. But this one looks very healthy. You have taken good care of him." He squinted his eyes and looked at Thao. "If this was just an ordinary prisoner, he would have been put with other Americans. Why has he been separated and given a spe-cial escort? He must be worth a lot of money."

Thao lit two cigarettes and pushed one between Muong's lips. "You're right, he's special. He's got a date with General Van Giap himself. All Hanoi awaits his arrival."

Thao could sense by the way Muong was rubbing his face and from the look in his eyes that he had plans of his own for the American. "You know," he said softly, "I'm not a rich man, but I do have about five hundred dollars in gold. You give me the American, you can have the gold, and you and your men can go free. You tell your commander that he escaped and ran off into the hills and could not be found. It has happened before; there are many places to hide."

Thao threw back his head and laughed. "I walk in and tell the General that with four men in my command, the American escaped. I wouldn't get much of a chance to spend that five hundred. We'd all be shot. Besides, what would you do with him? He eats a lot."

Muong's face lit up. "I would take him to the capital of Vientiane. Americans bring a high price, especially officers. They can use him to bargain with the Americans. I could get enough money to buy arms and ammunition for my men so we can continue our struggle against the imperialists. I would say I found him wandering in these mountains. I get what is needed, and who cares what happens to him.

"You know," he added sharply, "I could kill all of you and just take him. But I'm an honorable man. What I take, I pay for. It is not right to steal from a friend."

Thao played in the dirt with the toe of his boot as he digested Muong's proposition. "Yes, I guess you could do that," he finally replied, "but you'd never live to get him to Vientiane. I was on a radio just two days ago to a battalion not far from here. They know approximately where we are. You take that American, and they'll have a division here within a day.

"As it stands right now, we just consider you an insect, like the mosquito. You bother us and make us uncomfortable, but you're no real threat. Like I've already told you, there are some who just want an excuse to clean these mountains out. I think it rather foolish that both of us should die for him, and that's exactly what would happen should you take him."

Muong thought for a few minutes before answering. "Comrade Thao," he said happily, "I have thought it over. If that American is so important to my Vietnamese brothers, it would be wrong for me to take him from you. Therefore, as my contribution to the war effort, I will allow him to go with you. But before you are allowed to leave, I have one request." He walked over to where the packs had been put into a pile and kicked them to make sure they were full. "You have many supplies in here," he called out. "As you can see, we are far from a supply area and do the best we can with what we have. I sometimes think that our Russian and Chinese friends forget that we are also fighting against the Americans. It takes much food and ammunition to keep this area liberated. And you can tell by the looks of my men, there are many things they need. Maybe there are some things in those packs that could make life a little more comfortable for them."

Muong turned and looked at his men, and then back at Thao. "I'm afraid that if you tried to leave with these packs, I may not be able to hold them back. Even I have my limits."

They all closed in around Muong. Looking at the blank, starving faces just waiting for the word, Thao knew Muong was right. There was no way they were going to let them leave. They could have cared less about the American; it was Muong who wanted him. But there was food in those packs, and they looked desperate enough to kill for it.

Thao took a deep breath and sighed. "Okay," he replied reluctantly. "Tell your men to go through the packs and take what they need."

When Muong called out the order, they swarmed over the packs like hungry wolves. They ripped the ammo belts from the Chieus and took anything that wasn't attached. All the Chieus had left when Muong's men were finished were their uniforms and boots. Picking up the weapons and packs, Muong's men dumped the contents onto the ground in front of him. Looking down at the pile, Muong ordered everybody to stand back.

Bending down, he sifted through his newfound booty. He grabbed food rations and cooking utensils and started throwing them in the air. It was like a basketball game; when he'd throw something there would be thirty hands trying to catch it. The lucky one would clutch his newly found wealth against his body and start running for the nearest cover.

Muong had to stop his search when two men got into a fight over a blanket and threatened each other with a knife. As soon as that fight was broken up, another broke out over a cooking pot. As he moved to separate the two men, another two started. Pulling his pistol, he fired three shots into the air. "Stop this," he screamed. "I will shoot the next man who starts a fight. There's enough here so that everybody will get something. Now, everybody drop what they have on the ground, and move back. I will divide it up later."

When order was restored, he picked up the last pack and dumped it. Courage and Thao glanced at each other when the blanket was picked up and the camera and civilian clothes dropped out. Picking up the clothes, Muong held them up to check the size. Satisfied they were too large for him or any of his men, he tossed them to Thao. "You can have these, they're no good to us." His eyes beamed when he saw the camera. "What have we here?" he asked, lifting it gently from the ground. He held it up for his men to see. They all had a bewildered look. They had never seen anything like that before. "This is a camera," he called out. "And a fine one at that. It takes pictures."

As he held it to his eye and pointed it at some men close by, they cowered down and covered their faces as if it were a weapon.

"Don't be afraid," he called out. "This does not shoot bullets." Turning to Thao, he asked, "Where did you get such a fine camera?"

"It was in the possession of the American when he was captured. Although he was dressed in his Army uniform, the camera and clothes were in his possession. Our intelligence people believe that he was going to change into these clothes and then use the camera for spying. We are taking them along to be used as evidence at his trial."

"Trial!" he scoffed. "Lieutenant, your people will take this man, get a confession out of him, and then kill him. You don't need evidence for that. I believe the clothes are enough. I'll keep the camera. We'll say it's a present from you to me."

Sticking it in his shirt, Muong continued rummaging through what was left in the packs. When he was finished he looked up at Thao. "I'm sorry that we need so much of your equipment, but you are close to home and your people will replace what we have taken."

Muong glanced at Thao's watch, but when he saw the look in the taller man's eyes, he knew the watch was going to stay. "Comrade," he said smartly, "I admire your watch, but it would be wrong for one officer to steal from another. It is yours to keep." Reaching over, he patted Thao's holster. "You may also keep your pistol. It is of little use in these mountains, but it could protect you from some of the dangerous people who roam these hills."

As Muong continued to talk, Thao pushed his hands away. "Is there anything else you need?"

"No, Lieutenant," he replied with a bow. "You and your people are free to go. If you walk east for about five kilometers, you'll hit the border."

As they turned to leave, Muong called out for them to wait. "Here," he said, tossing three blocks of C-4 explosives and a roll of the det cord at Thao's feet. "You can have this back. My men are foolish enough with rifles. I don't want them blowing themselves up with that stuff. Have a safe journey, and tell our brothers in Hanoi that we are continuing the struggle."

More fighting and arguing broke out, and Muong had to make a hasty retreat to break up the combatants.

"Let's get out of here," Thao whispered, "while they're still busy."

They started moving, occasionally looking over their shoulders to see if any of Muong's people were following. When they were back in Vietnam, Courage called for a halt. As he sat down and relaxed against a tree he glanced up at Thao, who was studying the map.

"About how far are we from Dien Ban?"

Thao looked around, trying to coordinate exactly where they were. "I'd say about eight or nine clicks. If we head in a northeasterly direction, we should be there by late this afternoon. But I'm afraid, Mr. Burt, we're going to have to put off the operation for at least a day. Our friends took everything, even our mosquito netting. I'll have to go into Dien Ban and get some supplies."

Courage looked up and shook his head. "What are you going to use, your American Express card? We need a lot of everything."

"Ah, Mr. Burt, I'm very good at bargaining. Our honorable Laotian friend forgot to take my wallet. I have about twenty dollars in North Vietnamese currency. There is a thriving black market in the village. I should be able to trade my Russian watch for whatever else we need. And with all of the military units in the area, scrounging up weapons and ammunition shouldn't be too difficult. I'll have to see what I can do when I get there."

Thao was right on target. Two hours before sundown, he pointed to the east. "There it is," he called out. A red and blue Viet Cong flag fluttered in the breeze. "That's Dien Ban. It's about three miles from here. Now let's find a place to stay the night."

As they made their way around the mountain they discovered that there was no shortage of caves. They needed one that was large enough to accommodate six and would give them a view of anyone who might approach. When they found a cave halfway up the mountain that suited them, they moved inside. After darkness settled in, one of the Chieus gathered some dry wood and started a fire.

It was damp and the night brought on the cold, so they gathered closer to the heat. "I'm afraid it's going to be a long night, with no blankets and nothing to eat," Courage commented. As he used a stick to prod the fire for more heat, he thought about the runny eggs the first morning at the Duc, which he had pushed away. He wished they were in front of him now. Even the thought of Thao's mixture of dirty water and rice paste made him feel hungrier.

Thao threw some more wood on the fire and sat down beside him.

"How long will it take to get to Dien Ban?" Courage asked.

"If I leave after first light, I should be there by mid-morning. I could make it faster, but I want to make sure I'm not seen. With any luck, I should be back by late afternoon."

They settled in for the long, cold night.

# EIGHT

As the morning light broke through the entrance, Thao nudged everyone awake. "I'm leaving now," he said as he straightened and brushed off his uniform. "I'll be back soon."

It was still cold and damp, and one of the Chieus gathered some wood to start a fire. Burt told him there would be no fires. Smoke could bring visitors; they would have to wait until dark. He then told one of them to stand guard at the entrance, but he wondered later what the hell good does it did to put a guard at the entrance. They didn't have anything to defend themselves with anyway.

The hours passed. The cave quickly filled with darkness as the sun went down, and Burt told the Chieus that it was safe now to build a fire. They were just getting it started when the guard at the entrance whispered that someone was coming. Looking around for something to use as a weapon, Burt picked up a rock and moved over next to the guard.

Whoever it was, they were now close enough that Burt could hear panting and grunting—apparently it was hard getting up the hill. As the sounds approached the cave's entrance, Burt brought back the rock, ready to strike. When he caught the outline of Thao's face, he angrily threw the rock on the ground.

"Damn it," he cursed. "Why the hell didn't you call out? You damned near got your head busted in."

"I'm sorry, Mr. Burt," Thao replied between breaths. "I sort of lost my way, and with all of the caves around here, I wasn't sure this was the one."

Now Burt knew why Thao was out of breath. His arms were piled high, and he let out a grunt as he dumped everything on the ground. "I've got a few items here that should make things a little more bearable. There are blankets, food, a cooking pot, netting, and some salt tablets. I also picked up a few weapons and some ammunition. They're hidden at the bottom of the mountain. They were a little too heavy to carry up here. We can pick them up on the way out."

As one of the Chieus prepared the food, Thao briefed Courage on what was happening in Dien Ban. "There are more troops there now than the last time I was there. In fact, there are some camped just a few miles from here, but they are city boys and would be afraid to wander in these mountains. We're safe here for the time being.

"It's about a half mile to the bottom of the mountain. There's an old road that runs close by. It was built by the French to haul ore. It hasn't been used in a long time, and it's overgrown in many spots, but I should be able to drive a truck over it."

When the rice was ready, the Chieu handed each of them a bowl. "It appears that your people were right on target," Thao continued. "I overheard two officers talking at one of the local tea houses. One was complaining that his unit had just arrived and that in about a week they would be heading south. I figure that Huy will meet with the Generals in about five days."

"Humph," Courage responded, as he handed his bowl to the Chieu for a refill. "Yeah, we've got to get him before that meeting. How about the other things we need?"

"Well, I've already got a truck. The sandbags, shovels, and casket I'll get tomorrow."

"You got a truck already! How the hell did you do that?"

Thao cleared his throat, seemingly pleased with himself. "There are a lot of trucks in the area. Many of the drivers are peasants who have never seen a motor vehicle in their lives. When a truck breaks down, they don't know how to fix it, so they just leave it. I found the perfect one with a canvas cover and tank full of gas, near the marketplace. I pulled the distributor cap. When the driver returned and tried to start it, he gave up after a few minutes and left. I walked over and took the keys. I'll pick it up tomorrow morning."

Courage nodded his head. "All right, it looks like we've got that taken care of. And tomorrow you'll get the rest of the stuff."

Reaching over, Burt scooped his bowl into the pot. "This is pretty good," he commented. "I'll try some more. I see there's even a little meat in here. It's sort of stringy and sweet, but it's the best I've had since we left Danang. What kind is it?"

When he didn't get an immediate answer, Burt looked at Thao. There was an expression on his face that said, you really don't want to know, do you? "I see, I'm going to get that silent treatment," Burt said. "It doesn't matter; I've had it all, over here—snake, water buffalo, tiger, and on a few occasions I didn't bother asking."

Then it hit him. "Ah yes, we're in North Vietnam. I should have known. I've got a feeling we're eating the family pet. You know, the one that barks. The one that's called 'man's best friend.'"

He didn't need an answer; he could tell he was right by the expression on Thao's face. "Well," Thao finally answered with a half smile, "I was going to wait until you were done before saying anything. I know you Americans are kind of squeamish about eating dogs. I was afraid if I told you, you wouldn't eat it. It's important that we all keep up our strength. The most important part of the mission is coming up."

"Ah, hell," Burt responded quickly, "I've eaten a lot worse than a little dog meat. I'm not saying I like it, but like you said, the tough part is coming up."

The next morning, before he left, Thao made sure to leave the breakaway canteen with the syringes and pistol behind.

Courage would check them out. It would give him something to do.

At dusk they started the fire, figuring Thao would be back by the time they started to eat. When they were finished, Burt took his tea and moved up to the mouth of the cave to wait. He was expecting to see the lanky frame appear at any minute.

The warming rays of the sun brought him out of his sleep the next morning. Rubbing his eyes, he looked around. "Damn," he mumbled. "I must have fallen asleep. I guess Thao didn't want to disturb me." As the light filled the cave Burt could see the Chieus still sleeping, but there was no one on Thao's blanket.

Damn it, Burt thought. Where the hell is he? He should have been back last night. Something must have happened.

His pacing awakened the Chieus, and they started talking among themselves about what could have happened to their leader.

Burt walked to the entrance and looked over at the flag waving in the distance. As he stared at it, ideas started racing through his mind. Thao may have been picked up for asking too many questions. Maybe somebody had recognized him and they were interrogating him now. Then there was the thought from before the operation began—what if he was a double agent working for the NVIS? He could bring an army back with him. Nah, Burt thought, pushing that quickly from his mind. If Thao was going to do that, they would have been here yesterday.

He kept a vigil, waiting for Thao's return. By the middle of the afternoon he was contemplating what they would do if Thao didn't come back. There wasn't too much time left. Huy had to be taken before the meeting, and that was just a few days away. As he picked up stones and pitched them against the wall, Burt knew that he would have to come up with a new plan.

Without Thao there was no chance of getting the old man out alive, Burt figured, and he didn't come halfway around the world to get within three miles and turn back. But if he could take that old bastard out, maybe he could put an end to this insanity, if only for a little while.

Different ideas raced through his mind. His first was to have one of the Chieus steal a truck, come back, and pick them up. Then, with him concealed in the back, they would ram through the front gate. By the time the guards figured out what had happened, they could be at Huy's house. He could run in, shoot him, and then jump over the wall.

He quickly put that one aside. There were troops inside the compound. They'd never make it to the house. It would be suicide. He then thought about the original plan of throwing the blanket over the top of the wall and making his way to the house. There were six rounds in the pistol. That should take care of everybody in there. When he returned, they would head down the trail until daylight, and then it would be everybody for themselves.

He called for the Chieus to gather round. It was the first time he had ever had any real dealings with them. As he told them of his plan, they started talking among themselves, shaking their heads.

"Look," Courage said angrily. "There's no other way. And I'm not going back without finishing the mission. None of you will get any of the money unless we succeed."

The one who looked the oldest held up his hand for silence. "Sir, we are not disobeying you, or saying your idea is crazy. But there is no way that we can steal a truck. None of us know how to drive."

Burt just looked at them, trying to think of something to say. "That's just great!" he shouted, throwing a handful of rocks against the wall in frustration. "Here the top men in the Agency come up with an operation and tell me that every little detail is covered—the biggest operation of the war! And now

I find out that the only one who can drive is missing. Now what the hell are we going to do?"

Because of the tone of his voice and the fact that he was using English, the Chieus thought he was mad at them. "No, no," Burt reassured them. "It's not your fault. I'll think of something else. Go ahead and start building a fire. It'll be dark out soon."

He stared into the flames thinking about what move he would have to make the next day when the Chieu on guard whispered that someone was coming. Then they heard Thao's signal.

It seemed like the weight of the world had just been lifted off Burt's shoulders, and he let out a sigh of relief. He watched Thao walk through the entrance with a smile on his face and a backpack slung over his shoulder.

Burt looked at him and shook his head. "If I wasn't so happy to see you, I'd chew your ass out for scaring us like this!"

They sat next to the fire and Thao emptied the contents of the pack. "There should be enough food here for our return. The truck is parked at the bottom of the mountain with the shovels and sand bags. The casket is in the back. We should be able to move at first light.

"Now, to explain why I'm over a day late. When I arrived in the village, I had to find an insignia for my uniform from a unit that had recently arrived. I didn't have any problems, but a senior officer, seeing it, told me that all new arrivals had to attend a briefing at the District Headquarters. It wasn't that important, but it took most of the day. During the last hour, Mr. Huy made an appearance. He didn't say anything; he just sat on the stage.

"Once it was all over, I didn't have enough time to get the shovels, the sandbags, or the casket. I had to wait until this morning."

Taking the pot from the fire, he poured himself a cup of tea. "By the way," he continued, "it looks like Mr. Collins came through. There was an air strike just south of here a few days ago. From the rumors going around, there wasn't much damage, but it was the first time in a number of years this area was bombed. It must have made a few people nervous. I saw anti-aircraft guns being tested, and they are reinforcing many of the bunkers. This will help us get into the compound."

Thao reached into the bottom of the bag and pulled out a bottle. "Here, Mr. Burt, this is for you. I know it's not Jack Daniels, but it is liquor."

Taking the bottle, Burt held it close to the light, trying to make out the Russian writing on the label. "Well, I'll be damned. How in the hell did you find Russian vodka out in this goddamned wilderness?"

"Black market," Thao replied.

"Black market," Burt repeated as he unscrewed the top and took a sniff. "I never thought Uncle Ho would allow someone to sell booze in his territory."

"Ah," Thao chuckled. "You should see the things they have for sale, even in Dien Ban, if you have the money. Watches and cameras from Russia and China, binoculars from East Germany, French perfumes, and American cigarettes, if you know who to ask. They sell for five dollars a pack. I was tempted, but it was too risky. If someone saw an officer buying them, it would be a sign of a capitalistic habit, and could arouse suspicions."

As Burt took a drink of the potent vodka, he could feel the warmth surging through his body. "Whew," he said hoarsely. "That's what I call strong." Before taking another swallow, Burt held the bottle up in a toast. "Thao, my boy, I never did care for them goddamned Ruskies, but I gotta admit, they sure know how to make vodka."

When he was finished, he tossed the bottle in the corner. "Now, that's what I call an after-dinner drink."

Courage called everybody to gather around. "Okay, it looks like tomorrow is the day. From the time we leave here until we get to our destination, things are going to be hot and heavy. I doubt any of us will get much sleep. But if everything goes according to plan, it should only be a few days. Let's get the weapons cleaned and everything packed. Don't leave anything behind." He turned to Thao. "How many sandbags are there on the truck?"

"Five hundred," he replied. "If we leave here at first light, we should reach the truck by six o'clock. I figured that by working in shifts we can fill about a hundred an hour. One man holds the bag, one fills it, the other ties it and hands it up to the one on the truck. With a ten-minute break every hour, we should be finished by eleven o'clock. With the traffic, I esti-mate that from the time we leave until arriving at the District Headquarters, it'll be just over an hour, sometime after twelve. That's when the old man goes to the house."

"Well, if we could get there a little after twelve, that would be perfect. How about the guards at the gate, they any differ-ent from the last time you were here?"

"Not really. They lay around in the little guard shack. I don't even think their weapons are loaded."

While the Chieus worked on their weapons, Burt took the breakaway canteen and removed the contents. He carefully filled the syringes, remembering what he was taught at the Embassy. "This should keep the old geezer on ice for a while," he remarked, placing them gently back inside the canteen.

Next Courage picked up the pistol, screwed on the silencer, pointed it at the ground, and squeezed the trigger. There was a sharp pop, but they were in a cave. It would hardly be heard outside. He hoped it would never have to be used.

# NINE

Before leaving at first light, Courage took off his Army uniform, buried it, and put on the civilian clothes. They were a little loose from the weight he had lost, so he had to pull in his belt another notch.

They went single file down the side of the mountain with Thao in the lead. The light was just breaking through the trees when he held up his hand for everyone to halt. "The truck is over there," Thao whispered. "Let me make sure the area is clear."

When he was satisfied, he waved for them to follow. When all of the camouflage had been removed from the truck, he jumped up on the back and threw down the sandbags and shovels. "Mr. Burt," he called out softly, "you come up here and wait in the back in case somebody comes by. You can help stack the sandbags. I figure at fifty per row, we can make it look full. First we'll line the bags around the inside; if somebody lifts the canvas to check, all they'll see is sandbags."

Everything went according to plan for the first hour, but the heat and humidity slowed down the pace after that. They were now taking ten-minute breaks every half-hour.

Thao wiped the sweat from his eyes and looked up at the sun, which was almost directly overhead. "How many rows do we have, Mr. Burt?"

"Just about nine," he replied after a quick count.

"That's close enough. It's nearly eleven-thirty; we're running about a half-hour late. Crawl over the top and sit on the casket. We'll fill in the space from this side."

As they moved slowly down the old road, Courage could have sworn they hit every rut and hole. Suddenly the engine was gunned, and they were going up a steep incline. He grabbed onto the side to keep his balance, thinking they were going to lose some of the sandbags. As he reached over to balance them, the bouncing was over. They were on a smooth surface.

The flap behind the driver's seat was closed, but there were a few small holes that he could see through. They were on a main highway now, and by the dust being kicked up he wondered if this was the famous Ho Chi Minh Trail he had always heard about.

There were trucks passing them, heading south. As they got closer, he could hear horns. Now it was stop-and-go. Courage wiped the sweat from his brow. It had to be over a hundred degrees, with the sun beating down on the canvas. At least there was a breeze when the truck was moving.

His attention was quickly diverted from the heat by a sharp rap on the flap. "We're almost there," Thao whispered. "The main gate is straight ahead."

Thao brought the truck to a stop in front of the barbed wire that was stretched across the entrance. He tapped his fingers nervously on the steering wheel as the guard finished his mango, wiped his hands on his shirt, got up from his chair, and slowly walked over to the truck.

"Hot day, Lieutenant," he said in a leisurely manner as he looked the truck over. "What have you got here?"

"Sandbags," Thao replied quickly. "I've got orders to repair the bunker near the house in the back."

"Hah," the guard laughed. "I don't know why anybody would want that one fixed. By the time that old man got there, the danger would be over and besides, he has left orders not to be disturbed."

Thao opened the door, jumped from the truck, and walked up to the guard. He grabbed his collar and pushed it close to his face. "You see how sweaty my uniform is?" he screamed. "You'll notice that the three sitting on the tailgate are also drenched. The reason for this is that we've been working our asses off since early this morning to fill all of these bags. I received an order from my Commanding Officer this morning that the bunker would be repaired and the truck returned no later than three o'clock. He becomes very angry when his orders are not followed. Of course, we could unload all of the bags here, and you could get somebody to help you carry them to the house."

That brought an immediate response. "No, no, there are only two of us here, and we must guard the gate." When the guard was finished walking around the truck, he looked at Thao and rubbed his face. "Well, okay," he said reluctantly. "I'll let you in. But if the old man complains, you tell him that the guard at the gate didn't want to let you in, but you gave him a direct order."

Thao looked at the guard and smiled. "Don't worry, he won't even know we're there."

The guard motioned to his companion to pull back the wire. Tipping his hat as they drove through, Thao moved the truck slowly across the soccer field towards the small house tucked beneath the trees in the far corner.

Reaching the house, he backed the truck along its side, between two of the trees, so only the front was visible. He then hit the flap with his fist. "Okay, Mr. Burt. Let's go."

They would need a space big enough for Courage to crawl over and drag Huy to the front of the truck. Thao and the Chieus started pulling bags from one side and Burt pulled from the other. They were just about through when a voice from the rear of the truck stopped all activity.

"What's going on here?" the voice demanded.

Thao turned quickly. There, at the back of the truck, was an old man wiping his hands on an apron. Dropping the sandbag he was holding, Thao walked to the rear of the truck and jumped to the ground. "I have orders to repair this bunker," he said, wiping loose sand from his uniform.

"Well, you can't do it now," the man whispered angrily. "Mr. Huy is not feeling well and left orders that he did not want to be disturbed. You and your men will have to go. You can come back after three o'clock."

With his humped back, bald head, and bowed legs, he had to be at least seventy years old. By the smell of his clothes, Thao figured this was the cook. "We're not going to make any noise," he whispered back. "All we're going to do is unload the sandbags and place them near the bunker. I'll instruct my men to be extra careful."

"No, no, that will not do," the man whispered harshly, shaking his head. "He is a very light sleeper and would be very angry at me if he found you here. Now," he said, shaking his finger in Thao's face, "you and your men get on that truck and leave here immediately, or I will report you to your Commander."

Thao looked at the old man and shrugged his shoulders. "It's okay with me if you want us to come back later. But someone has to sign my release. I guess that'll have to be you."

"Yes, yes, Lieutenant," he replied quickly. "Give me your paper and I will sign it. Then be on your way."

Reaching in his pocket, he pulled out a piece of paper and slapped it down on the tailgate. After writing "released from detail" on it, he handed the pencil to the old man. "Sign here, and we'll be on our way."

As he leaned over to sign the paper, Thao stepped back, reached in his shirt, and removed the pistol with the silencer. After taking a quick look around to make sure there was no one watching, he aimed the pistol two inches above the old man's left ear and squeezed the trigger. There was a low moan as the lifeless body slumped to the ground. Death was swift—his eyes never closed.

Thao pointed at two of the Chieus to help, and they lifted the body onto the back of the truck.

"It's all clear," he whispered. "Let's go."

In a few minutes there was enough room for Courage to crawl over the top of the bags. As they jumped from the back of the truck, Thao gave him the pistol with the silencer and took his own pistol from its holster.

He then pointed to an open door. "I think that's where the old man came from," he said softly. "It should lead to the kitchen. Let's go in that way." Signaling to the Chieus to watch the front and rear of the truck, Thao and Burt walked slowly towards the door. Peering around, they saw a hallway about twenty feet long with another half-open door at its end. With Thao in the lead, they tiptoed down the tiled hallway. When he reached the door, Thao slowly pushed it open and looked in. This was the main dining room.

Courage looked around. It was like many of the other French-designed houses he had been in. The dining room was in the middle, with everything else branching off from it. The only sounds were the steady ticking of an old clock in the corner and the swishing of the ceiling fan. In the middle of the room was a large table that would seat at least twenty people. This would be where Huy entertained his guests. On the wall next to the clock was a Viet Cong flag and a portrait of Ho Chi Minh.

Burt was tempted to go over and write "yellow power," or "Ho sucks" on the picture, but that would be a dead giveaway that there was an American involved, and could jeopardize the operation. He was also aware that the Agency didn't share his sense of humor.

As they were contemplating their next move, they heard the sloshing of water somewhere off to the right of the dining room. As they looked at each other, Burt nodded. They would check it out.

When they reached the doorway, Courage slowly looked around the corner. Whoever it was, he had his back to them and was washing something in a large tub on a table. He moved quickly to the other side of the doorway and Thao moved up to where he had been. He still had his back to them as he continued noisily moving something up and down in the water.

Thao looked over at Courage. Thao pulled his knife. Slowly, he stepped through the doorway and moved towards the figure who was still busy with his hands in the tub. The room was darker than the others they had been in, and he didn't see that there was a chair in front of him. When Thao hit it, the figure turned quickly around.

He was a young boy wearing an Army uniform. He must have been the servant boy they had been told about, washing dishes in the tub. He was completely startled by the man standing a few feet away with a knife in his hands. He stood there, his eyes bulging in fright, staring at Thao, wondering what he was going to do.

Neither of them moved; they seemed frozen. Courage watched. Kill him, kill him, he wanted to scream out. What the hell are you waiting for? If he screams, he'll let everybody in the house know we're here. As the soldier started to back up, Burt knew he couldn't wait any longer for Thao to act.

As he stepped into the room, the terrified eyes moved quickly to him. Seeing Thao may have frightened the boy, but seeing an American made his eyes bulge more and his mouth fall open. If he was going to cry out, he never got a chance. Courage raised the pistol and hit him with a shot through the heart.

Although he never made a sound, the impact knocked him backwards into the tub and stand, sending all of it crashing to the floor. It sounded like a thousand dishes breaking at the same time. It was loud enough that if there was anybody in the house, they would have heard it.

Moving back through the door, they hid in the shadows of the hallway with weapons ready, waiting for someone to investigate the noise. The five minutes they spent pressed up against the wall seemed like five hours.

When Burt was satisfied that no one was coming, he motioned for Thao to follow him. Back in the dining room, he noticed a darkened hallway off to the right. This would be where the bedrooms were found, and the cook did say that the old man was sleeping. He must be a heavy sleeper, Burt thought, if that noise did not wake him up.

Walking to the first door, he put his ear against it. He then looked up at Thao and shook his head. At the second door he could hear a ceiling fan. Someone was in there, but who? The third door was the same as the first—quiet.

Burt pointed at the second door, thinking, that's where he's got to be. Handing the syringe and the chloroform to Thao, he pulled back the hammer of the pistol with his right hand and wiped the sweat from his left hand onto his pants. Taking a firm grip of the door handle, he pushed the door open a few inches. When he was satisfied it was not locked, he nodded, and they walked quickly into the room.

The room was dark, but there was just enough light coming through the windows that they could see the outline of a bed against the wall. Courage walked over and sat on the edge of the bed, looking at the curled-up figure.

It took his eyes a few seconds to get used to the dark. He thought for sure that they would have awakened him, but the man just lay there snoring. Looking down, Burt shook his head. So this is the famous Mr. Huy, he thought. His frail old body couldn't weigh more than a hundred pounds. How could something so small and wrinkled cause so much misery in this world?

Courage put up his right hand and Thao placed the chloroformed pad in it. Huy would have to be awake for the drug to work. Taking the pistol, he put it between Huy's eyes and gave a slight nudge. The snoring stopped and his eyes opened quickly.

Huy looked up and blinked a few times, as if his eyes were playing tricks on him. He had to be seeing things. How could a foreigner be sitting on his bed with a gun pointed at him?

When he finally realized that there was nothing wrong with his eyes he tried to sit up, but he was no match for Courage, who forced him back down and put the pad over his face. Turning on his side, he pushed the pad away. "Please, please," he pleaded. "Kill me if you have to, but don't harm the girl. I will do anything you ask, just spare her."

Grabbing the old man, Burt turned him over and pinned his arms against the wall. "What the hell is this guy talking about?" he whispered, as he picked up the pad and tried to put it over Huy's face. Huy continued to turn his face from side to side, calling out to spare the girl.

"Thao, hold his head in place so I can get this stuff in him."

As they held him down, Courage saw something coming towards the bed. Before he could move, it had jumped onto the bed with them. It was a small girl. She couldn't be more than three or four years old. She threw her arms around the old man, burying her head in his chest.

"Who the hell is this?" Burt demanded.

Huy slowly looked up at the American. "She is my grand-daughter," he answered angrily. "She is the most precious thing in my life. I know what you've come to do to me. I can accept that. But she knows nothing, there is no need to kill her. Please, I beg of you." Even through the look of defiance, his eyes filled with tears as he held her close and stroked her long, black hair.

"We're not here to kill you," Burt said. "You're not that lucky. We're going to go on a little trip together. You cooperate with us, and I'll see nothing happens to the girl. You screw up one time, and she dies. So starting right now, her life is in your hands."

Huy continued stroking her hair as he listened to Courage. After a short pause he looked up. "I guess I'm in no position to argue right now. What is it you want me to do?"

Taking the syringe from Thao, he grabbed the old man's arm. "I think this will be a little more effective. I want you to relax. I'm going to give you a shot. It won't hurt you, it'll just make you sleepy."

The hardest part of administering the shot was finding a vein in the small arm. There was no resistance as he inserted the needle and slowly pushed the plunger. By the time he pulled it out, Huy was fast asleep. Pulling the girl away, Burt handed her to Thao.

"What are we going to do with her?" Thao asked. "We sure can't take her along. She'll slow us down."

"Well, we can't leave her here. She's old enough to tell what happened, and could identify us. I figure we can take her along until we ditch the truck. Then we can drop her off in some village." Burt could tell by Thao's expression that he wasn't pleased about taking another passenger along.

As Courage picked up the limp body and threw it over his shoulder, he turned to Thao. "I know that when you agreed to join this operation, the plan was only to bring him back. There was nothing said about any of his relatives. The only other choice we have is to put a bullet through her head. After what he did to your family, if anybody has the right, I guess you do. But it wouldn't bring any of them back, and you wouldn't be any better than this old man on my shoulder.

"I think I've gotten to know you pretty well since we started out together. I know we're from different cultures and he stands for everything you hate, but the way he pleaded for her life, he's not going to try anything that will jeopardize it. I say she comes with us."

Thao listened carefully, his eyes darting between Courage and the girl he was holding. He had heard how the old man begged for her life. "Okay," he answered. "You're right, he owes me. But the future of my country rests in getting him back. I'll get my revenge someday. Okay, we'll take her along."

After chloroforming the girl, they went back through the dining room and out the door to where the truck was waiting. After putting Huy and the girl on the tailgate, Thao told one of the Chieus to get the body from the kitchen.

After Huy and the girl were lifted over the sandbags and placed in the corner, they all started replacing the bags. One of the Chieus reported that there was a well in the backyard. When all of the bags were in place, Thao ordered that the two dead bodies be dumped in the well.

When they were finished, Thao jumped in the front and peeked through the flap. "Are we ready, Mr. Burt?"

"Ready. They'll be asleep for hours. Just get us through that front gate."

The same soldiers were still drilling on the soccer field as they lumbered by. "You're finished so soon, Lieutenant," the sentry joked as the truck came to a stop. "You've got a lot of bags left."

Thao looked at the guard and laughed. "It wasn't the old man, it was his cook, and I wasn't going to argue with a meat cleaver. I dropped just enough bags and told him to fix it himself."

"I told you so," the guard smiled, pulling back the wire. "That old man doesn't like anybody disturbing his sleep."

Pulling through the gate, Thao turned down the main street. It was nap time, and with the exception of just a few vendors peddling their wares, the street was deserted. For the first time, Thao wished he hadn't sold his watch. He needed to know what time it was.

Glancing up at the sun, he figured it wasn't quite one o'clock. With Huy not being missed until after three, they had two hours to put some miles between them and Dien Ban.

At the edge of town was a checkpoint with a manually-operated gate. As he brought the truck to a stop, the guard in the small hut walked towards him. "If you were supposed to be in that last convoy," he called out, "they left over an hour ago." Jumping up on the running board, he looked inside the truck. "Are you carrying food or something else I could use?" he asked.

"No," Thao growled. "All we've got are sandbags that we're hauling south of here, to repair bunkers. If you want to eat one of them, help yourself."

After peering under the canvas, the guard was satisfied. "How about some cigarettes? You got any you can spare?"

Reaching in his pocket, Thao grabbed a pack and angrily threw them on the ground. "Damn it," he screamed. "I'm already an hour behind and it will take the rest of the day to catch up, and you stand here asking me stupid questions! You get your ass over there and lift that gate, or I'll report you for trying to steal government property and being disrespectful to an officer!"

Jumping to the ground, the guard scooped up the cigarettes and opened the gate. "Thank you, Lieutenant," he called out as they drove through.

When they were out of sight, Thao rolled up the small flap. "I know it's hot back there. I'll leave this open so you can get the breeze. But I'll have to drop it if we see anything."

From the little Burt could see, the Ho Chi Minh Trail looked like an expressway compared to the other roads around there. It must have been a main road at one time, between the North and South when the French were in charge. High trees lined both sides, making it virtually impossible to see from the air. That had to be the reason they were running convoys in the daytime.

It was clear ahead and Thao put the pedal to the floor. There was a lot of dust being kicked up, forcing Courage to cover his mouth. "Now I know why they call this the 'Yellow Brick Road,'" he coughed.

Twice they had to slow down to ford a stream, and once they were flagged down by a unit stopped alongside the trail. The Sergeant said that one of the men had shot himself in the foot and he wanted to know if they had any medical supplies. Thao explained that all they had were sandbags, and they moved on.

An afternoon downpour grounded some of the dust and cooled off the inside of the truck. Burt checked their passengers' pulses every half-hour. After all they had gone through, he didn't want Huy to die from an overdose. There were more troops walking south, but they moved out of the way as the truck drove by.

When the sun started to duck behind the trees, Burt mentioned to Thao that they should start looking for a place to camp for the night. They had made good mileage that day, and there was no sense in pressing their luck. A lone truck traveling at night could easily be stopped and searched.

Coming into a clearing, Thao saw a long stretch of elephant grass on the side of the road. Making a sharp turn, the truck crashed through the brush. It was taller than the truck, and the brown blades slapped against the windshield. He couldn't see where they were going, and he had to struggle with the steering wheel to keep going forward.

When he estimated that they were about a quarter of a mile from the road, Thao began driving in circles, matting down the grass. Once the area was flat enough, he turned off the engine. "How's this, Mr. Burt?"

"Good enough," he replied. "Let's start pulling bags so we can get out of this sweatbox."

When there were enough bags removed to provide a crawl space, Courage gently handed Huy and the girl through, and then crawled out himself. "Whew," he said, wiping his face. "It's hot back there."

"How are they doing?" Thao asked.

Burt looked down and shrugged his shoulders. "Well, their pulses are strong. From what we gave them, I figure they should be coming around in a little while. In the meantime, why don't you put the Chieus out? Take them about a hundred yards in each direction. Give them their can and string, but tell them to pull it only if they see or hear somebody. There is to be no noise. Give them their rations before they leave."

It was almost dark when Thao returned. Burt had the tailgate of the truck down and was sitting on the back, eating out of a can with his knife. "Jump up here," he called out. "We're having the blue plate special tonight—rotted rice with meat. At least, that's what I think it is. The meat part is the one that crawls around."

As Thao jumped up on the back, Burt tossed him a can and then placed the lantern between them. It wasn't bright enough to light up the area, but at least they could see what they were doing.

They were almost finished when Huy moaned and moved his arm. "Well," Burt remarked, "it looks like our guest is finally waking up."

As Huy slowly opened his eyes, the top of the truck came into view. Although he was still disoriented, he knew he wasn't in his bed. As the drug started to wear off, he remembered what had happened. His eyes now focused on the two figures sitting on the sandbags, eating and looking at him.

"Where is my granddaughter?" he screamed in a high, squeaky voice. "I demand to know what you've done with her!"

Courage was close enough to reach out with his size eleven boot and push it up against Huy's throat, pinning him to the floor and cutting off any further conversation. "Shut up," he whispered. "She's right over here. She's still asleep and should be coming out of it in a few minutes. When she does wake up, she's going to be one scared little girl. You had better make sure she doesn't scream or cry. If she does, it won't last long. Need I say anymore?"

Burt could tell by the look in Huy's eyes that he had gotten the message. "Now," he said softly, "I'm going to take my
foot away. If you talk any louder than I'm talking right now,
the foot goes back for the rest of the night. Do we understand
each other?" Huy gave a short nod, and Burt pulled the boot
back.

Squinting through the poor light, Huy could make out his
granddaughter's form on the other side of the truck. Moving
on his hands and knees, he picked her up and cradled her in
his arms.

"May I have some water?" he asked.

Burt reached down, picked up a canteen, and handed it to
him. Huy tore off a part of his shirt, poured some water on it,
and then carefully patted her lips.

"Why have you done this to us?" Huy asked as he moist-
ened the cloth again. "I'm just an old man, living out the last
few years of my life with my only living relative. We're of no
importance to anybody."

Courage, who was eating another can of rice, chuckled at
the remark. "An old man," he repeated. "You think I walked
through this shit hole to bring back some old croaker who was
only a low-level party member? You don't give us very much
credit, do you? I know who you are. I've read your file, from
the first time you and Ho were in the slammer together to
when you liquidated millions of your own people. I know goddamned well who you are."

The girl was starting to respond. She rolled her head from
side to side and started to cough. "There, there," Huy said softly. "It's all right, Grandfather is with you. There's nothing to be
afraid of." He gave her a few small sips of water from the canteen, which she swallowed freely.

"You remember what I told you," Burt advised. "She's got
to stay quiet."

Huy slowly looked up at the American. "You don't have to
worry about her making any noise. She hasn't cried or spoken

a word since the day her parents were killed. She was two when it happened, and now she's three and a half. It's been a year and a half since she's uttered any noise at all. She's been to the finest doctors. They say time is the only cure."

Reaching into a backpack, Burt found a can of rations, opened it, and handed it to Huy. "Here," he said. "Try and get her to eat some of this. It tastes like hell, but it's filling."

The girl's face wrinkled after the first spoonful, and she tried to spit it out. The old man told her that she had to be a good soldier, that they were going on a journey, and that if she didn't eat, she would get sick. He promised her that if she ate all of her food, he would give her anything she wanted when they returned. When the last of it was forced down, he praised her for being such a brave little girl.

She soon closed her eyes and started falling asleep again. Courage threw him a blanket, and Huy made a bed for her. He only had to sit by her for a few minutes before she was fast asleep. Bending over, he kissed his granddaughter on the forehead and stood up. Reaching in his shirt pocket, he pulled out a pair of wire-rimmed glasses and put them on. It was about time he got a better look at his captors.

As he moved towards them, Burt now understood why the operation called for Huy to be transported. His body was bent and his legs wobbled when he walked. He wouldn't be able to walk a hundred yards on his own.

Huy looked at the American and forced a smile. "From what has happened today, I presume that we will be together for a while—that is, until our forces find us. In the meantime, would you like me to call you 'Mr. American,' or do you have a given name?"

"Oh, I'm sorry. How inconsiderate of me," Burt answered smugly. "Here I go, snapping up somebody right from his bed and I never even introduce myself. You can call me Burt or Courage, whichever suits you best."

Huy continued studying the American. "You speak our language very well. You are one of the few foreigners I have met who can speak our dialect. I wonder how a young and intelligent man like yourself could be convinced by your CIA to try something as foolish as kidnapping me. What kind of madmen do they have in Langley these days?"

Tossing the empty can on the ground, Burt stood up and looked down at the old man. "What makes you think I'm with the CIA?"

Huy laughed. "Mr. Courage, as you can see, I'm old and can't get around as well as I used to, but I'm not senile. I've been monitoring your operations since you were in Laos. I must admit that your Phoenix program has met with some success, but that will be short-lived once you leave. No, only the Agency would know who I am and where I was located. Your bumbling military could never have pulled this off. Even with the most modern equipment in the world, they would have found some way to screw it up. I must congratulate you. As foolish as this entire plot is, I would never have expected it.

"So, now that we know each other, where do we go from here?"

"Who I work for really doesn't matter," Burt replied. "What matters is that I have you, and you're coming back with us. You can make it easy or difficult; it doesn't matter to me."

Huy's expression quickly vanished. "Temporarily," he added sharply. "We are still a long way from your lines. Once I am reported missing, liberation forces will search this area. This foolish plan has no chance of succeeding, and you're going to die for nothing."

"Well, before all that, I want you to meet the man who will take over in case something happens to me." He called for Thao to join them.

As the American's cohort approached, Huy squinted at the figure. He remembered that there had been two people in his room, but it was dark and he never got a good look at the other person. The first thing Huy recognized was the lapel of his uniform, with the rank of First Lieutenant. The old man's eyes burned with hatred as he looked into the face of his countryman. The American was a capitalist and was doing this for money, but this man was betraying his country.

"You are a traitor to your country," Huy screamed in a high-pitched voice. "You shall have your tongue cut out!" He then spit in Thao's face.

Huy may have talked to Generals and party members in that manner when he was in Hanoi, where he wielded a lot of power, but here, he was just an old man in the back of a truck. If there was anything more he wanted to say, it was cut short as Thao grabbed him by the throat, lifted him off the floor, and slammed his body against the side of the truck.

"You call me a traitor," he answered softly. "You murdering son of a bitch. You turned my country into a cemetery, and now you want to do the same thing down here. You're lucky this American is along, or you'd never have made it out of that bed."

The old man was kicking his feet and trying to pull Thao's hands from his throat, but he was too weak.

Courage came up behind Thao and grabbed his wrist. "For Christ's sake, let him go. I didn't go through all this to have you kill him. You gave me your word when we left that you would do everything possible to bring him back. That's the objective of this operation. Now let him go."

Thao was still staring at the old man as he released his grip and pulled his hands away.

"Why don't you go for a walk, Thao? You look like you could use some fresh air."

As Thao jumped off the truck and disappeared, Burt walked over and helped the gasping Huy sit up on the sandbags. "That is a very violent man," Huy said, rubbing his throat. "He would have killed me if you hadn't pulled him off."

The old man was still having trouble breathing. Courage handed him a canteen and told him to take a few swallows. When he was finished, Burt reached into his pocket and offered him a cigarette. Huy's hands were shaking so badly that Burt had to hold them steady to get it lit.

"He's got a good reason to hate you. You killed most of his family in one of your purges. He holds you personally responsible. If something ever happened to me, he'd drop both you and the girl before I even hit the ground. You had better hope that I stay healthy."

It took two more drinks of water and another cigarette before Huy regained his composure. Looking over the top of his glasses, he studied the American's face. "Mr. Courage," he finally said. "It appears that we have a unique situation here. If you die, I die and she dies. I don't care about myself—I've dedicated my life to the revolution and am prepared to die for the liberation of my country. But the little girl over there is all I have in the world. Her father was my only child. He and his wife were killed in one of your air strikes. She was there when it happened and was the only survivor. She hasn't spoken since that day.

"I would do anything in the world to assure her safety. But, if something should happen to you, I'm sure your friend Mr. Thao would take great pleasure in killing both of us. And like you said, he feels it is his right. Therefore, I am willing to make a bargain with you."

"A bargain, huh? What kind of a bargain?"

"When we start off tomorrow, you leave her along the trail where she can be found. That way she won't be with us in case something happens. In return, I'll go anywhere you want willingly. I won't give you any trouble, and I promise I won't try to escape."

Burt looked down at the old man, pulled out two cigarettes, lit them, and shoved one between Huy's lips. "Bargain," he scoffed. "That's no bargain, that would be suicide if something went wrong. We've got a long way to go and things could get a little hairy. She's the best bargaining chip I've got. You don't think I'm just going to drop her off and let her describe what happened. We wouldn't get more than five miles. No, she goes all the way."

Huy looked at the American and nodded his head. "I see," he replied. "It appears that you have me, what you Americans say, over a barrel. How ironic that under different circumstances we would kill each other. Now, to survive, we must make sure each of us lives."

"Those are the fortunes of war," Burt replied, picking up a blanket and some netting and tossing them to Huy. "Here, you can sleep next to her. Put some of the netting over her or the mosquitoes will eat her alive."

As Huy curled up next to the girl, Courage sat in the darkness, thinking. Once they left the truck, Huy would have to be drugged before being placed in the casket. There wouldn't be enough room for him and the girl. They had no other choice; she would have to be chloroformed and left in some bushes. If she was dropped off in a well-traveled area she would be found in a few hours, and they could put a lot of miles on in that time. If not, she would die.

As he jumped down from the truck, Burt could make out Thao's outline leaning up against the side. "Have you checked the map?" he whispered.

"Yes, Mr. Burt," he whispered back. "If we make the same mileage as today, we should hit the area where we leave the trail by tomorrow afternoon. If we put the beeper out, which has a range of twenty miles, we should be picked up the next day.

"The only problem I foresee," he continued, "is that once we leave the truck and start heading east, we're bound to run into some local force or NVA units. Now, we can get by with the story that the casket contains the remains of a political party member being brought back to his native village for burial. I can talk us through that. And all of the journalists want to see what's going on at the front; you look enough like an East German not to arouse any suspicions, plus you have papers. But we can't take the girl along, even if she can't talk. There could be some questions that I wouldn't have any answers for. And like you said, getting him back is what this operation is all about."

"I know," Burt sighed. "I've thought about it and decided that as soon as we leave the truck, we should give her a little whiff and stash her in the bush. We should be safely back at the Special Forces camp before she even wakes up.

"Now, let's get back in the truck and get some sleep. We've got a long day ahead of us tomorrow."

# TEN

At first light Thao left to bring in the guards. Courage awakened the old man and the girl, and gave each of them a rice cake and a cup of water. "Eat this before we leave," he ordered. "There won't be anything to eat or drink while we're traveling."

When Thao returned, Huy and the girl were placed up front with Courage, and the sandbags were replaced. The old man looked at the casket, then at Burt. "I presume that's for me?" he asked. His question went unanswered.

When all of the bags were in place, Courage sat across from the old man and his granddaughter. Holding up the syringe, he looked at Huy. "I can use this stuff to knock you both out, but it's not very comfortable. If you promise to just sit back and stay quiet, I won't use it." Pulling the pistol from his belt, he waved it towards them. "On the other hand, if you make one move to give us away, I'll shoot her between the eyes and you in both kneecaps. Then, just before they take us, I'll finish you off. But you'll see the girl die first."

Holding his granddaughter close to his chest, Huy stared at the American. "I guess," he replied, "that anybody who would go on a mission like this would be crazy enough to follow through with such a threat. You have my word; we'll remain silent."

The trail was clear as they drove away from their camp and headed south. With the flap open, Burt could see that the farther south they went, the less tree cover there was. The breeze through the small opening helped cool off the small area they were confined to. As they followed the winding trail through streams and up and down mountains, Burt thought about how lucky they had been so far. With few exceptions, everything had gone according to plan. Within a few hours they would be home free.

After going through the daily afternoon downpour, Burt had just leaned back to relax when the truck started to slow down and there was a rap on the canvas.

"Mr. Burt," Thao called out, "there is a convoy of trucks stopped just ahead. It looks like some of them are stuck in the mud. It's too narrow to pass. What should we do?"

"Damn it," Burt swore under his breath. It could take the rest of the day to get them moving, and a truck carrying sandbags this far south would stick out like a sore thumb.

"Okay," he sighed. "We can't do anything until the road is cleared. Pull off to the side and turn the engine off."

Thao was just about to do as Burt said when the trail before them burst into flames with a deafening roar. His eyes widened, his mouth dropped, and both hands froze to the wheel. Courage saw the same thing. They were transfixed as the massive explosions came at them faster than the eye could see. They were caught in the middle of an air strike, and there wasn't a damned thing they could do.

The explosions ripped the ground, splintered palm trees, and disintegrated the trucks ahead of them. "Holy Christ," was all Burt got out before ear-shattering explosions on both sides sent pieces of canvas and sandbags catapulting through the air. Burt could feel the truck starting to roll and the weight of the sandbags hitting his body—then there was nothing.

Thao held on tight to the steering wheel as they rolled down the embankment. The truck rolled over twice before stopping on its side. When they were sure it wasn't going to roll anymore, Thao and a Chieu crawled out through the passenger-side window.

Running to the rear, they found that two of the Chieus had been thrown clear. They had a few cuts and bruises and said they were okay. The other one had landed in the path of the truck and it had rolled over him. He was conscious, but complained that he had no feeling in his legs.

Huy and the girl had also been thrown clear and appeared to be uninjured, but there was no sign of the American. Looking around, Thao decided that Burt had to be under the pile of sandbags. "He's got to be under here," he called out to the Chieus. "Let's start pulling these bags off!"

They had removed about ten of the bags when Thao noticed a knee sticking up. "Don't worry, Mr. Burt, we'll get you out!" He ordered the Chieus to work faster, and breathed a sigh of relief when he heard coughing and spitting from underneath the pile.

Burt was still spitting sand when they removed the last sandbag. "Here," Thao said, handing him a canteen, "wash it out with this."

It took four mouthfuls of rinsing and spitting before Burt was able to talk. "Damn," he said, feeling a sharp pain in his left leg as he sat up slowly. "Did we lose anybody?" He looked around and saw that all but one were accounted for. "We're lucky any of us are alive."

Thao bent down and examined the injured leg. "It's lucky we happened to be at the end," he commented. "The ones ahead caught the brunt." Looking both ways to make sure there was no one within listening distance, Thao looked at Courage. "It looks like everybody is all right, except one of the Chieus. The truck rolled over him. He has no feeling in his legs, and there is no way he can be moved. Other than that, it's just a few scratches and bruises."

Burt's knee was now throbbing with pain. "Okay," he said, gritting his teeth. "Get me to my feet. I want to see if I can walk."

When they slowly stood him up, the pain was so bad, he wished he was unconscious again. "Damn!" he screamed, falling back and grabbing his knee. "I think something's broken."

Thao carefully rolled up Burt's pants leg and began squeezing softly, starting at the ankle, and working his way up. As he reached the knee area, Courage bit his lip. "That's it, right there."

Thao leaned back and rubbed his face. "I'm no doctor, but it's my guess you have either a broken or badly bruised kneecap. I've got some aspirin here to give you for the pain, but you're not going to be able to travel. We're at the bottom of an embankment. We can rest here for a while."

Looking up, Burt shook his head. "Are you kidding? We can't stay here. This place will be crawling with people in a little while, looking for survivors. We've got to get out of here. Help me get up there and we'll see what we've got."

Every movement sent pain through his body as they labored to the top of the embankment. Burt knew there was nothing more devastating than a B-52 strike, and this was no exception. As they looked down the trail, thick black smoke hung in the air. As far as they could see, the area was a smoldering heap of upturned earth, splintered trees, and burning trucks. Bomb craters were everywhere, and there were secondary explosions still sending flames fifty feet into the air from the ammunition in the vehicles. If there was anybody still alive, they were staying under cover. There was no movement to be seen.

Burt looked over at Thao and shook his head. "There's no way we could even attempt to get through there. Trees ripped up by their roots—it would take a half a day to go a hundred yards through that stuff." Another explosion made them cover up.

Thao agreed. "Not to mention that we could also get blown up. Let's get out of here."

When they reached the bottom of the embankment they decided that there was only one alternative. "I figure if we move about a mile east," Courage said, "we can rest up and wait for the trail to be repaired. I don't know how the hell we're going to get another truck though. Maybe we can pick off a straggler."

Thao said that he would carry the girl and lead the way. One of the Chieus could carry Huy, and the other two could get on each side of Burt and be his crutches. As long as he could hobble on one leg, they could at least be on the move.

As they gathered up what would be taken along, Courage looked over at the injured Chieu lying motionless in the grass, staring at the sky. When they were ready to leave, he waved his hand for Thao to come over.

"I'm sorry," Burt said sadly. "I wish we could take him along, but we're going to be slowed down enough, and if he's got no feeling in his legs, his spine is probably severed. We can't take the chance of leaving him here alive. Make it look like he was killed in the air strike."

"I will take care of it, Mr. Burt," Thao replied. "It's a task I'm not looking forward to, but he knew the risk just like the rest of us. He'll just want to make sure his family is paid."

"You can tell him I'll see to it personally."

They had gone a short way when Thao announced that he had left something back at the truck and he had to go back. When he returned, he gave Burt a nod to show that it had been taken care of. The three Chieus looked at each other, and then at Burt and Thao. They knew what had happened. They also knew there was nothing else that could have been done.

"Let's move out," Thao called, picking up the girl.

For the first fifty yards there was tall elephant grass which looked at least eight feet high. They had to move slowly, gently pushing the razor-sharp blades aside. Then they came to bamboo thickets and thick, tangled vines. Thao had to set the girl down, cut a fifty-foot path with the machete, return, pick her up, and carry her to where he had finished cutting. Then he'd put her down and start over again.

The Chieus who were helping Courage walk were both about five-foot-seven; trying to support Burt's six-foot frame while carrying equipment, they were having a hard time keeping up.

Thao figured they had been moving for about an hour when he called a halt. Dripping with sweat and exhausted from swinging the machete, he signaled that they would take a fifteen-minute break. He walked back to where Burt and the Chieus lay exhausted on the ground, and checked Burt's knee.

"Let me wet some palm leaves and wrap them tightly around it. They may help bring down the swelling."

"How's the old man?" Burt asked between breaths. "It's got to be over a hundred degrees in here. Make sure he's got enough water."

When Thao was finished dressing the injury he checked on Huy and gave him water. They were just about ready to move out when they heard the sound of a truck stopping near the area they had left an hour ago. The voices were faint. After a few minutes they heard the doors slam, the engine start, and the sound of the motor fading into the distance.

"Okay," Thao whispered. "Break's over, we gotta move."

With the intense heat they had to stop every fifteen minutes. Everyone had been bitten by so many insects that they weren't even swatting them anymore. There were still a few hours of daylight left when Thao found a small stream. Setting the girl down, he dropped the machete and collapsed on the ground.

Courage let out a groan of relief as the Chieus eased him down and propped him against a tree. "Damned Agency," he mumbled to himself. They could have asked the military to postpone air strikes on the trail for a week or two without giving the operation away. There wouldn't have been any questions. Now here they were in the middle of nowhere, with him unable to walk.

Loosening the compress made by Thao, Burt exposed his swollen knee. His kneecap was now as big as a baseball, and sent a sharp pain up his leg when he touched it.

Thao and the Chieus cooled off in the stream. Afterward, Thao ripped the bottom of his shirt off, dipped it in the water, and walked over to where Courage was sitting. "It doesn't look good, Mr. Burt," he said, gently wrapping the new compress around his knee. "You're not going to be able to travel until that swelling goes down. If you try in this terrain and humidity, you'll be dead in a few days." He looked over to where Huy and the girl were slumped against a nearby tree. "By the looks of him, he won't make it much longer either. This area is pretty desolate. We're safe here for a little while."

As Thao finished with his knee, Burt had a decision to make. He was right, there was no way they could move like this. It would take months to get back. His knee would eventually get better, but the way the old man was breathing, he wouldn't last a week. There had to be a better way.

"Okay," he said, reaching into his pocket and pulling out a cigarette. "At first light tomorrow, take one of the Chieus and go back to where the air strike was. Maybe there's some way we can go around. I doubt there's anything left that's driveable, but see what you can find."

"Very good," Thao answered. "We're going to need supplies anyway. There should be some things I can pick up. We should be back before dark."

It was a sleepless night for Burt. The netting kept insects away, but any slight movement sent sharp pain streaking through his body, waking him instantly.

Before leaving in the morning, Thao dipped the compress into the water and rewrapped Burt's knee gently. "It looks like it hasn't gotten any worse," he commented. When he was finished, he pulled out his pistol and dropped it at Burt's side. "Just in case you get a few visitors," he said.

After they disappeared into the bush, Courage looked around. There was enough bamboo here to make himself a crutch. After one of the Chieus cut him a five-foot piece, he started smoothing off the rough edges with his knife.

He was still cutting away when Huy opened his eyes. "Mr. Courage," he said softly, "I was wondering if you could spare some food and water for us."

Reaching into the pack, Burt grabbed two cans of food and a canteen and tossed them over. "Here, help yourself."

Huy woke his granddaughter and they ate in silence. When they were finished he put the blanket around the girl and crawled over to where Courage was leaning against a tree. Huy handed him the canteen and, picking out a tree opposite Burt, he leaned back and watched curiously as the arm support was tied to the top of the makeshift crutch.

"You're looking pretty good today," Burt joked, breaking the silence. "That cool night air has you looking much better."

Huy slowly bowed his head and smiled. "I wish I could say the same for you," he replied. "It appears that your injuries will prevent you from going much further, and that thing you're putting together will be useless in this terrain. I would say, my American friend, that this suicidal plan has ended in failure. And the amusing part is that it was your own people who caused it. It's hard for me to believe that your CIA would allow such a blunder. Such a well-executed plan—you knew exactly where I was, and when to strike. And then to have your hopes dashed by American bombs!"

His eyes narrowed as he looked at Burt. "But on the other hand, maybe you weren't supposed to get back. Maybe that air attack was supposed to kill all of us. It wouldn't be the first time they sacrificed one of their own. You are nothing to them—just a pawn to be used in one of their games.

"We could return to the liberated area. You would receive the best of medical attention, and I would grant you political asylum. You have proven that you are brave and dedicated, but in your condition, and with liberation forces searching every-where, it will only be a matter of time before we are found, and you will be killed. You are still a young man. I'm offering you life instead of death in this stinking jungle. Besides, if you saw how happy people are in the liberated areas, it would change your perspective."

Using thin strips of vine, Burt secured the top of the crutch. He eased himself up, and put it under his right arm. "Not too bad," he commented as he hobbled around in a cir-cle. "At least I can get around."

Looking over at the old man, he smiled. "Liberation forces, liberated areas. Where the hell do you get off using the word 'liberated'? I happened to be in Hue after your liberated forces left. I happened to see a few of the mass graves of the ones who were liberated. Thousands of men, women, and children; entire families butchered. Is that what you call liberation?"

"They were traitors to the revolution," Huy shouted, shak-ing his fist. "They were corrupted by you Americans. They had to be punished for their crimes."

"Crimes! What the hell crime can a two-year-old baby com-mit?"

"You will never understand because you are an American," he countered in his high, squeaky voice. "No revolution has ever succeeded that did not eliminate all of the opposition. Read your history, Mr. Courage. If even one element is allowed to exist it will rise up and the revolution will fail. It's just like your body when you are sick. You take medication to kill the germs. If you don't take enough and they are not all killed, the disease will return. You will only get better when they have all been destroyed. All of the germs in this country must be destroyed before we can get well. And that is what this war is about."

Limping back to the tree, Burt eased himself down to the ground. "If I take about an inch off the bottom, it should be just about right." As he started to cut, he glanced over at Huy.

"So, you've got to get rid of all them germs, huh. I guess that's the part you like best. Then you've got your buddies, the Khmer Rouge in Cambodia. They're even worse than you when it comes to brutality. I wonder how many germs they'll have to kill if they ever take over?"

"How dare you lecture me on morality," Huy interrupted angrily. "I am well versed in your history. Your race has been responsible for more death and destruction than all others combined. You have used war and killing to satisfy the ruling class, to steal land and enslave its people back in your history to the Inquisition, when people were tortured and put to death if they didn't believe in your God. And the two World Wars killed millions, but still you did not learn.

"And you Americans are the worst. You were the only people to ever use nuclear weapons, not only on military targets, but on civilian-populated cities—hundreds of thousands of innocent people vaporized at the snap of a finger.

"Then when the war is over, you conduct trials for the war criminals and make them into a big media event. The Americans want to show the world that there will be no mercy for those who have committed crimes against humanity. I believe they were called the Nuremberg trials.

"What about the crimes against the innocent people of Nagasaki and Hiroshima? Was that fewer people than the Nazis killed?" Huy paused and smiled. "But, as the fortunes of war go, there are never any criminals on the winning side. You foolish, foolish Americans. You believe that everything should be done your way. You push your way into a country uninvited, your pockets bulging with money. Then, when all else fails, you say that what this country needs are free elections." Leaning over, he spit on the ground. "There are no such things as free elections. There is nothing free in this world.

"America may possess the latest in modern warfare equipment, but you'll never win this war. I have an inexhaustible supply of people who are willing to die for the revolution. And

that, my American friend, is why you'll leave here the same way
as the French did, with your tail between your legs."

Leaning back against the tree, he continued, "You have to
admit that your own God once said, 'the meek shall inherit the
earth.' Or don't you read the Bible?"

Courage stopped cutting and thought about the question.
"You're right," he replied after a short pause. "But I don't
think he meant they were going to do it with AK-47s."

"Ah," Huy scoffed. "You joke now, but when you are tracked
down and killed by our forces, we'll see how funny you are
then."

Burt turned quickly and pointed at Huy. "Until that happens," he said sharply, "I'm in charge. And if I have to take you
with one crutch or no crutch, you're going with us. Now if you
don't mind, this capitalistic warmonger would like to get a little snooze in before Thao gets back. Why don't you move back
to where your girl is. I think she's awake."

* * * * *

It was late in the afternoon when the Chieu on guard signaled that Thao and one of the Chieus were back. Courage
thought they were making a lot of noise until he saw Thao
leading a water buffalo. Where the hell did he find that? Burt
wondered.

After tying the animal to a tree, Thao walked over to where
Courage was resting, threw off his helmet, and wiped his forehead. Picking up a canteen, he took a long drink, and what
water was left he poured over his head.

"Well," he said after a minute's rest, "we can forget about
going south. The area is a mess. From what I could see it looks
like an entire battalion was hit. It'll take at least a week to
clean up the bodies and debris. The bridge was also
destroyed." Thao drew the map from inside his shirt. "It looks
like the only way back is to head east. This is pretty desolate

territory and it's off the main infiltration routes. I doubt we'll see very many people for a while."

Courage looked over at the buffalo, slowly swishing its tail and grazing lazily on banana leaves. "I suppose," he sighed, "we're all going to ride on the T-bone express. Hell, I'll be older than the old man by the time we get back."

"Mr. Burt," Thao replied, somewhat offended. "My people have used this animal for centuries as a means of transportation. They are sturdy and good on narrow trails. I worked many years in the rice paddies with them, and they are easy to handle if you know how. After I've rested, we'll make a bamboo stretcher large enough to carry you and our guests and all of our supplies. It may be a bit primitive, but he'll be able to drag it through anything."

"Where the hell did you find him?" Burt asked.

"He was wandering around near the strike area. They were probably using him to carry supplies. In all of the confusion, he just wandered off. He must have been pretty close—he got a few cuts. But that won't slow him down."

By the time the sun went down, Thao and the Chieus had put together a stretcher using belts, strings, and vines. Thao had the three Chieus sit on it while he led the water buffalo around in a circle to make sure it was strong enough.

They left at first light. There were only a few areas along the way where Thao had to use the machete. When they stopped that night, he figured they had made ten miles. "That's further than we'd have gone waiting for the trail to be cleared," he said.

★       ★       ★       ★       ★

He was right about the area being desolate. They traveled for five more days without seeing a living soul. Bananas and mangos were plentiful, and Courage started to wonder if they were still in Vietnam.

On the sixth day they came across a trail with fresh foot-prints, and that night the sound of a plane could be heard in the distance.

Thao, ready for his nightly check of Burt's knee, tilted his ears towards the noise. "We must be getting closer," he said. "And by the prints we saw today, we'll be running into civi-lization pretty soon. Let's see how your knee is doing." Carefully unrolling the compress, he took a long look. "Well, it looks like the swelling has gone down. How does it feel?"

"Not too bad. I can put a little weight on it, but I'm still not ready for a foot race." He then looked into Thao's eyes. "That's why we've got to do some serious talking. I know that once we get closer to the lines, we're probably going to have to make it on foot. If and when that happens, and I can't make it, you take Huy, the girl, and the Chieus and make it back to friendly lines. Tell them where I am, and they'll send out a rescue team to pick me up."

He stiffened as Thao tightened the bandage a bit more roughly than usual. "This must be another one of your American jokes," he replied.

"It's no joke," Burt snapped. "The primary purpose of this operation is to get that old man back. We're all aware of the risks, and I can't allow my handicap to jeopardize the success of this mission. Hell, I can survive out here. I've done it for years."

Thao finished with the wrapping, stood up, poured two cups of tea, and returned. "Leave you behind," he said sarcas-tically, handing Burt a cup. "Let's say that we followed your orders and hid you out someplace and did make it back to friendly lines. If it was a South Vietnamese unit, we'd be shot just from the uniforms we're wearing.

"Now let's assume we get really lucky and make it to an American unit. I tell them that this is the Vice President of North Vietnam and his granddaughter and that there is an

American CIA Agent hiding out in the bush who would appreciate having a chopper sent out to pick him up.

"Knowing the Americans like I do, by the time they finished laughing I'd be in a prisoner of war camp, they probably would let the old man go, not knowing who he is, and you'd be old and gray before you ever saw a rescue team.

"Besides, you yourself said that there had to be an American present from start to finish. Those are the orders and that's the way we're going back. You should at least be able to walk in a day or so."

Burt sipped his tea as he listened to Thao. He was right; being off course like they were, without an American to do some talking, they'd never make it. "All right," he said reluctantly. "We'll play it by ear. But if it ever comes down to the jumping-off point where either one of us could prevent Huy from reaching safe hands, I'll make the decision on who goes and who stays. And that's final."

Thao lit up two cigarettes and handed one to Burt. "Agreed."

The next afternoon they found an abandoned cart with a broken wheel alongside the trail. Thao estimated that it would take about two hours to fix. With a cart they could move four times faster than with the clumsy stretcher. It would also be a lot more comfortable for them to ride in.

When they were finished with the wheel, they filled the cart with straw and leaves. "There, Mr. Burt," Thao said, bowing. "Now you can ride in comfort—no more bumps."

As they were about to lift Huy and the girl into the cart, the old man turned to Courage. "May I ask you a favor?"

"You can ask for anything. What is it?"

"I know that we are getting close to the front and will soon be stopped at checkpoints. This foolish plot will be exposed at the first one, and you will all be killed. I don't fear for my own safety, but my granddaughter is of no military importance to you. I only ask that she is not placed in the cart. Let one of the soldiers carry her. Please. I don't want her in the line of fire."

For the first time, the old man made sense. They were sure to start making contact pretty soon, and although Thao was a good talker, there could be an alert out for Huy and the girl. Even with their antiquated communications system, the word could be out by now, given the time they had lost.

"You're right," Courage finally replied. "And I'm going to make sure that nobody makes any mistakes."

Reaching into one of the packs, he removed a few feet of cord, a detonator, and a hand energizer. Walking over to Huy, he held them up. "Do you know what these are?"

Huy looked at the white rope and shook his head.

"Well, let me show you how it works." Looking around, Burt picked out a bamboo tree about six inches in diameter. Limping over, he wrapped the cord around the tree, taped a detonator to it, and then returned. After attaching the energizer, he called to everybody to stand back.

"Watch what happens when I squeeze it," he said to Huy.

The explosion echoed through the hills, and pieces of wood scattered in every direction. There was only a jagged stump where the tree had stood. Moving over to the backpack, Burt took out three white blocks and held them up.

"This is C-4," he announced.

Wrapping the cord around the blocks, he pulled himself onto the cart, buried them under the straw and leaves, and attached the energizer. After lowering himself to the ground, he walked slowly over to Huy and looked deep into his eyes.

"I think you're right," he said sternly. "We're bound to be stopped at some checkpoints. You had better be very convincing, because I'm going to have that energizer in my hand. If I don't like the way you blink your eyes, pick your nose, or scratch your ass, I just give it a little squeeze and we'll all go up.

"Now, the three of us are going to be in there together. We may find out just how much you're willing to give to the revolution. I have no doubt you're willing to give your life—but how about hers?"

Huy closed his eyes and his face tightened as anger and hatred for this American surged through his body. "You have no right to do this," he shouted angrily. "She is an innocent civilian. I beg of you, don't put her in the cart!"

He was still shouting and screaming as they loaded him into the back. Every time they hit a bump Huy cringed and held the girl tight until Courage finally assured him that the only way the C-4 would go off was if the energizer was used. As he looked over at the old man he felt a small sense of relief. They were getting closer to home, and there was no way Huy would jeopardize the life of that little girl.

Huy was silent most of the morning and only spoke after Burt offered him a cigarette. "I've been thinking," he said, taking a long puff, "even if you were successful in delivering me to your people, what good is it going to do? You'll get nothing out of me. If you have studied my background, which I'm sure you have, you know that I've been in both French and Japanese prisons. I've been tortured by the best, and have never uttered a single word. You'll get nothing out of me."

Courage looked over and gave a friendly wink. "Hey, they don't torture people anymore. Pulling out fingernails and beating on the bottom of feet went out with bow ties. They use drugs now. They just stick a needle in your arm and start the truth serum going. You just lay there and answer any question they ask. Yep," he sighed, "once the old juice starts flowing, you've got no control."

As the old man slowly stroked the girl's hair he peered at the American. Was this another one of his jokes, or was he telling the truth about the use of drugs? He remembered a KGB Colonel once telling him that they had used drugs in an interrogation. The patient had died, but they had gotten the information from him first.

So that's what the Americans had in store for him. They were going to drug him. If only they hadn't taken the girl along, it would have been so easy. There were two things that were important now. The girl had to be kept alive, and he must never be turned over to the Americans. He would have to make a move shortly.

# ELEVEN

When Thao started seeing more evidence of recent traffic in the area, he put one of the Chieus on point ahead of them. As the cart creaked along the winding trail, the faint sound of artillery could be heard in the distance.

Burt looked up at the sky and figured it was just about noon when the Chieu on point came running down the hill waving both hands. Thao stopped the cart and went up to meet him.

After a short conversation he turned and told Burt that something on the other side of the hill had to be checked out. He told the Chieus to be alert; there were people nearby.

When they returned in a half-hour, Thao stepped up on the wheel of the cart.

"What have we got?" Burt asked.

"An NVA hospital just over the hill," he replied, taking off his helmet and wiping his forehead, "and this trail goes right through the middle. I checked it out. There's no way around."

"From what I saw, the only soldiers there are sick or wounded. Including the hospital staff and the patients, it looks like there are about forty or fifty people. Of course I couldn't see inside the hospital. There could be more in there. I think that if we take it really slow we could walk right through without arousing any suspicion."

Courage reached down and adjusted his bandage, contemplating their next move. "How about weapons? Did you see any laying around?"

"No, I didn't see any at all. Weapons are scarce and are badly needed at the front. There could be a few around, but if anything should happen, we've got the element of surprise."

"Okay," Burt replied, "but I don't want any shooting unless it's absolutely necessary. If we have to kill one of them, we'll have to take them all out. That's going to attract people, so let's be careful."

They had an extra AK-47 which Courage had buried in the straw. He reached over and placed the girl on her back, and moved Huy closer to him.

As Thao led the buffalo up the trail towards the complex, Courage checked for any large antennae indicating they had a communications center. Three long platform buildings, sitting among the trees, looked like places where the wounded would be recuperating.

The winding road led to a large white building at the top of the hill and then made a sharp right turn back into the jungle. It reminded Burt of an old southern plantation, nestled among the large trees.

His eyes carefully scanned each building for any signs of communications equipment. As they drew closer to the main building he could make out two bunkers on the front porch and a few people milling around. They would have to go right by them. This would be the test. If the word was out, this was how they would know. Reaching his hand through the straw, Burt snapped the safety off the AK.

The white majestic building seemed out of place in the sprawling jungle, but he had seen many like it before. They were old French rubber plantations that were taken over by the Vietnamese when the French left. This one must have been converted into a hospital.

They passed within twenty feet of the platform buildings, and could see the wounded laying on mats inside. As they passed the doorway of the last one, two wounded soldiers with their heads wrapped in bandages gave them a casual glance.

On the front porch, they saw a group of six soldiers playing cards. The guards seemed more interested in the game than in the cumbersome cart going by.

They had just passed the main entrance; in another hundred yards they'd be back in the bush. Suddenly a voice from behind the group of soldiers called out, "Excuse me, may I be of some help?"

Stopping the cart, Thao watched as a young officer dressed in a white jacket made his way down the stairs. The insignia on his collar indicated he was either a doctor or on the staff.

"I'm the doctor in charge of this hospital," he said, stepping on the wheel of the cart and looking inside. "It appears that you have some wounded people here, Lieutenant," he continued as he checked the bandages on Burt's knee. "These bandages are filthy, and the man and girl appear to need medical attention."

Courage looked at the doctor, who reminded him of Thao—smooth olive skin, that distinguished look, and pearl-white teeth.

"Who are you people, anyway?" the doctor asked.

Thao moved up to where he was standing. "We're on our way back to our unit. We had to escort a wounded Colonel back to the trail where he was put on a truck and sent home. The Caucasian is an East German journalist on his way to the front to report on the war. He happened to get caught in an air strike a few days back and injured his knee. The unit he was with suffered a lot of casualties and is still back in the mountains.

"He could have waited until they were ready to move, but no, he had to get to the front as soon as possible. So the Commanding Officer told me to take him with us." He looked at the doctor and winked. "I'll bet when he gets there, he'll wish he was back in the mountains."

The doctor continued to work on Burt's bandages as Thao talked. "Yes," he replied, "I'm sure you're right."

"The old man and the girl are from one of the liberated villages south of here. They were also in the strike, but were not injured. There was room in the cart, so I figured we could take them along."

As the doctor examined the girl, he turned to Thao. "It appears that she has a few cuts on her leg. Let me take her inside and clean up the wounds and insect bites. We can take the German also, and I'll change that compress."

As the doctor reached over to pick up the girl, Courage noticed that somehow she had gotten the detonator cord wrapped around her leg. The doctor would know something was wrong if he saw it. Feeling around, Burt slid the hidden AK so that the barrel was pointed right at the doctor's chest.

Huy had noticed the same thing, and as the doctor started to put his hands underneath the girl to pick her up, Huy quickly pushed him away. "Please, doctor," he screamed. "I don't want her moved. She complains about her back hurting. She could have a serious back injury, and moving her could make it worse. She is comfortable on the straw. I'll take care of her."

"I'm sorry," the doctor said, pulling his hands away. "I don't mean to put her in more pain. But if she has a back injury, she should be taken to a hospital in the North. There are no facilities where you are going."

"I'm aware of that," Huy answered sharply. "But she is my granddaughter and I know what's best. Our village is a day's journey from here. Once she is rested and ready to travel, I'll get to a hospital that will treat her."

The doctor then turned his attention to Burt. "I'd like to ask him how he's feeling, but I don't speak German."

"That's all right, Doc," Burt answered quickly. "I speak your language, and to answer your question, I feel fine. The knee's still a little sore, but in a few days it should be good as new."

The doctor looked at Courage with a sense of disbelief. "You speak our language very well," he replied in amazement. "It is not often that I have met a foreigner who has spoken our language as well as you. Even the French who have lived in Hanoi for many years have not mastered our language so well. You are to be complimented."

"Well, Doc, it's kind of hard reporting on a war if you can't speak the language of the people fighting it. I want to make sure that all of my articles are accurate and correct. I want to talk to the soldiers at the front. The whole world is watching what's going on here, and I don't want to miss anything.

"It's like I told the Lieutenant when he suggested that I should wait until the unit caught in the strike moved south. I explained that I didn't come halfway around the world to see our comrades fighting for their homeland to be slowed down by a few American bombs. When the American warmongers are pushed into the sea, I want to be there."

"You are also a very brave man," he replied, patting Courage's knee. He then stepped off the wheel and turned to Thao. "You and your people are welcome to rest here if you wish. I'm sure you're not that anxious to get back to the front."

"I wish we could, doctor," Thao replied. "But we should have been back two days ago, and we've got a Company Commander who frowns on people who are late. I'm going to have a hard time explaining why we're so late as it is. We'd better be moving on."

The doctor asked Thao to wait for a few minutes. When he returned, he handed him a satchel. "Here," he said. "Inside you'll find some aspirin and clean bandages. Give the German and the girl two or three each day to keep their temperatures down. And make sure you change that bandage on his leg. If infection sets in, he'll be going nowhere."

After thanking him, Thao threw the satchel into the cart, grabbed the lead rope on the buffalo, and started towards the jungle trail. When they were out of sight, Burt took in a deep breath and let it out slowly. "You did pretty good, old man. I guess you were telling the truth when you said you'd do anything to save her life, because that's what you just did."

The further south they traveled, the wider the trail. It was now wide enough to accommodate trucks. Thao kept to the left side and moved out of the way of the wounded being carried towards the hospital. Even Courage was surprised that no one looked up at them as they passed. He figured they must have other things to worry about.

They pulled off the trail just before dark and set up camp for the night. It was too risky to build a fire, and after Thao put out the Chieus he and Courage sat in the dark, planning what they hoped would be their last day in the bush.

Burt listened to the faint sounds in the distance: boom, boom. "Those are 105s," he whispered. "American 105s. I figure they're no more than five or six miles from here. And with the artillery behind the grunts in the field, we're about two or three miles from the front. We should be close sometime tomorrow morning. The hairy part is getting from one side to the other. Maybe we'll luck out and run into some friendlies."

Thao opened a can of rations and handed it to him. Burt couldn't see it in the dark, but he could smell it. "This is one thing I'm not going to miss," he joked softly. "By this time tomorrow night, I'll be dining on American food and washing it down with aged whiskey."

The artillery continued through the night, and there was the occasional sound of small arms fire. They were close to home.

# TWELVE

At first light they were traveling again. In less than an hour they had counted over a hundred wounded being carried up the trail.

As they rounded a sharp bend, they saw that the trail dipped down and went straight ahead along a tree line, as far as they could see. There was the sound of small arms fire straight ahead. As they studied their next move a shell landed close by, and the buffalo started to spook. Thao had to hold on to the rope with both hands.

Courage climbed up to get a better view from the top of the cart. As he surveyed the area ahead he noticed a small trail branching off to the left. There was also one leading off to the right, but that was where the sound of the rifle fire was coming from. Thao looked up at him for a decision on which way to go.

"Thao," he called, "keep going straight for about fifty yards. There's a small trail leading off to the left. It looks wide enough for the cart." A shell landed a hundred yards away and the buffalo started trotting with Thao hanging on.

As they turned onto the trail, Burt spotted an open area off to the left. There, through the opening, was a dry rice paddy. It had to be at least two hundred yards across. On the other side was a steep embankment.

"Hold it," he called out, pointing to the paddy. "There's our way home. Let's go."

His eyes were fixed on the paddy, and when the cart didn't move he glanced down, ready to holler at Thao to ask what he was waiting for. But that wasn't necessary. He was looking at

a full squad of North Vietnamese soldiers who had the cart surrounded. He could tell by their blank faces and mud-caked uniforms that these were hard-core veterans. They all had their
weapons at ready.

Courage and Thao exchanged glances as an NVA Captain
with his pistol drawn walked slowly towards them. He stopped
near the cart and looked up at Courage. He then looked at
Huy and the girl. His deep-set eyes, high cheekbones, and
faded uniform told Burt that this guy was nobody's fool. When
he was finished staring at their passengers he walked over to
Thao, who snapped to attention.

"What the hell are you doing in this area?" he screamed.
"Can't you see this is a combat zone? There are enemy soldiers
within less than a mile and you bring these people here.
What's the matter with you?" He walked back to the cart with
Thao in close pursuit. "Who are these people?" he demanded.

"The tall one is an East German journalist," Thao answered
quickly. He indicated to Burt to show his papers. As they were
being handed down the Captain looked at Huy and the girl.

"And who are they?"

As the captain looked over the papers, Thao explained that
he and his men had been assigned to bring a wounded Colonel
back to a hospital and when they were ready to leave they were
ordered to take along the journalist who had been injured in
an air strike, and to bring the old man and the girl to a village
that had been liberated.

"What unit are you assigned to?" the Captain demanded.

"B Company, 326th Battalion, 26th NVA Division," Thao
replied sharply.

"You're a little bit north, aren't you, Lieutenant?"

"You could be right, sir. I must admit that we could have
made a few wrong turns."

Courage studied the Captain as he talked to Thao. He could
sense that he wasn't buying Thao's story. When Thao was finished, the Captain crumpled the papers and threw them on the
ground.

"Take their weapons," he screamed. "Shoot any who resist."

The Chieus were quickly disarmed and pushed together against the back of the cart. The Captain then reached over and took Thao's pistol from his holster and stuck it inside his own shirt. Stepping on the wheel, he ran his hand through the straw until he felt the AK. He picked it up and tossed it to one of the soldiers. "I don't think our German comrade will be needing this," he remarked.

Stepping down from the cart, he walked over to Thao. "There is something very wrong here. I don't know what it is, but I don't believe a word you've told me, Lieutenant. A few days ago my Adjutant received a message from Division Headquarters. I was too busy to pay attention, but I do remember that there was something about an old man and a girl. It's back at my command post. I believe that we should all go back there and read that message. That should clear this matter up."

After looking around, he shook his head. "That thing will never make it through. The people in the cart will have to walk."

"I'm sorry, sir," Thao replied, shaking his head. "None of them are able. The girl and the journalist have broken legs and the old man is too weak."

The Captain looked at Thao and then up at the people in the cart. Then he looked at the brush and rubbed his face. "Perhaps you're right. I could make it there and be back in ten minutes by myself. Dragging that through would take an hour. The next attack will be in a half-hour, and I've got to be here."

After a moment's thought, the Captain ordered Thao and the Chieus to squat and put their hands behind their necks. "You two," he called out to some soldiers nearby, "you stand guard over these people. If any of them make a move, you are to shoot them. If you allow them to escape, I'll have you shot. Do you understand?"

The two young soldiers looked nervously at the Captain and shook their heads. "Yes, sir," they answered in unison.

"The rest of you, be on the alert for any enemy movement. Take cover if necessary. I'll be back in a little while."

As he passed the cart, the Captain stopped and looked again at Huy. He studied the wrinkled face. He knew that face from someplace, but where?

"You look familiar. Haven't I seen you before?"

Huy wanted to scream out what was going on, but out of the corner of his eye he could see Courage's hand tightening around the energizer. It would all be over when the Captain got back anyway. Why risk their lives now?

"I'm sorry, Captain," he replied slowly, shaking his head. "You must have me confused with somebody else. I've not been to very many places outside of my village."

"Humph," he answered. "I still think I've seen you before, but perhaps you're right."

As he disappeared into the brush, Huy moved over next to Courage. "You should have listened to my advice a long time ago," he whispered. "At least you would have had a chance. Now when the Captain returns, he'll bring more soldiers. You have no weapons and you can't run. Let's face it, Mr. Courage, there is no escape."

Huy slowly moved his hand towards the energizer. "Why don't you just give me that device, then nobody will get hurt. You can come back with me and spend the rest of the war in comfort. You know I've got a lot of influence." He looked into Burt's eyes. "You have already proven your bravery. And I must admit, you almost succeeded, but you must now realize that it's over. It would be foolish for you to die for nothing."

As he felt the old man's hand near his, Courage quickly grabbed it hard enough that he saw pain come to the old man's face. "You make one more move," he whispered through his teeth, "and it's 'good morning, Buddha.' You got that?"

Courage let go and looked dejectedly at the rice paddy. "Son of a bitch," he said to himself. "Come all this way, and get caught two hundred yards from home. Two hundred yards," he sighed. It may as well be two thousand miles, he thought. Once that smart-ass Captain gets back, it'll be Hanoi Hilton time. We've got to do something before then.

The artillery that had been silent was now firing again. A round hit about a hundred yards away out in the paddy, sending pieces of shrapnel flying overhead. Those who weren't hidden quickly jumped behind trees or moved further back in the brush. But not the two guards. They stayed close to the cart and kept their weapons on Thao and the Chieus.

Another round landed a hundred yards to the rear, sending pieces of wood and leaves catapulting through the air. It made them duck, but they kept their eyes and weapons on the prisoners.

"We can't stay here," Thao called out to the guards. "We're in the open; they're firing at us. The next one will be right on top of us."

The younger guard, who was no more than seventeen, looked nervously at the older one. He wanted to agree with Thao and move the cart out of the line of fire, but the older guard shook his head. The Captain had ordered them to stay put, and that's where they would stay.

The next round was close enough to send dirt and pieces of wood over the top of the cart. The buffalo started to bolt.

When two more rounds exploded nearby, the older soldier finally realized that they had to get out of the open or they would all be killed. "OK," he called out, pointing his rifle at a large tree surrounded by grass high enough to provide cover. "We'll move over there."

When they were safely there, Thao and the Chieus were told to squat once more at the rear of the cart. After a few more rounds, the artillery stopped.

One guard watched them in back while the other held the buffalo at the front. They both looked intently across the paddy, watching for any movement. "They have stopped shelling," the older one called out. "They may be ready to attack."

Burt figured time was running out. He looked at where both guards were standing and decided they were too far away for him to try and jump them. Even if he jumped one, the other one would see him do it. Damn, if he only had a gun.

Then it hit him like a kick in the stomach. The gun in Thao's canteen flashed through his mind. But how many rounds were left? They didn't bring any extra ammunition. He tried to remember how many shots had been fired. He remembered firing one in the cave—or was it two? Then he'd used one on the cook and one on the servant boy. There should be at least two and possibly three rounds left.

The guards had their eyes glued to the paddy, expecting to see a thousand American soldiers at any second. Courage leaned over the side of the cart and waved his hand at the soldier guarding Thao and the Chieus.

The guard kept his rifle trained on Courage as he walked up to the cart. "Excuse me, Private," Burt said, wiping his mouth. "The Lieutenant is the only one with water. Would it be all right if I got down and took a drink from his canteen?"

The guard looked up at him with distrust.

"Look, I've got a bad leg. I'm not going anywhere. And you've got enough soldiers around here to kill all of us if I do anything foolish. Please, I only want some water."

"Okay," the guard said after a few moments. "You can get down and take a drink, but then you get back up there. If you make one wrong move, I'll kill you."

Easing himself over the side, Courage kept the energizer in his left hand and slid it through the straw, keeping a close eye on Huy. As Courage reached the back of the cart, Thao rose slowly under the watchful eye of the guard, fingers still inter-locked behind his neck.

With Thao blocking the guard's view, Courage snapped open the canteen with his right hand. There was the gun, han-dle up. He reached in, slid it out, and pulled back on the ham-mer.

"Hurry up and get that water," the guard called out, his eyes dancing between the paddy and the prisoners.

"Here, have a drink yourself, asshole," Courage burst out, stepping from behind Thao. Turning quickly, the guard caught sight of the pistol. He tried to bring his rifle around, but he never had a chance. The bullet smashed into his forehead, com-ing out the back of his head with such force that it sent his hel-met and spattering blood flying through the air.

He still stood there with his head rolling and his mouth open. Even in death he attempted to do what he was trained to do—kill the enemy. He tried to turn his rifle, but there was nothing there. Staggering to the left, his knees finally buckled and he fell to the ground.

Knowing the guard at the other end would be coming to investigate, Burt quickly jumped underneath the cart. When he saw the guard's legs go by, he rolled out and stood up behind him.

In three quick steps he closed in and shot him in the back of the head, but the helmet deflected the bullet. The impact sent him sprawling to the ground, stunned but still alive.

With a dazed look the guard searched for his rifle. He didn't see the American standing over him. The last round finished his search.

Huy couldn't see what was going on, but after hearing the shots he knew that Courage couldn't be holding the energizer anymore. Pulling on the cord, he lifted it back into the cart. As soon as it was safely in his hands, he started screaming. "Kill these people! They are traitors, and the foreigner is a CIA spy! I want him alive!"

He didn't know it, but his pleas were falling on deaf ears. The two soldiers were dead and the others were too far away to hear him.

Thao picked up the two AK-47s and threw them to the Chieus as Courage ran over to the cart. "Let's get the hell out of here," he cried as he handed the girl and the still-screaming Huy to the third Chieu.

There was now gunfire coming from the thicket. The Chieus with the rifles ran up to provide some cover fire. Burt took Huy over his shoulder and gave the girl to Thao. "Let's make a run for it. Tell the other two to stop firing and come with us."

As Thao turned to call them he saw one go down, and then the other. "Let's go, Mr. Burt. They won't be coming."

The Chieus had done their job. Burt and Thao were fifty yards out in the paddy before the soldiers reached the cart.

Courage could see the dirt kicking up around him and could hear the whiz of the bullets screaming over his head. Looking over at Thao, he told him to start zigzagging. "It'll make us a little harder to hit," he gasped.

He felt a round go through his pants leg, and then a burning sensation in his thigh, but those were the least of his problems. His knee was now throbbing and the left side of his body was in agonizing pain.

Running as hard as he could, he felt his leg go numb, and he and the old man went sprawling to the ground. Thao, sensing that Burt had been hit, handed the girl to the Chieu and told him to go to the top of the embankment and wait.

Burt was still face down when Thao reached him and turned him over. "Where are you hit?" he asked between breaths.

Courage shook his head. "I'm not hit," he replied, his chest heaving and gasping for air. "My leg gave out. Just help me get to my feet and I'll be okay." There were still rounds kicking up the dirt, but they were just about out of small arms range.

They ran another thirty yards, and then there was a fifty-foot embankment to climb. With Thao carrying the old man, Courage hobbled close behind. He slipped and fell twice before they finally reached the top.

Collapsing on the ground, Burt rubbed his knee and groaned. "Thao," he called out. "I can't move. Look back and see if they're behind us."

Thao wasn't in much better shape than Courage as he gasped for air on his hands and knees. Slowly turning, he looked across the open paddy. "There's no one coming," he spurted between breaths. "They're afraid that if they come out the artillery will catch them in the open. They won't move until they're ordered to."

A mortar round slammed into the embankment, showering them with dirt. As Courage rolled over to see what was on the other side, he banged his fist into the ground. "Shit!" he yelled. "Another paddy, and this one's full of water. It would take us two days to cross it."

Another round hit, sending a fountain of water and mud into the air. They were on a four-foot-wide berm that separated the paddies, right out in the open. "We've got to get out of here," he shouted, scrambling to his feet. "We're sitting ducks out here, and they'll walk that mortar right in on top of us."

As he looked around he saw a tree line to the south. It appeared to be about three hundred yards straight down the berm. There was nothing to the north, and east and west were out of the question.

He knew that narrow dikes were a favorite place for "Charlie" to place booby traps, but it was either that or wait for the mortars to finish the job. "Okay, we're going to head for that tree line. Stay in single file, and don't stop for anything."

Biting his lip to distract himself from the pain, Courage limped as fast as his body would allow. There were still mortar rounds landing, but they were now on the move and not such an easy target.

They were halfway down when Thao called out, "Mr. Burt, look up in the sky; there's an American plane right above us. Should we signal him?"

Courage stopped and looked up. "No," he sighed, "that won't be necessary. That's a spotter plane and he's already seen us. You can bet your ass there's a fighter close by, just looking for a target. We'd better find some cover in a hurry."

Quickening his pace despite the pain, Courage hurried along keeping one eye to the sky. Suddenly he caught a glimpse of the fighter jet off in the distance, banking to the left. He was coming in for the first pass.

They'd never make it to the woods. The twenty-millimeters on that fighter would cut them to pieces. Looking for a place to run, Burt noticed a small pond of water at the bottom of the embankment. It must be an offshoot from the water-filled rice paddy. There had to be a culvert between them. "This way," he said, waving his hand.

Halfway down, he fell again and rolled to the bottom. As he scrambled to his feet, the fighter roared overhead, close enough for him to see the pilot's green helmet. "He's just going to turn around," he called out. "He'll be back in a minute."

With mud up to his knees, he slogged his way toward the source of the water. The entrance was covered with weeds and tall grass. He and Thao worked quickly to clear the opening. It was about four feet high and half-filled with water.

Bending down and backing in, he told Thao to hand him Huy first and then the girl. Then he moved far enough back for Thao and the Chieu to get in. "Is everybody in?" he asked.

"We're all in, Mr. Burt," Thao panted.

They could hear the scream of the fighter as it got closer, and then the impact of the twenty-millimeters as they thumped harmlessly into the ground outside. "It's a good thing we found this place," Thao blurted. "He won't be able to get us in here."

He didn't say anything, but Burt knew better. That was just the first pass, the strafing run. The next one would be the big stuff. From what he remembered about F-104s, they either carried napalm or five-hundred-pounders. If this guy was packing napalm, they were goners. Anything dropped close by would go right up the culvert. If the flaming jelly didn't burn them to a crisp, it would suck the oxygen out of the air, and they'd suffocate.

As he held Huy's head above water, waiting for the plane's return, he thought back to the time when his unit had trapped an NVA company whose only option was a small wooded area surrounded by fields. After sealing off all avenues of escape, they had called in air strikes to finish the job.

He remembered sitting on top of the Vietnamese Armored Personnel Carriers, drinking cold beer and toasting each time one of the fighters circling overhead dove in to drop its load. When they were finished they had turned a small patch of woods into a lumber pile.

Sweeping through the area after the strike, they found where some of the soldiers had tried using their rifle butts to dig a hole. Others, with dirt clenched in their fists, had tried using their fingernails to escape the death from the sky. But there was nowhere to hide, and the entire company was wiped out.

Now, up to his neck in stagnant water, he knew what it felt like to be on the receiving end, trapped with no way out. All he could hope for was that the pilot was new in the country. But most of the jet jockeys he knew could drop a five-hundred-pounder in a garbage can from five thousand feet.

Hearing the roar of the engine as it got closer, he pulled the old man close and braced his back against the wall.

Screams filled the culvert as the concussion from the explosion surged through followed by a tidal wave that washed everybody on top of Courage and the old man. They were all temporarily under water until it receded.

Coughing and gagging, Burt frantically felt around in the darkness for Huy. Feeling his arm, he worked his way up to his head and lifted it above the water. Huy was coughing and trying to get his breath.

Courage felt like his head had been in a vice and one of his eardrums had been punctured. "Is everybody all right?" he gasped.

There was a period of silence before Thao answered. "We're okay," he called out with pain in his voice. "The Chieu was buried up to his waist when the ceiling collapsed, but I think he'll be all right. I'll dig him out."

Courage looked down to where Thao's voice was coming from. There was total darkness. The explosion must have caved in the entrance. There was light at the other end. He hoped the fighter didn't see it, or he'd close it, too. Thao was still straining and groaning, trying to free the Chieu, when Burt heard the screaming of the engines as the plane approached. "Don't get too comfortable back there," he called out. "He's got one more for us. Brace yourself!"

This one wasn't as close, and the blocked entrance absorbed most of the shock. They did feel some of the concussion and more dirt fell from the ceiling, but it wasn't as bad as the first round.

"That should do it," Courage sputtered, spitting out dirt and water. "He's dropped his load. He'll be heading home now."

The plane made two more passes overhead, but there was no more firing. Then the noise from the engine disappeared into the distance.

"Okay," Courage called out. "We're going to move towards that light at the other end. Move slowly, to keep the wake of the water down. And watch the ceiling—it looks like it could fall at any time."

With his knee and head pounding, Burt started crawling with his left arm while using his right to keep Huy's head above the water. The old man was still coughing and gagging. He kept calling out, "Mai, Mai." This was the first time he had spoken his granddaughter's name. "Mai!" he called out again. "Where is she?"

"She's all right," Courage assured him. "She's a little scared, but she's safe. You can see her when we get out of here."

After twenty agonizing minutes that seemed more like twenty hours, they reached the other end. Pushing the grass aside, Courage poked his head through and checked out the area. Off to the right, not more than thirty yards away, was the wooded thicket they had been heading towards. Glaring at the massive entanglement of trees and jungle, he wondered what was waiting for them in there. But with no other place to go, it was their only choice.

"Thao," he whispered after pulling back into the culvert. "I know it's got to be a hundred and some degrees back there and you're not getting much air, but it's too dangerous to move right now. We've got to wait until the sun goes down. Then we'll head for that wooded area. Can you hang on for a while?"

"I think so," came a weak reply. "The girl and I are all right, but the Chieu was buried for a long time. When I went back to get him his head was underwater. I can't feel a pulse."

"Damn it," Burt cursed. "I wish there was something we could do now, but we can't risk exposing ourselves."

As Courage lay there in the murky, dung-smelling water, there wasn't a bone or muscle in his body that didn't ache. Sweat rolled down his forehead into his eyes as he strained to keep the old man's head above water. He splashed water into his eyes every few minutes to relieve the stinging. Every time he started feeling sorry for himself, he remembered what the ones behind him had to be going through. At least he was breathing fresh air.

Once the sun had dipped below the horizon and the sounds of the crickets filled the air, Courage poked his head through the opening. "Okay," he whispered. "It's clear. Let's ease out of here."

There was a small platform outside the entrance that was used to control the water flow between the paddies. After propping Huy against one of the boards, Courage crawled back to help get the others out. Reaching in, he grabbed the girl first. She was covered with dirt and there were signs she had been crying, but other than that she seemed alert. When he put her next to Huy, she threw her arms around him.

When Burt pulled his partner out, Thao was barely coherent, with his eyes rolled back in his head. He immediately started sucking in as much air as his lungs would hold. When he stopped coughing and spitting out water and his breathing returned to normal, he wiped some mud off his face and looked up at Courage. "Another half-hour and we'd have all been dead."

Courage helped him over to where Huy and the girl were and then went back in for the Chieu. He had only gone a few feet when he felt a cold, lifeless arm and saw the Chieu's head under the water. His face was ashen gray when Burt pulled him out. He'd been dead for hours. He must have died when the ceiling caved in on the first bombing run.

As he knelt before the body, Burt bowed his head. He didn't have the strength to move him anymore. He gently picked up one of the Chieu's arms and laid it across his chest, and then moved the other, positioning him as if he were lying in state.

"I'm sorry," Courage said softly, "but this is the best I can do. You did a good job, all that was expected of you. That goes for all of you. Maybe nobody else will remember what you did, but I will."

Burt paused and looked to the sky. "We can't stay here. We're still out in the open."

Thao was sitting up and drinking from the canteen when Courage joined them. "I'm afraid the Chieu is dead," Burt said somberly. "It looks like he's been dead for a couple of hours."

"I'm sorry, Mr. Burt," Thao replied. "I tried to dig him out, but he was under the water for too long."

"It wasn't your fault. It just happened. It could have been any one of us." Taking the canteen from Thao, he took a long drink of water. "As much as I'd like to stay here and rest for a while, we've got to make it to that wooded area. Dusk is the best time to move, and I figure we have about a half-hour before dark sets in."

Mustering all of their strength, Courage put Huy over his shoulder and Thao picked up the girl. "Okay," Courage whispered. "I want you to walk right behind me. This area could be loaded with mines. Watch where I put my feet, and put yours in the same place."

As they broke through the tree line, he stopped and looked around. It looked like a hell of a battle had been fought there, and not long ago. Uprooted and broken trees littered the area; wrecked sandbags and milky white globs from napalm explosions were scattered as far as he could see.

Stepping slowly and cautiously, putting each foot down gently, Burt searched for a crater big enough for them to stay in until morning. Out of the corner of his eye he caught the silhouette of what looked like an old bunker. As they moved closer, he saw he was right. The roof was gone, but the sides were still standing. They had to clear away a few branches and vines from the entrance. Courage let out a groan as he lowered Huy down and sat him against the wall.

There were rusty cans and American ammunition belts scattered on the floor. It must have been a South Vietnamese area at one time, he thought, picking up a few C-ration cans to see if there were any that had not been opened.

When he finished checking all of the boxes and cans, he kicked one in frustration. "Nothing," he said disgustedly, "not a single grain of rice. They didn't leave anything."

Moving back to where the others were, he slid down next to Thao. "Well, it looks like we're getting closer anyway."

Thao turned his head slowly, struggling to keep his eyes open. "Closer to what?" he asked weakly. "Do you have any idea where we are?"

Burt looked around at the darkness now moving in. "Well, from where the artillery was coming from and where we left our Captain friend, I figure we're right in between the two. But which one we're closer to, I don't know. I can tell by the junk I found around here that this is an old ARVN bunker. It looks like they left in a hurry—they didn't leave much. Have we got anything to defend ourselves with, just in case?"

Thao slowly shook his head. "We did have a rifle until the culvert caved in, but there was no ammunition left in it anyway. What did you do with the pistol?"

"Hell, I pitched that when we started across the paddy. It's a good thing you didn't waste the girl. That would have been the fourth round, the one that finished off the guard. That round was the difference between us being here, and dining with our NVA friends tonight."

The mud covering his body was now dry and he started peeling it from his face and hair. "Well," he continued, "instead of figuring what we don't have, let's see what we do have."

Thao reached behind and pulled out a canteen. "This is it," he replied. "It's about half full. Not much for four people, especially in this heat. We'll have to ration it."

"Yeah, you're right," Burt answered. "There's water in the bomb craters, but it wouldn't be fit to drink. Give me that beeper. I'll put it out in the morning. Maybe somebody will pick it up."

With the beeper in his pocket, Burt picked up the canteen and moved over to where Huy and the girl were sitting. Much to his surprise, the old man's eyes were open. He was having problems breathing, but after what he had gone through they were lucky he was still alive.

"Mr. Courage," he whispered, weakly grabbing Burt's wrist. "I can't go on. You can kill me if you want, but I'm not going any further. I can't breathe with these chest pains."

Holding the canteen to his lips, Courage told him to drink slowly. "You'll make it," he assured him. "You're one tough old bastard. If the French and the Japanese couldn't kill you, what makes you think I can?"

"Please," he pleaded, his voice starting to strain, "just leave me here to die. But you must promise me that you will send Mai back home. You and I may disagree on many things, but that has nothing to do with her. From one man to another, give me your word that you will see that she is safely returned."

After giving the girl some water, Burt turned to Huy. "I'll take care of it. You've got my word. But that's not going to happen. We're all going to make it."

Burt placed the girl on Huy's lap and whispered that she should get some sleep. He would try to find food in the morning. As he moved back to where Thao was slumped against the wall, he knew the old man was right. He was getting weaker. If he didn't get some help, Huy wouldn't make it another day.

Reaching into Thao's pocket, Burt pulled out a pack of cigarettes. They were soaked all the way through, and he squeezed the pack until the water ran out. Then he threw it into the darkness. "Ah, what the hell, I was trying to quit anyway," he sighed.

Courage stared at the stars through the roofless bunker and rubbed the side of his head. It was still numb from the explosion in the culvert. The throbbing pain was persistent in his ear, and he pulled out dry blood with his finger. Damn, I hope that thing isn't punctured, he thought to himself.

After reviewing all of their options, he decided that they would have to stay put for at least a day. Everybody was physically spent, and with the area probably booby-trapped it was no place to be wandering around.

Looking over at Thao's sleeping form, he realized someone should remain awake in case they had company. Reaching over, he pulled some of the dried mud from his partner's face. "You're a good man, Mr. Thao," he whispered. "You sleep. I'll keep an eye on things."

Leaning back against the wall, Burt watched the full moon above. Boy, he thought, I sure could use a cocktail right about now.

# THIRTEEN

Having intended to stay awake in case something happened, Burt was angry with himself when the morning sun made his eyes snap open. Quickly looking around, he saw that Thao, Huy, and the girl were still asleep.

Okay, he said to himself, reaching in his pocket and pulling out the beeper. I might as well go out and find someplace to put this sucker.

Emerging from the bunker, he wished he had the machete. Pushing and pulling broken branches and twisted vines, he was making enough noise to be heard a hundred yards away. Spotting a small clearing, he snapped the switch to the "on" position and tossed the beeper into the middle.

As he was about to turn and head back to the bunker, Burt suddenly froze. He heard the snap of a twig and felt the presence of somebody behind him. As he started to move his head, he felt a cold metal object behind his left ear. He didn't have to see it to know it was the barrel of a gun.

"D-D-Don't move," a shaky voice said, "or I'll blow your f-f-fucking head off."

Courage felt the tension drain from his body. The man spoke English, and with a southern accent. "Take it easy, soldier," he said slowly. "I'm an American."

"I ain't no soldier," the voice replied angrily. "I'm a Marine. Now put your hands behind your neck and turn around, real slow. You make one false move and you're dead."

Doing as he was instructed, Burt found himself looking down the barrel of an M-16 with a baby-faced grunt Marine on the other side. He didn't seem to be more than eighteen years old. His lips were nervously twitching and sweat poured down his face. He was gripping the M-16 so tightly that his knuckles were turning white. Burt wanted to tell him that his was the prettiest face he'd seen in a long time, but by the way he was running his finger around the trigger and blinking his eyes, he figured the less he said at this time, the better.

"Now, y'all stay put and don't move," he ordered. "Jackson, Jackson!" he called out. "I got something over here you ain't gonna believe." When there was no response, he called out again. "Jackson, goddamn it, where the hell are you?"

Before he could call out again, the bushes moved, and out walked a tall, lanky black man, dressed in his Marine jungle uniform. Courage watched as he moved closer. He had to be at least six-foot-six and couldn't weigh more than a hundred and thirty pounds. There was a large pink and purple plume protruding from the top of his helmet and a patch on his flak jacket that read "Kill a Commie for Mommie."

With his M-16 at ready, he moved cautiously towards Burt. "Keep your weapon on him," he called to the other Marine. "I wanna get a better look at this dude."

As was seldom the case, Burt had to look up. The Marine's eyes widened; through the dirt and mud he could make out brown hair and blue eyes. "Hey," he shouted. "This motherfucker is a round-eye!"

"I know," the other replied. "He told me he's an American, but it could be a VC trick."

"No sir, Dexter, my man," Jackson laughed. "There ain't no slope-heads with blue eyes. No way this man is from Vietnam. But what he's doing out here where there ain't nothing but gooks is something we got to find out. I better get the Sarge down here right away. We got something big here. Did you search him yet?"

Dexter shook his head. "I ain't had a chance. I didn't want to take any chances out here by myself. Should we do it now?"

"No, let's wait until the Sarge gets here before we do any-thing else."

Noticing the Corporal's stripes on Jackson's collar, Courage looked up at him. "Corporal Jackson, I can assure you I'm an American. If you'll get me back to your unit, I'll explain every-thing to your Commanding Officer."

First Jackson smiled, and then he rammed the butt of his M-16 into Courage's stomach with a force that made him dou-ble over. "Hey, man," he screamed. "Don't you be telling me what I should do. I'm the one with the fucking gun. You ain't going nowhere until the Sarge gets here." Stepping back, he called to Dexter. "I'm going back for the Sarge. If this moth-erfucker moves, waste his ass."

Burt's knee was starting to throb. He wanted to ask if it would be okay to sit down, but the way Dexter was pointing the M-16 at him, he decided it was safer to put up with the pain.

It wasn't very long before he heard loud noises coming from the brush, and then he was surrounded by a squad of Marines. Looking around, it didn't take long to figure out who the Sarge was. He seemed to be in his mid-twenties, while the rest of them were in their teens. Square-faced, and with a solid two hundred pounds on him, he was about as tall as Courage. His chest was too big for his flak jacket and he had nothing on underneath. The sweat rolled down his large biceps as he stopped in front of the prisoner.

"Well, well," he said slowly, tipping his helmet back and wiping the sweat from his face. "It looks like we got us a pris-oner, and a dirty one at that."

"Maybe he's a Russian advisor," one of the Marines called out.

That brought laughter from everybody except the Sarge, who turned angrily. "All right," he screamed, "this is no time for jokes. This is enemy territory, goddamn it. Spread out and check the area. He's probably got friends nearby."

They all moved out with the exception of Dexter, who continued guarding the prisoner. "Did you search this man?" he was asked.

"No, Sergeant, I didn't," he replied meekly. "I was by myself and was afraid he'd try something."

The Sergeant looked at the young Marine and shook his head. "'I was by myself and was afraid he'd try something,'" he mimicked in a boyish, squeaky voice. "Let me tell you something, boy," he bellowed. "If you don't want to go home to your mama in a box, you better start learning how things are done out here.

"Now, the first thing you do when you capture somebody is search him from his asshole to his elbow, like this." He stuck his boot between Burt's thighs and moved it quickly to the left, spreading Burt's legs. After patting him from the crotch to the waist, front and back, he took a rope from his belt and tied Courage's hands behind his back.

When he walked around to the front, Burt noticed the name tag on his uniform. "Sergeant Rucker," he began, "this isn't necessary. I tried to explain to the Corporal that I am an American. If you'll—"

"You shut your fucking face," the Sergeant interrupted, screaming at him. "I'll do the talking! You just stand there and keep your trap shut."

Pulling a soggy piece of paper from Courage's shirt pocket, he opened it slowly. "What the hell kind of language is this?" he asked, turning it in his hand.

"That's German, and there's an explanation for that."

The Sergeant smiled as he folded the paper up and put it in his pocket. "I'm sure there is," he answered sarcastically. "I'm sure there is."

He looked directly into Courage's eyes. "You know something, dirt ball? We've known for a long time that there was an American running with the gooks. They say it's been going on since '65. There are even rumors that there was a reward for this traitor, dead or alive. And do you know something? I think I've got the dirty little bastard standing right in front of me. Now, what do you think about that?"

Courage glared at him. "Listen, you stupid asshole," he shot back, "I'm no traitor and I'm not a deserter. Now, why don't you be a good Marine and get me back to your headquarters instead of playing your cat-and-mouse games with me?"

If he had any more to say, Rucker's fist put the words to an abrupt end. He could feel the left side of his face go numb from the force of the blow. Falling to the ground, the pain shifted to his ribs as he felt the full force of a combat boot crunch into his side.

As Burt lay on his back, trying to get his breath, Rucker knelt down beside him and grabbed his hair. "I told you to keep your goddamned mouth shut, didn't I!" he screamed, pulling Burt's head back. "You give me any more shit, you Commie-loving son of a bitch, and I'm going to kill you right here."

He pulled Courage's face up to his. "I've lost a lot of friends over here. It's bad enough when they get it from the slopes, but when they've got an American helping them, it makes me want to kill somebody. Right now I'm on the edge, so don't push it."

He still had him by the hair when one of the Marines returned with the beeper and handed it to him.

"What were you going to do with this, comrade?" the Sergeant asked, shaking his head. "I suppose you were going to turn it on, and then when a chopper picked up the signal, you and your slope-head friends would spring a little ambush."

He slammed Courage's face into the ground angrily and stood up. "Dexter," he yelled. "Get the radio man over here. I've got to get a hold of the battalion and let them know about this. Move out now."

As Rucker waited for the radio man, Courage rolled over onto his back. "Look," he said painfully between breaths. "I've got three people in a bunker not too far from here. They don't have any weapons. They're probably aware you're here, but are afraid to come out. They've got to go back with me."

The Sergeant rubbed his chin, contemplating the request. "Okay," he finally replied. "You can call your pals out. But you tell them there's a platoon of Marines here and that they're surrounded. If they make one false move, they'll get their asses blown away—and you'll be first."

The squad returned, and the Sergeant ordered two of them to help Courage to his feet. Close behind with their weapons at ready, they followed him through the thicket to the entrance of the bunker.

"Thao," Burt called out in Vietnamese. "Can you hear me?"

"I hear you," came a faint reply.

"I want you, the old man, and the girl to come out, but make it real slow. There's a bunch of trigger-happy Marines out here just looking for an excuse to shoot somebody. So take it slow and easy."

Carrying the old man and leading the girl by the hand, Thao slowly emerged from the bunker.

As the bunker was being checked out, Rucker looked over at Courage and laughed. "This is it? This is who you're running with? I can see the NVA dude, but what's with the old rice burner and the little rug rat? You using them for bait?"

Burt turned to Rucker and wiped the blood from his mouth. "Well, to tell you the truth, I'm very sentimental. I'm taking the old man to a retirement home and the girl to an orphanage."

The smile quickly disappeared. "You can come out with your smart-ass answers out here, but you'll be singing a different tune when they get you back to the battalion."

"Miller," he called out, "have you got them on the horn yet?"

"Yes, sir," he replied quickly. "They're on the line now."

Grabbing the receiver, he placed it in his ear and covered the other side of his head with his hand. "Sergeant Rucker, First Platoon, Bravo Company here. I need to talk to S-2."

After a short while he began talking again. "Major Curley, sir, this is Sergeant Rucker. We've found something out here that I believe you intel people would be interested in. We've captured one Caucasian, approximately six-two, a hundred and eighty pounds, with blue eyes and, through the mud, looks like brown hair."

There was a pause as the party on the other end spoke. "Yes, sir," he continued. "He's Caucasian all right, and we caught him right out here in the middle of 'Charlie' country. He says he's an American, and he speaks Vietnamese and English. He has some type of papers that are written in German. I believe he's that American who's been running with the Viet Cong. What do you want us to do?" He paused. "Uh-huh, uh-huh," he replied. "Yes, sir, we can have them ready by the time the choppers get here. There is also an NVA Lieutenant, an old man and a girl. Do you want them all?" Another pause. "Okay sir, I'll give you the coordinates and we'll throw green smoke when the choppers get here."

Handing the receiver back to the radio operator, he waved his hand in a circle above his head. "Okay, people," he shouted. "We've got a chopper due here in about ten minutes. I want these people ready to go. I want their hands tied and bags over their heads." He paused and looked at the girl. "With the exception of her. Now let's move—we ain't got all day."

Although he ached in his ribs, head, and knee, Burt took in a deep breath. It was a long trip, but they had made it. As they were tying up Thao, he called over, "Is everybody all right?"

Thao nodded and smiled. "We're all okay."

"Knock it off," Rucker shouted. "I don't want any of you people talking to each other." Looking at Thao with that smile on his face made the Sergeant even madder.

"I don't know what you're smiling about, you slope-headed son of a bitch. Once they stick you in that ARVN prisoner-of-war camp, we'll see how funny it is.

"And you," he said, walking over to Courage, ready to put the hood over his head. "I hope they put your ass against a wall and shoot you."

Before he put it over his head, Burt moved away. "Before you do that, I want to tell you something. You're pretty brave with my hands tied and a squad of men behind you. Next time I see you, you'll be the one lying on the ground."

"That's mighty big talk," came the reply, "but if they don't shoot you, I'll be an old man before you walk the streets again." He jerked the hood over Burt's head and tied it tightly so he could hardly breathe. "How do you like that, big mouth?" he laughed.

They were led to a clearing and ordered to sit. It was difficult to breathe through the burlap and although he couldn't see, Burt knew they were in the sun. He could feel the sweat running down his face, stinging his eyes. But with his hands tied, all he could do was keep them closed and endure the pain. That was something he was getting used to.

"Here it comes," a voice shouted. "Let's get 'em ready."

They could hear the chopper coming closer, and soon felt the dust being kicked up by the rotor blades. As they were lifted onto the floor of the chopper, someone called out, "All right, we've got four of them. Are there any more?"

"No, that's it. S-2 has already been alerted. They'll be waiting for you. They've already been briefed."

As the chopper lifted off, Burt could tell that he was near one of the doors. He could feel a breeze, which helped him cool off under the hood. It was a strange feeling, not being able to see. You knew you were moving, but you couldn't tell in which direction.

Using increments of one second, he had counted to three hundred and fifty when the chopper touched down. A few seconds later the engines were shut off. They had been closer than he'd thought.

He could hear voices in the distance, but he couldn't make out what was being said. Then he felt himself being lifted from the chopper and heard someone say, "Take the tall one to the S-2 shack and the others to the infirmary."

There was someone supporting him under each arm as he was guided to the intel building. "Step up," a voice said on the right side. "There's three stairs ahead." Burt's leg almost gave way, but there was someone to catch him.

They were walking on wood, and he heard a screen door close as they passed. When they stopped he was told to sit down in the chair behind him. In the next five minutes the door was opened and closed four times. He would hear footsteps come close and then go away.

Then he heard the door slam. Two sets of footsteps came towards him and stopped in front of him. He heard them slowly walk around him in a circle, stopping every few feet.

"Whoever the hell you are," Burt called out, "would you mind taking this damned thing off my head? I can hardly breathe. You've got my hands tied, and with the condition of my leg I can assure you I'm not going anywhere."

They must have been taking his request into consideration. After a whispered exchange, he felt fingers at the back of the hood untying the rope, and it was slowly lifted from his head.

Taking a gulp of the fresh, cool air, Burt looked up at a Marine Captain and a Major. "Thank you," he said, taking in another deep breath. "I never knew how hot it could get under one of those things."

"Yes," the Captain replied, tossing the hood on the floor, "I imagine it is quite uncomfortable, especially in this climate."

The Captain was about Burt's size and age, with a bronzed, square face and that professional Marine look. The Major was a good six inches shorter and looked to be in his late thirties. His round, white, pudgy face and small potbelly were definite signs that he wasn't a field Marine. He had to be the Regimental Intelligence Officer.

"Let me introduce myself," he said politely, pulling up a chair across from Courage. "I'm Major Hunter, and this is Captain Pierce. We're from Regimental S-2. If you know anything about the American military, I'm sure you know what that is."

Courage looked at the Major and nodded. "I know what it is."

"Good, then we are starting off on the right foot. I must say that by the looks of you and where you were captured, there are a lot of questions that need to be answered."

Leaning over as far as he could, Courage looked into Hunter's eyes. "Before I answer any questions, I wonder if you could do me a favor."

Hunter thought for a few moments before answering. "Well, if it's within reason, I might consider your request."

"The same jerk that tied that hood over my head also tied my hands. He tied them so tight, I can't feel any circulation in my fingers. I'd appreciate it if you would untie them."

Hunter looked up at the Captain for his opinion.

"Look," Burt continued. "You've got two armed guards over at the door. You've got my word, I'll sit right here."

Nodding his approval, Pierce walked behind him and cut the ropes.

"Now that we've made you a little more comfortable," the Major replied, "maybe you could answer a few questions for us, the first being who are you, what were you doing in a VC-controlled area, and what about these papers identifying you as a Hans Kreuger, journalist for an East German newspaper?"

Still rubbing his wrists, he looked first at Pierce and then at Hunter. "Well, my name is Burt Courage and I work for the U.S. Agency for International Development program. The German papers were a cover. What I was doing out there with the other people you picked up is classified, and I'm not at liberty to discuss it with you or anyone else."

The Major leaned back in his chair, rubbing his chin with a look of skepticism. "You say you work for USAID?" he asked. "I wasn't aware the USAID program had people running around in enemy territory with NVA officers and civilians. I thought you people were strictly in the pacification program—you know, building schools and helping the local farmers with their rice crops. The area you were picked up in is not very suitable for rice, and that NVA Lieutenant was no farmer. I'm afraid you'll have to come up with a better story than that.

"But before you go any further, I want to advise you that I'm familiar with all of the USAID Chiefs in I Corps. Can you tell me which one you work for?"

Courage took a long look at the Major. He didn't want to blow Mac's cover, but if he didn't come out with a name, they'd never get out of there. "Okay," he sighed. "If you'll call the USAID Compound in Hoi An and ask for Mac Andrews, he'll verify who I am."

Hunter leaned back in the chair, with a bewildered look on his face. "Mac Andrews," he repeated slowly. "Mac Andrews, I've heard that name. In fact, I've met him." Suddenly his eyes widened and his jaw dropped. "Mac Andrews!" he shouted. "He's CIA! Are you telling me this is a CIA operation?"

Burt looked up at the Major, who was now on his feet, standing right over him. "I'm not telling you anything," he replied after a short pause. "I'm just telling you he'll verify who I am. If you'll get on the phone and call him, it'll save us both a lot of time."

Hunter's eyes darted nervously between Courage and the Captain. He was going to have to make a decision. "Okay, Mr. Courage, we're going to check you out."

He pointed to one of the guards at the door. "You, get on that phone in the corner and contact the USAID Compound in Hoi An. Let me know when you've got them on the line."

He tapped Pierce on the shoulder and told him to come over to where they could talk in private.

"Captain," he whispered, "I want you to get back to Division and report directly to General Sampson. Explain that we've picked up what looks like a CIA operative in our area. This can be a touchy situation if that guy's telling us the truth. See what they want to do, and get back here as soon as possible."

Hunter paced back and forth until the Marine informed him that they had the USAID compound on the line. Turning his back to Courage so that his conversation could not be heard, five minutes passed before Hunter held out the phone to Burt and told him to come over. Sitting for such a long time had stiffened Burt's knee, so he had to limp over to the phone.

"It looks like your story checks out," Hunter said, handing him the receiver. "But you're not out of the woods yet. You can talk to Mac Andrews for two minutes."

"Mac, is that you?" Courage called out.

The connection was not very good, and there was a lot of static, but the voice at the other end was definitely Mac's. "Burt, you son of a bitch," he yelled, "it's good to hear from you! We gave you up for dead when you never showed up at the camp. I thought we'd never see you again. But how the hell did you wind up with the Marines?"

"It's a long story, and when we sit down over a cocktail, I'll give you all of the details." He looked around to make sure the Major wasn't too close. "How soon can you get me out of here?" he asked softly. "These people are asking a lot of questions, and I think they're calling in the big brass."

"You tell them nothing," Mac replied sharply. "You tell them that you have direct orders from me. I've got a chopper standing by. I figure with flying and driving time, I should be there in an hour. By the way, did we get what we wanted?"

"You bet we did. A little weak from the trip, but alive and kicking."

"That's great. I'll let Saigon know right away. I'm sure they'll want to pass it on to Headquarters."

The Major pulled the phone from his hand. "Your time's up." He put the phone to his ear. "I'm afraid, Mr. Andrews, that if you made any plans to pick up Mr. Courage, you'll have to put them on hold. I'm sure the I Corps Commander will have a number of questions that he'll want answered, given that Courage was picked up in his area. I'm afraid he'll have to remain in our custody until the General is satisfied." Slamming the phone down, he never gave Mac a chance to reply. He ordered Courage to return to his chair.

The Major walked over to the desk near the front door and sat down. He kept his eyes on Burt, nervously tapping his fingers. Every few minutes, he would glance down at his watch. He was waiting for somebody.

The clock on the wall showed that a half-hour had passed when the sound of a jeep stopping out front had the Major on his feet and out the door. Burt could hear voices outside, and the one doing all of the screaming was not the Major's.

"These goddamned CIA spooks," came a deep, booming voice. "Who the hell do they think they are, running an operation in our area without permission? I'll get to the bottom of this damned quick."

Storming through the door with Hunter in close pursuit, the man with the booming voice stopped to scrutinize Courage, who was looking up from his chair on the other side of the room.

The man was a full Colonel. Tall and lanky, with a twinge of gray showing from beneath his hat, he was one hundred percent Marine, from the top of his head to his spit-shined boots. His tough, leathery skin gave him the look of having put a lot of years in the Corps, and he was nobody to screw around with.

"Oh no," Burt mumbled, "here we go again."

Courage watched him walk quickly across the room and stop in front of his chair. For a minute he just stood there, looking down at Burt and slapping his swagger stick against his leg.

"Son," he said, finally breaking the silence, "from the looks of you, you've had a pretty rough time out there. Now I can get you some medical help, but it all depends on you."

Looking over at one of the guards, he snapped his fingers and pointed at a chair. It was quickly carried over, and he sat down in front of Courage.

"You see," he continued, removing his hat and wiping his face, "we've got a problem. I've got a three-star General who's fit to be tied, and with good reason. General Sampson is the I Corps Commander. He's in charge of everything up here. Nothing, and I mean nothing, goes on in I Corps without his knowledge and approval."

He leaned forward and managed a smile. "Now, if you'll cooperate and answer all of my questions, I may be able to calm him down a little bit, and we can get you patched up. I might even be able to talk him into releasing you back to whomever you belong." The smile quickly disappeared and his eyes narrowed. "But you tell me one goddamned lie or hedge on anything I ask you, and I'll personally throw your ass in the brig. Do we understand each other?"

Easing back in his chair, Courage studied the hardened face. "The only thing I understand, Colonel, is that I'm a civilian, and you have no authority over me. I'm not about to tell you anything. Now, you can go back and tell your General that."

Burt could see the Colonel's anger starting to build. He clinched his fists and the veins on the side of his neck bulged. Pushing himself up slowly, he took his frustration out on the chair, kicking it across the room.

"Listen, you smart-ass son of a bitch," he screamed, pointing the swagger stick in Courage's face. "I don't care who you are—CIA, USAID, whatever—you don't come into our area of operation without clearing it with us first. That may be all right down South, where the Army is in charge, but when you're in our backyard, you'll play by our rules."

"What the hell are you talking about?" Courage argued back. "Your area, my area. I thought we were all on the same side. I wasn't aware they had divided the country up like a pizza. This is mine, don't step foot in it—it's no wonder we're losing this goddamned war!"

"You shut up and listen to me," the Colonel yelled even louder. "You know damned well what I mean! Now if you want to play hard-ass, I can accommodate you. I'll have your ass interrogated around the clock. We'll see how tough you are. From the looks of you, you won't last a day. I haven't been in the Corps all these years and been promoted to Colonel because I was a quitter. I'll get the information one way or the other. I can make it mighty rough on you."

Looking up, Courage eased himself out of the chair, cringing as pain surged through his ribs and knee. He looked at the Colonel. "Rough," he repeated, talking slowly between his teeth and holding his ribs. "Let me tell you about rough.

"I had a gun put to my head by some NVA Colonel who wanted to see what my brains looked like. Then there was the gold-toothed bastard who wanted to take me to some place in Laos and trade me for weapons. I've been caught in the tail end of a B-52 strike and been shot and mortared at more times than I can remember. I laid in a culvert up to my nose in shit-water while the U.S. Navy dropped five-hundred-pounders on me.

"Then I figured we lucked out when we finally reach friendly lines, and what happens? Some redneck Sergeant of yours with the IQ of an ice pick decides that I'm a traitor and tries to rearrange my face and ribs. Then I'm tied up like a side of beef, have a hood thrown over my head, and I wind up here.

"I've lived like a rat for so long, I wouldn't know what a decent meal looks like. The side of my face is numb, and I may have a concussion. I know my ribs are cracked, and my knee hurts so bad, I can hardly walk on it."

Courage moved back and sat in the chair. "Colonel," he continued, "you don't know the meaning of the word rough. But I'm going to give you some information. Then I'm going to give you some advice.

"This operation is under the direction of the U.S. Ambassador. Now, if I know my chain of command, he's the top man in country. I mean he's over everybody, military and civilian, and that includes your General Sampson. So, now, if by tomorrow myself and the three Vietnamese who were picked up with me are not on our way back to Saigon, you and your General are going to get busted down to your starched shorts.

"Now for the advice. This is way over your head. I suggest that you get back in your jeep and tell General Sampson that if he is that interested, he can call the Ambassador."

The Colonel stared curiously at the mud-caked figure in the chair, slowly tapping his swagger stick against his leg. If what Courage was saying was true, maybe he had better back off. He had put in a lot of hard years in the Corps and was up for promotion to Brigadier. Making enemies in high places was something he didn't need. And this operation looked like something the CIA would pull. Them with their little spy games—why don't they leave the war to the people who know what's going on?

He was still contemplating his next move when shouting from outside captured his attention. "You can't go in there, sir," someone called out. "That's a restricted area."

"Restricted, my ass," came a loud reply, and Burt recognized Mac's voice. As he pushed his way through the door, the two Marine guards tried to restrain him. "Get your goddamned hands off me," he ordered.

The Colonel held up his hand. "It's okay, men, you can let him pass. Then go on back outside."

From his protruding lower lip, glazed eyes, and red face, it was evident that Mac was angry. As he brushed the dust from his shirt and pants, he glared at the Colonel.

Then he spotted Courage on the other side of the room. He walked over to him, still staring at the Colonel. "Damn," he said, lowering his eyes to look at Burt. "You sure do get dirty in your work."

Mac grabbed Burt's face and carefully turned it to the side. "By the looks of that eye, it'll be swollen shut in a little while. Other than that, you don't look too bad."

Courage looked up at Mac. "That," he replied, rubbing his face, "was compliments of the U.S. Marines."

"Well," Mac whispered with a wink, "sit tight. I'll have you out of here in a few minutes."

Walking casually over to where the Colonel was standing, Mac extended his hand and said, "I'm Mac Andrews from USAID."

The Colonel was a good foot taller than Mac, and the last thing in the world he wanted to do was shake hands with him. After some hesitation, he slowly put out his hand.

"I'm Colonel Painter, Division S-2," he said coldly. "You don't have to pull that USAID crap with me. I know who you are and what you do. I only wish you would do it some other place. Maybe you people don't know it, but there's a war going on around here. We've got enough to do without you people playing your little spy games."

Mac looked up with a puzzled expression and rubbed his face. "You know, Painter, you're right. I did notice that. In fact, I've been noticing it for the past three years. I'd like to sit around and talk to you about it, but I'm rushed for time. The only thing I want to know is, are you going to release Mr. Courage and the people brought in with him?"

Painter stiffened at the request. After a few moments of thought, he looked at Mac. "I'm sorry. I don't have the authority to release him, and you don't have any authority to take him. They'll all stay in our custody until General Sampson makes a decision."

Mac thought for a while. "So," he responded, "you want authority. I'll get it right from the top. May I use that phone in the corner?"

"Go ahead," Painter replied. "I don't know what good it will do you. The General has the final say in this area."

It was a long ten minutes before the connection was made, and after a few more minutes of conversation, Mac turned and held the phone out. "Colonel Painter," he called. "It's the Ambassador. He'd like a word with you."

A look of surprise crossed Painter's face, and he instinctively snapped his heels together and took the receiver. Mac moved over next to Courage and gave him a nudge. "He won't have an ear left when the Ambassador is finished," he whispered.

They watched for the next few minutes as Painter squirmed. They heard "Yes sir, Mr. Ambassador," three times, followed by a "what about the General," then "yes, sir, Mr. Ambassador" twice more, and a final "yes sir, it will be taken care of immediately."

After replacing the receiver, Painter looked over at them. By the frustrated look on his face, it was obvious he wanted to vent his anger on someone, as he slapped his swagger stick against his leg.

"Captain Pierce, Major Hunter," he screamed. "Get over here right now."

They were through the door in seconds, and snapped to attention in front of the frustrated Colonel.

"Major," he said, gritting his teeth. "I want these people off the base. You and the Captain will personally escort them to the main gate."

"Don't forget the Vietnamese that were brought in with me," Courage reminded him. "I'm sure the Ambassador meant all of us."

Fearing he might lose his temper, Painter looked at the floor. "Make sure the Nationals are with them."

As Mac helped Courage to his feet, Painter looked on. They had made him look bad in front of his men, and he wasn't about to let them go without having the last word. As they reached the door, he stepped in front of them. "Before you leave, I'm going to give you some advice.

"You may have used your clout to get out of this one," he said, shaking his stick angrily in front of Burt's face, "but be advised: this is our area, and if I ever catch you in I Corps again, not even the President will save your ass."

Courage pushed the swagger stick aside. "Get that god-damned thing out of my face, you jerk. You can pull that crap on some seventeen-year-old recruit, but I'm not in your precious Corps, so get the hell out of my way."

Sensing there was going to be trouble, Mac jumped between the two. "All right," he shouted, "that's enough, Burt. Let's go, there's a jeep outside. And Colonel, you have my word, you'll never see this guy again."

Painter had plenty more to say as he followed them outside. But when Burt turned to answer, Mac grabbed him by the shoulders and pushed him towards the jeep. "Don't even bother answering that asshole," he whispered. "We've got more important things to worry about."

The Major came over and told Mac to follow him. He'd take them to where the Vietnamese were being held.

Following the lead jeep, Mac kept looking at Burt out of the corner of his eye, shaking his head and laughing. "I know it's not funny," he chuckled, "but you sure are a sight. I've had some people come back from operations looking bad, but you take the cake."

Leaning back in the seat, Burt looked at Mac. "Yeah, well, it's a long story. I'll brief you tonight."

"I think the first thing we should do is get you to a hospital and have a doctor take a look at your leg and head. You're going to need some X-rays, and they may want to keep you around a few days for observation."

"That's exactly why we're not going there," Burt responded sharply. "The first thing I want to do is go back to your place and have a cocktail. Then, if it's the last Saturday of the month, I need to take a shower. I'm not going to spend my first day back in humanity lying in a hospital bed. I've got a steak and a bottle of Black Jack coming, and a little pain isn't going to deprive me of that. I'll wait until we get back to Saigon, then I'll get checked out.

"But if you've got a hospital nearby, I'd like to take Huy there. We damned near lost him a few times on the way down. In fact, it's a good thing we got picked up today. I don't believe he would have made it much longer."

The jeep in front of them stopped beside a small building encircled by a chain-link fence and barbed wire, with guards at its entrance. Hunter called out that they would be right back.

In a few minutes Thao came out, carrying Huy, with the girl walking close behind.

"So that's the famous Mr. Huy," Mac commented. "He sure as hell doesn't look like any Vice President, does he? Who the hell is the little girl?"

"That's Huy's granddaughter. She was there when we snatched him. It was either kill her, or take her along. As it turned out, taking her along was the smartest move we made. We'd never have gotten back without her."

"I don't see any of the Chieus. They must be keeping them in a different area."

"No," Burt replied, bowing his head. "We lost them all. One got it during an air strike, two were killed by the NVA while covering us as we made a run for it, and the other one suffocated in a culvert. I'll tell you one thing—they all did good."

Thao was all smiles as they loaded into the back of the jeep. "I'll bet you're glad to be back, huh, Thao," Mac joked.

"Yes, sir," he replied happily. "It's good to see you again."

As Mac looked down at Huy's small, frail figure covered with dirt, he shook his head. "Geez, he doesn't look too good. You sure he's all right?"

"Ah, he just looks bad," Burt replied. "He's more dehydrated than anything else. We get him to a hospital, and he'll be fine in a few days."

When they reached the main gate, the Major's jeep pulled off to the side and they drove through. Mac was still glancing back at Huy. "God, who'd ever believe that something like that could be responsible for keeping the entire U.S. military at bay for all these years?"

"Don't let his looks fool you. That old bastard has more blood on his hands than Ho Chi Minh himself. And if we hadn't gotten him when we did, there would be a hell of a lot more."

It was a twenty-minute ride through Danang before Mac turned into a driveway blocked with barbed wire. The two guards, recognizing the jeep, ran from the bunker and pulled it back.

Burt looked around as they drove into the compound. There were sandbag bunkers every fifty feet, connected by trenches that circled the entire area. There was a chain-link fence in front of each bunker to deflect rockets, and each was manned by three thirty-caliber machine guns. On the outside was a field of fire for at least five hundred feet, laced with barbed wire, claymore mines, and booby traps.

"You've got a fortress here," Burt remarked. "It would take a small army to penetrate it."

Mac looked over and smiled. "Well unfortunately, the enemy knows more about us than our friends do. They know this is the center for the Phoenix program in this area. They bypass military installations to hit us—it's happened four times in the last six months. I guess that sort of tells us something. We must be hitting them where it hurts. That's why they want to put us out of business.

"Then you get some Marine Colonel who comes down, scratching his head and wondering why the Viet Cong are attacking a civilian compound. The last time they were here they found a map on one of the dead bodies with CIA houses circled on it. Some Captain, after looking at it, shook his head, saying he couldn't figure it out. He thought they must have hit the wrong place. It's no wonder I take a drink once in a while."

Stopping in front of the main house, he pointed to a small building off to the side. "That's our dispensary. I'll have Huy and the girl taken there. We've got a doctor and a full staff."

"Not bad—you've got your own hospital."

"We have to. Some of our guys get busted up out in the field. We sure as hell couldn't take them to a military hospital, and the civilian ones—well, I wouldn't put my dog in one of them."

Standing under the shower, Burt felt he had washed off half of Vietnam. After a shave and a change of clothes he was starting to feel like a human being again.

Mac was nursing a martini at the bar when Burt arrived in the dining room. "There's a bottle of Jack Daniels, compliments of Collins. Help yourself."

Filling a glass with ice, Burt slowly poured the amber fluid from the bottle, enjoying the crackling noise as the two blended together. "This has been a long time coming," he called out, holding the glass up in a salute. "What do you say we drink to a successful operation, and an end to this goddamned war?"

As he relaxed on one of the stools, Burt wondered why it was so cool. Then he noticed a large air conditioner in one of the windows. "Not bad," he commented. "Air conditioning, fancy bar, nice rooms. I could take this for a while."

"Ah," Mac shrugged. "When they put me in a hellhole like this, they'd better provide some of the comforts of life. After all, this is my home away from home."

Mac had gulped down three martinis before Courage had finished his first drink. "When you're ready to eat," he said, grabbing the gin, "the cook has our steaks ready to throw on the grill. Just give me a yell.

"By the way," he continued, dropping an olive into his glass, "while you were cleaning up, I got a hold of Collins at the Embassy. I briefed him on everything so far. I mean to tell you, he is one happy man. He wanted to talk with you, but he wasn't on the phone with the scrambler. He said he'll be waiting in Saigon when you get there.

"I also checked on our guests. The doctor said you got the old man here just in the nick of time. Another day or two and you would have had a dead body on your hands. They've got him sedated and are feeding him intravenously. He'll be good as new in a few days."

As Mac grabbed the bottle of Jack and started to fill his glass, Burt pulled it away. "I'm going to have to take it easy on that stuff for a while. For the past month, the only thing my stomach saw was rotten rice and bad water. It's going to take some time for it to get used to the good stuff. But if you want to tell your cook to get those steaks going, I'm ready to eat."

Over dinner Courage explained how the B-52 strike had prevented them from making it to the Special Forces camp, and then how they wound up in the hands of the Marines. When he was finished, Mac shook his head. "You're lucky any of you made it back. But maybe the Lord was on our side on this one."

After they finished eating, Courage limped over to one of the cushioned easy chairs and eased himself into it. "Ah," he sighed. "This is the softest thing I've put my butt on since leaving Saigon. You don't mind if I just sit here for a while, do you?"

"No, sit down and relax. How about another drink?"

"Nah, not right now," Burt replied. "I just want to rest."

Taking a deep breath, he closed his eyes, and for the first time realized that it was all over.

# FOURTEEN

The smell of fresh-made coffee filled Burt's nostrils and he opened his eyes quickly. He was still sitting in the chair. Mac, seated at the table, looked over his glasses as he sipped from his cup.

"Good morning," he shouted cheerfully. "I didn't mean for you to have to sleep sitting up last night. But as soon as you closed your eyes you were dead to the world. I tried to wake you, but it was no use. You looked comfortable enough, so I let you sleep."

As Burt got up out of the chair, Mac could see by the expression on his face that he was still hurting. "How're you feeling this morning?"

"A little better," Burt answered. "My ribs still ache, my ears are still ringing, and my knee still bothers me. But other than that, I'm all right."

As he sat down at the table, Mac poured him a cup of coffee. "How about something to eat?" he suggested. "We've got bacon and eggs, ham, pancakes—you name it."

"That's okay. Coffee is all I need right now. After that spread you put out last night, I couldn't eat anything just yet.

"By the way," he said, pouring some milk into his coffee, "how long are we going to be staying here?"

"You'll be leaving tomorrow morning at nine o'clock. There'll be an Air America plane that will take you directly to Saigon. It would have been here today, if it weren't for the bad weather."

"Do you think that's wise? I mean, if they're keeping the old man alive with a needle in his arm, wouldn't it be better to wait a few days until he's fully recovered?"

Mac looked over and took another sip of coffee. "It's not that I don't like your company, but we've got to get you out of here as soon as possible. Now, old 'Charlie' may not have the latest communications equipment, but he's got an intel network that won't quit.

"Take this place, for example. All of the guards are Chinese Nungs. The majority of them don't even speak Vietnamese, and they are completely loyal to the Americans. But there are also Nationals working in here as maids, cooks, and as orderlies in the hospital. I'm sure some of them are Viet Cong.

"Now, there's been no word out of Hanoi about Huy's disappearance, and we didn't expect there would be. But they know who has him. From my past experiences, I would guess that in two days they will know he was here.

"There are presently two NVA Divisions just west of here. They could probably take the city with that many men. And if they knew that their head man was here, I'm sure they'd try. The quicker you get back to Saigon, the better.

"Now," he continued, finishing his coffee and standing up, "I've got to run over to the MACV compound. I should be back around noon. Help yourself to anything you want—with the exception of the maids."

"Mac, before you leave, where can I find Thao?"

"He's down in the Nung shack. I asked him last night if he'd join us, but he wanted some hot Vietnamese food. I couldn't very well refuse him."

Burt took a walk across the compound to the smaller building that Mac had shown him. Thao was seated at a long table when he entered.

"Mr. Burt," he called out. "I think maybe you miss my cooking and came down here to have me fix one of my specialties, like I did in the field."

Glancing down at the ingredients in the bowl, Burt quickly shook his head. "No thanks," he replied. "I'm laying off the lizard tails and bat wings for a while, but I will have some of that tea you've got brewing on the stove."

After pouring him a cup, Thao sat down across from Burt. There was a full smile and a glow on his face that Courage had not seen before.

"You look like you're in a good mood," Burt said, taking a sip from the cup. "I've never seen you so happy before."

"Mr. Burt, I've got many reasons to be happy. We accomplished our mission, and now, for the first time in many years, I believe that the leaders in Hanoi will have to start serious negotiations with the Americans. They know we've got Huy and they will have to bargain to get him back."

Taking another sip of tea, Burt looked at Thao. "I don't know," he answered with a tone of skepticism. "You're putting a lot of stock in that old man. Do you really believe they would be willing to back down on some of their demands just to get him back?"

"You bet they will," Thao answered quickly. "If there is one thing that you Americans have never understood, it is the leadership in Hanoi. They operate strictly by plans and discipline. To your people, Huy was a military target. But to the North he is more than that. He is the eye and the mind of the revolution. He runs the war machine. Without him, the North is leaderless. Without him the war will come to a grinding halt. Ho is only the spiritual leader. He can only rally the people. Huy knows how to use them. With him in American hands, you have the best bargaining chip at the peace table. When they realize that a military victory is not possible, then, and only then, will they agree to a treaty. Then this terrible war may end."

Burt finished his tea and sighed. "I hope you're right. We've done our job. We delivered him in one piece. Which reminds me, we've still got to get him to Saigon. They're sending a special plane to pick us up. We've got a flight time of nine tomorrow morning. Be ready to leave at eight. Any questions?"

"No problem. I'm like you, I travel light. I'll have everything ready."

Burt traveled back across the compound. As he walked into the dispensary, he could see through the mosquito netting that Huy and the girl were still asleep. Sitting on the edge of the bed, he peered through the netting and looked at the old man. He had been cleaned up, and there was a little bit of color in his face, but his breathing was still labored and he was a long way from being out of danger. Pulling back the netting, Burt reached down and touched the small, wrinkled hand. The eyes of the old man twitched. He knew someone was touching him.

"How are you doing, old man?" Burt whispered, holding the hand softly. "You're looking a little better than you did the other night in that bunker. I thought for sure you'd never see the sun come up. You just hang on. We've got some good old American doctors who will have you back on your feet in no time."

"I see our patient has a visitor," came a voice from behind him. Burt turned and saw a white coat and stethoscope—this had to be the doctor. "He's a remarkable man," the doctor said, softly shaking his head. "Anybody else with a heart that weak would have been dead by now. Even at his age, he has a strong will to live.

"I'm Doctor Lawrence," he said to Burt, picking up Huy's slender arm and checking his pulse. Burt moved out of the way, so the doctor could sit on the bed. "It's still weak," he continued, "but it's much better than when he was brought in."

Courage stood nearby as he continued his examination. "You know, Doc, we've got a flight out of here tomorrow morning. Do you believe he'll be able to travel? I mean, if there's any chance he's not ready, we can always wait a day or so. The most important thing is to get him there alive."

After pushing back each of Huy's eyelids and checking his eyes with a penlight, the doctor stood up and replaced the netting. "I don't believe moving him will have any effect," he sighed, looking at Burt. "He'll be on intravenous from the time he leaves here until the time he arrives in Saigon. I do kind of wish he was a little stronger, but I understand that time is important. There will be a doctor and an ambulance ready to meet you, and there are better facilities there than here. I believe everything should turn out all right. I'll check him before you leave in the morning."

Burt looked over at the girl in the next bed; she was still sound asleep. "How about her?"

"She's no problem," the doctor answered quickly. "I checked her out thoroughly, and with the exception of a few bruises and a little dehydration, she should be back to normal in a day or so. She's young; all she needs is rest. I wish I could say the same for him."

The next morning, Mac drove them out to the Air America hangar. The sun glistened off the twin-engine Cessna parked on the tarp. There had to be at least a full platoon of Chinese mercenaries all around the aircraft, kneeling with their weapons ready. Nobody was going to get close to that plane unless they were ready to fight.

Burt looked over at Mac, who gave him a broad smile. "With the kind of cargo we've got in the back, I'm not taking any chances of anything happening. Once you're airborne, you'll be out of my jurisdiction. But until that time, I'm not taking anything for granted."

Recognizing Mac, the guards waved them through. The crew members, dressed in their gray uniforms, waited in anticipation at the bottom of the stairs. They must have been told that whomever they were transporting was a VIP. When Mac brought the vehicle to a stop, they helped carry the stretcher up the stairs and into the aircraft.

"Now that's what I call the red carpet treatment," Burt commented, jabbing Mac in the side. "You think they'll serve the customary two drinks on the way back?"

"I don't know about the accommodations going back," he replied. "But I'll bet it will be a lot more relaxing going back than it was coming here."

"You've got that right," Burt answered cheerfully. "Mac, I just want to thank you for all of your help. Everything didn't go as planned, but the end result was a success, and that's the important thing. I don't know what I would have done without you."

"Ah, come on," he replied, pushing Burt out of the jeep. "I just helped out with some of the logistics and happened to be at the right place at the right time. You, young man, were the one who made it a success. I've been around for a number of years, and this had to be one of the hairiest operations I've ever been involved in. If it ever gets declassified, I'd like to tell my grandchildren about it—that is, if I ever have any.

"Now," he commanded, pointing at the plane, "you get on that aircraft, get that old man back to Saigon, and see if we can put an end to this war. I'd like to get the hell out of here in the next year or so."

With a final wave of his hand, Courage boarded the plane. Mac was right about one thing, he thought, as he eased back into the soft seat. It's going to be a much better trip going back.

Huy had an attendant on each side of his bed monitoring his vital signs. As Courage got up to stretch his legs, he noticed that the old man's eyes were open and he seemed to recognize him.

"I see you're awake today," Burt commented as he walked by. "That's good, I want you to be alert when we arrive in Saigon. You always said you'd be in Saigon someday. I'm just getting you there a little faster." Huy glared at Burt, then quickly turned away.

When the plane touched down and taxied to the end of the runway, Burt could see the reception committee all lined up in a row. There was a jeep, an ambulance, and two limos behind them.

As the door was opened, Burt took in a deep breath. The same old bitter smell, but it was home. Poking his head through the door, Burt saw Collins at the bottom of the stairs with his hands in his pockets, pacing back and forth. He had to be the worst dresser in Vietnam, in plaid slacks, a yellow shirt, sunglasses and a solid red tam on his head. He looked like he just walked off the golf course. There he was, waving his hands, with a smile from one ear to the other.

The smile became even larger as Burt emerged from the plane. "Courage, you're the prettiest sight I've seen since I arrived in this country," he called out, shaking his fist in the air.

When Burt reached the ground, Collins embraced him with a hug of such force that it lifted him off his feet. "Damn, it's good to see you again," he said. He stood back and looked into Burt's eyes. "I'll admit I had my doubts about this operation, but with you in charge, I knew it would succeed."

"Thank you, John," Burt answered. "And now," he said, pointing to the top of the stairs, "I have a present for you."

As the medical people gingerly carried the stretcher bearing Huy down the stairs, Burt watched Collins' eyes follow the procession. "I can't believe we finally got him," he said, as if in a trance. "This is the guy who has caused all this grief over the last twenty years."

Thao emerged next, carrying the child. "That must be the girl Mac told me about," Collins said. "She is his granddaughter?"

"That's her," Burt replied. "We almost didn't take her along, but it's a good thing we did. We wouldn't be here today if it wasn't for her. But you'll be hearing about that later."

As they loaded into the limousine, Collins noticed the swelling on Burt's face. "Looks like you ran into a little trouble. I'll have a doctor take a look at that when you feel up to it."

He looked up at Collins and grunted. "Let me tell you, I got more lumps from our side than from the enemy." He gingerly rubbed his face. "This was from our friends—the U.S. Marine Corps."

"Well," Collins resumed, "the main thing is that you made it back in one piece and delivered the merchandise. It's too bad we lost the Chieus, but it's a small cost, given the results."

Reaching in his pocket, he pulled out a silver flask and tossed it into Burt's lap. It appeared to be the same one he had the night they left. "I feel a little Jack Daniels is appropriate at this time. I guess it's not too early, is it?"

"Are you kidding?" Burt laughed. Tipping the flask, he took a long drink. "Now," he said, handing it back to Collins, "that's the best one I've had today."

"You know," Collins marveled, putting the flask in his pocket, "you still have your sense of humor, and for all that you went through, you don't look too bad. It does look like you lost a little weight. I wish I could lose a few pounds."

"Tell you what, John. The next time Headquarters needs someone to go into North Vietnam, take the assignment. It's a fantastic way to lose weight. Better than any diet plan."

"Oh no," he laughed, waving his hands. "I'm a little too old for that. I leave the field operations to young people like yourself."

Leaning back in the seat, Burt put his hands behind his head and sighed. "Have you heard anything from Hanoi Hannah or seen any information about the old man's disappearance?"

Collins looked over and shrugged his shoulders. "They've been as quiet as a church mouse," he replied. "But I didn't expect them to tell the world that we snatched their right-hand man, the one who was responsible for kicking the French out of Indochina, the hero of the Tet Offensive. No, they know we've got him, and in a few days they'll know where he is. But even they know they couldn't muster enough forces to attack the Embassy. We've got them by the balls and they know it. We'll just wait and see what happens over the next few days."

Collins reached over and picked up the phone to give the driver instructions. When he was finished, he gazed out the window at the traffic. "I just told the driver to take us to the Duc. I'm going to drop you off there. I'm taking Thao to the Embassy, where he can be debriefed. He should be back at his old job in a few days.

"I'm going to give you tomorrow off to rest up. Your debriefing will start the day after that. I'd like to give you more time to get yourself together, but Headquarters already has two guys en route. They'll be here tomorrow night. I guess the Director wants your report ASAP. I'll have a jeep pick you up in the morning, at seven o'clock."

     ☆      ☆      ☆      ☆      ☆

The debriefing took place in the conference room at the Embassy. As Courage walked in, he saw two men seated at the end of the long table. One appeared to be in his early fifties and the other in his mid-thirties.

"Mr. Courage," the older one spoke, "it's a pleasure to meet you." Both men stood to shake his hand.

"As you've already been instructed," he continued, "you'll be going through a complete debriefing over the next few days. Now, there may be questions that you think are stupid or of little value. But every little tidbit is important to us. There is no such thing as unimportant information."

They never offered their names, and Burt didn't ask. He figured if they wanted him to know they would have told him. The older one asked all of the questions. The younger one took notes and operated the tape recorder.

Courage had to go into detail about every move they had made from the time they left Saigon until leaving Danang. They wanted to know everything, from the terrain of where they were dropped off to what Huy's house looked like and what kind of pictures there were on the wall.

By the afternoon of the third day they were finished. After reviewing all of their notes and tapes, they told Burt he did not have to return.

As he passed Collins' office on his way out, Burt saw him behind his desk. "John," he called through the open door. "Mind if I come in for a few minutes?"

"No," he said, "come on in and have a seat. I was wondering when you were going to stop by. How's the debriefing coming along?"

Slumping down in the chair, Burt let out a sigh. "I'm just glad it's over. If I had to go through another day of that I'd go crazy. I swear, I'd rather be out in the field."

"I know what you're saying," Collins replied, walking over to the coffee pot and pouring himself a cup. "How about you, Burt, you want some coffee?"

"No thanks, I'm just passing by. I was wondering about Thao, and the Chieus' families."

"We paid off the families, as promised," he replied, sitting back at the desk. "They didn't know anything about the operation anyway, so there was no problem with them staying here in Saigon.

"I offered Thao a nice bonus, but he turned me down. He said getting Huy back was payment enough for him. He did say, however, that he would like a few pairs of American jeans. I told him I'd take care of that."

Burt thought back to what they had been through together. "You know, John, if you'd told me a year ago I'd be going on an operation with five North Vietnamese, the people I've been killing all these years, I'd have told you that someone was putting something in your tobacco. But they had to be some of the bravest men I've ever served with. And without Thao, we would never have even come close. I just hope someday, if this war ever comes to a victory for the South, that somebody will remember what he did."

"I'm sure they will," Collins replied. "And don't forget, you were also an important ingredient. Without you, there wouldn't have been an operation. Let's just say that it was a team effort made up of former enemies joining together for a common cause. How does that sound?"

Burt thought for a while before responding. "That sounds good to me," he replied. "I guess when you think about it, it would never occur to anyone that the Agency would be using enemy personnel to conduct an operation so secretive that even the American military wasn't told about it. Just thinking about it boggles the mind. But if everything turns out as planned, maybe we can accomplish in one quick move what the military hasn't been able to do in the past ten years." He paused. "While we're on the subject, how is our guest?"

Collins wrinkled his brow, stood, and walked over to pour himself another cup of coffee. "The old bastard is still complaining about us not sending the girl back to Hanoi. He claims you promised to send her back once you reached your destination, and that's why he cooperated. Any truth to that?"

"Cooperated!" Burt scoffed. "Does he call blowing two of my men away and then trying to kill me cooperating? He's got nothing coming," he said sharply.

Collins had returned to his desk. "Don't worry about it," he replied. "He's a smart old man. He knows we're holding all of the cards. He's just trying a little diversion."

"Have you started any interrogations yet?"

"No," he replied quickly. "It's going to be a while before he's up to any type of questioning. He's still weak and being fed through a needle. The doctors say it will be at least another week before he can even take any solid food. With the key to the war in their hands, Headquarters doesn't want to take any chances. He still has a bad heart. Time is on our side now. We'll take it slow and easy.

"But enough business," he said, slapping his hands on the desk. "You've finished your debriefing and you have some time off. Knowing you, you'll find something or somebody to keep you busy. Now get out of here and have some fun. If I need you, I'll leave a message at the hotel."

# FIFTEEN

After a few more days of rest and relaxation, Burt was starting to feel good again. Most of his aches and pains were gone, though there was still some swelling in his knee. The doctor at the hospital told him that it was a severe bruise but there were no broken bones. He was told to get lots of rest and drink plenty of fluids. Burt explained to the doctor that he was already doing that. The doctor didn't get it. He just looked at Burt and nodded.

As he was walking to the restaurant the next morning, the desk clerk saw him and started waving his hands. "Mr. Courage, sir," he called out in his broken English. "I have message for you."

"Hmm," Burt said to himself as he opened the paper. "I wonder who's looking for me now?" It was from Collins, and he wanted to see Burt in his office no later than nine o'clock that morning. Glancing at the clock on the wall, he saw it was already twenty to nine. He'd have to hurry to get there in time.

He was a few minutes late when he arrived at the Embassy, and Brian told him Mr. Collins was waiting for him in the conference room. He suggested using the back stairs, as that would be faster than waiting for the elevator. Burt took two stairs at a time, knowing it had to be important if they were meeting there.

Collins was seated at the far end of the table, tapping his fingers, when Burt entered. He could tell by Collins' expression that this was not a social visit. His face was drawn and it looked like he hadn't had much sleep.

"Sit down, Burt," he said abruptly.

As Burt pulled up a chair, Collins quickly jumped up and walked over to the bar, returning with a bottle of Jack Daniels and a glass. He put them on the table in front of Courage.

Burt looked at the bottle and the glass, wondering what was going on. "You know," he finally said, breaking the silence, "it's not my birthday. And I know you didn't invite me up here to drink the Ambassador's booze. So something is seriously wrong, and the only thing I can think of is either the old man died, or we brought the wrong one back."

It broke the ice and brought a faint smile to Collins' face. "You're wrong on both counts," he answered. "We've got the right guy, and he is very much alive. But what I have to tell you will explain why I gave you the bottle. You may want a few drinks."

Collins took a deep breath. "What do you know of the Paris peace talks?" he asked, sitting back in his chair.

Burt thought for a few seconds and then shrugged his shoulders. "Nothing much," he answered, thinking it was a strange question. "I know they argued for three months over the size of the table to be used. Neither government recognizes the other, and they haven't accomplished anything. At least that's what I've read."

Collins listened intently until Burt was finished. "Well, you know about as much as the rest of us, that there hasn't been much accomplished since they've begun. But what many people don't know is that until the Tet Offensive, they wouldn't agree to any talks at all. They believed we were the French all over again and that they would just wear us down. After the losses they suffered in the offensive, they finally concluded that a military victory was not forthcoming, so they had to come up with a different strategy. Knowing how the Americans think, they decided to work on world opinion—you know, the big bully picking on a small, backward country that's trying to settle its own problems.

"All that bickering about the size of the table and who was going to sit where was just to get the TV cameras in there. It was their purpose to portray themselves as a peace-loving country invaded by a foreign country ten times their size. And all they said they wanted was a just end to the war. They are masters in front of a camera. They even went so far as to say that if there was progress made in the talks, they would consider releasing a few of the American prisoners they had been holding. Apparently there hasn't been enough progress, because they haven't made any mention of releasing them since. They are well aware of the hype surrounding the POW situation, and how tough it is back home. They play it up every chance they get.

"Now comes the reason I've called you here. Yesterday, our friends from the North announced to the foreign press that they are going to release five American prisoners of war they have been holding. The men will be flown to Vientiane, Laos, where they will be turned over to the International Red Cross. It was their feeling that these men had suffered enough and should be returned to their loved ones. This, they said, was their way of extending an olive branch to us, of showing that they are willing to take the first step in bringing peace to Vietnam and putting an end to this cruel and unjust war. This is the biggest thing to come out of the talks since they started.

"It was their contention that if the Americans were also pursuing a peaceful end to the war, they could show it by releasing some of the North Vietnamese they were holding in return. They reported that the Americans are presently holding a sick old man who only wants to come home to die. They said that if the Americans were not willing to trade one old man for five Americans, they were not seeking peace, and now the world would know it."

Burt could feel his heart pounding as he looked up, his eyes frozen on Collins. He was waiting for him to laugh and tell him it was a joke. But, he remembered, the Agency never joked. He tried to talk, but the words wouldn't come out. It was like his whole world had collapsed.

Leaning back in his chair, Burt covered his eyes. "We're not buying that story, are we?" he said, incredulous. "I mean, after all we went through to get that old man here, there's no way they would trade him back. They've got to do something to keep him."

He didn't have to wait for an answer; he could see it in John's eyes. "I'm sorry," Collins replied softly. "But the decision has already been made, and I mean all the way from the top. He's going back. I realize what a serious setback this is—"

"A serious setback!" Courage interrupted. "A serious setback!" he shouted, slamming his fist on the table. He stood up, leaned over the table, and glared at Collins. "Is that what they're calling it back at Langley? Is that what you call it? A serious setback! I wish everybody would read that debriefing statement to see what we went through to get that son of a bitch back here. I took this assignment because I was told that even though the odds were a thousand to one, if we were successful there was a good chance we could put an end to this lunacy. And I believed them. And I still believe it."

He reached over and put his hand on Collins' shoulder. "John," he pleaded, "you've got to do something. Talk to somebody. You're the head man in country. I know you've got a lot of connections. You can't let this happen."

It was more than a minute before Collins spoke. "Listen to me," he said softly. "No one is more disappointed than myself and the Director about the way things turned out. And I don't have to read a debriefing statement to know what you went through. I've been bumping heads with these people for more years than I care to remember. We pulled off the perfect operation and caught them napping. They had to hit back.

"They never had any intention of releasing those Americans. But when we made off with their top man, they had to do something fast. To show you how clever a move it was, I'll tell you this. At the time of their announcement, they provided a list of names of who was being released. Even as we sit here, those prisoners' families are being hounded by the national press. They stick cameras and microphones in their faces and ask them how they feel about their loved ones coming home. Then you've got every two-bit politician, afraid he might lose his job, demanding that we cooperate in every way to bring those boys home. They're claiming that the trade of five young soldiers for one old man is an admirable gesture by the North Vietnamese, and could be the first step in a negotiated settlement.

"I talked to Headquarters this morning. The White House has been flooded with calls. Over ninety percent of those people want the President to take personal action to assure that nothing interferes with the release of these men. These are the first men ever to be turned loose by the North Vietnamese, and they don't want any screw-ups. They want those people back.

"Meanwhile, the ones pulling the strings up North must be sitting there with smiles on their faces, just daring us to refuse. Can you picture the propaganda they would put out if we turned them down? Even our friends would start to wonder if we are seeking a peaceful solution. You know, I've got to give them credit. What they're doing is masterful. We could never have figured it would turn out like this. But," he sighed, "I've been in the intel game long enough to know that some days you get the bear and other days the bear gets you. That's the business we're in."

There was a long silence as Courage pondered what Collins had said. "Has anybody considered just telling the world who Huy is?" he responded, the anger still in his voice.

"It was discussed," Collins replied quickly, "and turned down. Don't forget, with the exception of a few of us, he's not known outside of North Vietnam. If we tried it, the North would just say it was another American trick to continue their aggression against the Vietnamese people. Believe me, the wires have been hot between here and Washington and every option has been discussed. The final decision was made to send him back, and there is nothing you or I can do about it."

Courage shook his head in disgust. "So we send the old man back. Then it's back to Dien Ban and business as usual. It seems to me we're right back where we started from."

Collins tapped his fingers nervously on the desk, searching for an answer. "I guess that's one way of putting it," he finally answered. "Without the information from the old man, we have no chance of destroying the infrastructure. And if we don't do that, we're just wasting our time.

"In the meantime, we continue to do our jobs. Who knows? Maybe by taking him out for a while we somehow screwed up their plans. I believe that we won't see the offensive they were planning, not when we had the original planner in our hands. That may be just enough to encourage the South Vietnamese to take more initiative.

"However," he added, "there is another point I'd like to bring out. In the 1950s Eisenhower warned against a military-industrial complex. To him it was a real threat. Now we've got the media complex. Ever since the Tet Offensive, the media has used its influence to dictate what will be the future for South Vietnam. Hell, we're the most powerful nation in the world. We brought the Japanese and the Germans to their knees, and they were strong countries. We could dump these chumps like yesterday's garbage, but when your own media doesn't want you to win, Congress won't let you win, and the Vietnamese government is afraid to win, you're fighting a losing cause. And I'm afraid that's the position we're in now."

Collins took another deep breath. "Now that I've got that off my chest, allow me to tell you the primary reason you were called in. When Huy was advised that he was going home, he told the Ambassador, or should I say he demanded, that you and Thao be at the airport when he leaves. He said there would be no exchange unless his demands were met. It would be my guess that he wants to tell you personally that you did all that work for nothing.

"The orders from the Director, who I assume was instructed by the President, are that we will comply down to the last detail. Nothing—I repeat, nothing—will be done to jeopardize the release. The American prisoners won't be released until he steps off the plane in Vientiane.

"There will be media people crawling all over the place. They'll turn it into a circus. There will be TV cameras from all over the world covering this exchange. Everybody is playing this up, and that's why everything has to run smoothly.

"When you and Thao arrive at the airport, you will not talk to anybody. I'm sure the old man will have some parting words for you. However, being the professional you are, I'm also sure you'll act accordingly. Because he requested that Thao be present, I assume he wants a few parting words with both of you. You may have to bite your tongue at times, but just remember who you are representing.

"And now," he said, pushing up from his chair and glancing at his watch, "I've got a meeting with the Ambassador and a number of calls to make." Pushing the bottle and the glass towards Burt, he nodded. "Have a few 'cocktails,' as you call them. We'll just put them on the Ambassador's tab. Turn off the lights when you leave, and I'll see you when you get back from the airport."

After Collins left, Burt slowly picked up the bottle and studied the label. "Seven years old," he read out loud. "That's about how long I've been in this hellhole." Unscrewing the cap, he tossed it in the trash. "We don't need that anymore," he called out. Filling the glass halfway, he held it up to the American and South Vietnamese flags hanging from the ceiling. "Well, here's to both of you. I hope you'll be hanging next to each other a year from now."

Burt didn't know what time it was when he left, only that the bottle was empty and it was dark outside. Driving back to the Duc, he went over in his mind how he was going to tell Thao. If they had to be at the airport the next day, he would have to be told tonight. Collins hadn't explained how to do that.

The bottle of Jack Daniels was starting to show its effects as Burt walked into the lobby. He staggered slightly as he made his way to the bar. Peering into the darkness, he couldn't see any customers at the bar, nor any seated at the tables. He could see Thao in his usual place, holding up glasses to the light as he carefully searched for a speck of dirt or a streak that would require that it be plunged back into the water for rewashing. "Still the perfectionist," Burt mumbled, sliding onto a stool.

Seeing Courage at the end of the bar, Thao grabbed a glass, filled it with ice, and poured it to the top with Jack Daniels.

"Good evening, sir," he said politely, placing the glass in front of him. As Burt reached for his money, Thao held up his hand. "No, you keep your money," he insisted. "This is, as you Americans say, 'on the house.'" Courage couldn't look up at him. He stared instead into his glass. "I've got something to talk to you about, and it's got to be done tonight. What time do you get off?"

Thao looked around to make sure there was no one within earshot. "Does that something you want to talk about," he said softly, "have anything to do with an Air France flight that's leaving in the morning for Vientiane, Laos?"

That brought Burt's head up in a hurry. "I should have known," he replied, taking a gulp from the glass. "You've got a better intel net than the Americans will ever have. What do you know so far?"

"I do have friends around town who keep me informed about what is going on," Thao replied in a soft tone. "But when the North Vietnamese announced that they are willing to release five Americans they have been holding for years and that there is a special flight from Saigon to Vientiane, I knew that something was wrong.

"I know the Communists from the North. They don't release Americans out of the goodness of their hearts. There has to be something in return. A friend who works at the airport tells me that the security has been doubled and that the flight for Vientiane has only a few passengers. One is an old man and another a young girl. Their names have been changed, but not their ages. I came to the conclusion that there is going to be a little trading going on, and the Americans are being swapped for Huy and the girl. It looks like they outsmarted you again."

"Don't rub it in," Burt snapped, finishing the drink and hammering the glass on the bar. "I don't like it any better than you do. I tried talking to Collins, but the decision has already been made. Thao, we're just a part of the puzzle. We completed our assignment and got him back alive. But, other plans have been made at the White House and there's not a damn thing we can do about it.

"Now that you know what's going on, let me inform you of what will be happening tomorrow. Our distinguished guest Mr. Huy has requested, or should I say demanded, that before departing he wants to see both of our smiling faces. He made it clear that if we're not there, there won't be any release. I've got orders that I would assume come right from the White House that this trade is to go off without any complications. We will be perfect gentlemen. We may have to restrain ourselves, but I gave Collins my word that there will be a smile on Huy's face when he leaves."

Having refilled the glass, Thao placed it in front of Burt. "I don't think I'll ever understand you Americans," he said, shaking his head. "We bring in the biggest prize of the war—they have in their possession a man more important than Ho Chi Minh himself—and what do they do? Send him back. They save five lives and lose five thousand more Americans. And if the war is lost, how many more Vietnamese will be killed?

"I knew as a young boy that if the Communists were to be defeated, the only country that could help us was America. I spent many years studying your language, your customs, and what America stands for. One thing I learned was that the Americans are not quitters. When they believe something is right, they follow through until victory has been accomplished. I have read many books. Your country has never lost a war. But now I see them appeasing the Communists. I hope this is not the first step in the Americans deserting us."

"We're not deserting you," Burt hiccuped. "It's just that people back home are being fed a daily dose of what's been going on over the past few days through their televisions. Every night they see pictures of the sickly-looking American prisoners who will be returned to their loved ones as a gesture of peace by the North Vietnamese. They're not told about the politics. And if they were, they probably wouldn't care. All they want is for those five men to be released.

"I don't have to tell you that the war is not very popular at home. We saw evidence of that out in the bush, at that propaganda meeting. The only morale boosters they had were the pictures from American magazines and newspapers of people carrying Viet Cong flags and burning the pictures of the President while demanding an immediate end to the war. This kept them going more than anything else."

Finishing his drink, he pushed the glass towards Thao. "Give me one more and I'll call it a night. And don't worry, we're not about to pull the plug. We've given too much to just walk away."

"I hope so," Thao replied, refilling the glass. "You have done a great service for my country. You risked your life. Many times I believed we would not make it. But, the bottom line is, when it's all over you can just leave, but this is my home. Where can I go, or the millions of my people who have sided with the Americans? If we are abandoned my people will ask, if they didn't come here to help us win, why did they come at all?"

"We're not over here to lose," Burt shouted, thrusting his glass in the air and spilling half the contents. "You know, wars aren't started by people like you and me. We're just the participants. We're the ones who kill or get killed and when it's all over, we don't have a thing to say. That's when the politicians move in. You and I were born thousands of miles apart, in different cultures, and the only thing we have in common is that we don't want the Communists to take over the South. I don't know what the final outcome will be, but you and I did all we could. And who knows, maybe we shook up the big wheels in the North enough that they may just want to call it a draw."

Thao stopped wiping down the bar and looked at Burt. "You may have slowed them down by taking Huy out for a while, but their plan of taking the South will never be changed unless they are defeated." Walking to the end of the bar, he finished drying the glasses and putting them away. He continued to talk, but when he walked back to the other end, he soon discovered his words were falling on deaf ears. Courage had fallen asleep.

When Thao had finished cleaning up, he picked up a tablecloth and draped it over Burt's shoulders. "Here, my American friend," he said softly. "This should keep the chill away."

# SIXTEEN

As they drove out to the airport the next morning, Burt kept rubbing his neck. "Damn," he complained, "my neck sure is stiff. I feel like I slept on a barbed wire fence. Why the hell did you let me sleep at the bar?"

"You were too drunk to wake up, and I wasn't going to carry you up three flights of stairs. Besides, you were safe in there. I'm the only one with a key."

He could tell by the expression on Thao's face that he was enjoying the fact that Burt was suffering from a hangover. "Well, maybe you were right. But next time try to get me to a bed!"

Arriving at the main gate, Burt saw that Collins was right. It was the tightest security Burt had ever seen. Usually the guard would just wave you through, but they were stopped and ordered out of the vehicle. The jeep was searched and they had to give their weapons to the guards.

Passing through the door of the main terminal, they saw a mass of people at the far end. As they drew closer they could see flashcubes blinking and TV equipment. Burt pointed to a corner in the back of the room. "Let's move over there where we can see what is going on."

"There he is," Courage whispered, nodding to where Huy was standing on a platform, talking into a number of microphones with a group of people surrounding him.

They should have had a taller platform—Huy was only visible from the shoulders up. "How does it feel to be going home?" someone called out. After his interpreter translated the question, Huy's face broadened and he waved. He whispered into the interpreter's ear, and the interpreter spoke into the microphone. "I am very happy to be going home."

"Who are you?" another called out, "and why were you being held by the Americans?" After a long conversation with Huy, the interpreter answered. "I'm just an old man. I have committed no crimes. I was arrested with my granddaughter and held for no reason. They are releasing me because I have done no wrong. I just want to go back to my homeland and spend the rest of my years with my family."

Collins was right about it being turned into a media circus. They were throwing questions faster than the interpreter could translate them. There were questions in French, German, and one that sounded like Japanese.

As Huy continued to answer questions, Courage noticed that he kept looking around, and he had a good idea who Huy was looking for. However, Collins had told them that they were to be at the airport. There were no instructions that they had to meet the old man face to face. Maybe if they kept a low profile in the corner, he wouldn't see them and would just leave when the plane was ready.

Searching back and forth, Huy finally caught a glimpse of Courage and Thao leaning against the wall. Squinting at the two figures to make sure his eyes were not deceiving him, he smiled when he was certain it was them. Holding up his hand, he told the interpreter to advise the media that the interview was over for now. He had some urgent business to take care of.

Telling the guards to make a path for him, he walked quickly to where Burt and Thao were standing. As the entourage started to follow, he turned quickly and held up his hand. He instructed the interpreter to tell the group that he wanted a private meeting with the two gentlemen in the corner. After he was finished, he would be glad to answer all of their questions. There was some grumbling, but they honored his request.

As Huy came towards them, Burt could see he still had a noticeable limp, and his steps were shortened. His smile was getting wider as he got closer. Burt took off his sunglasses and slipped them into his shirt pocket. He had to admit, the old man looked pretty good. He was wearing a new suit that was a little too big, a new pair of shoes, and a big white hat that covered most of his face.

"Ah, Mr. Courage," he called out. "I want to thank you for coming. After all the time we spent together, I wouldn't want to leave without saying good-bye to you and your friend."

Stepping in front of them, he quickly turned to Thao. "As for you, my traitorous friend, you have used your tongue against the Vietnamese people. I promise, someday you will pay for your treachery."

Burt watched as Thao clenched his fist and rolled his eyes. Not wanting a repeat of what happened that night in the truck, he put his hand on Thao's shoulder.

"Don't worry, Mr. Burt," Thao said, still staring at Huy. "I know he'd like to create an incident, but it's not going to happen. I have only one thing to say. The next time we meet, there won't be an American around to protect you. Then you'll be punished for all the death and misery you have brought upon our people. And I'll live to see that day."

After scoffing at Thao, Huy turned to Burt. "As for you and your bosses at the CIA, it appears that all of your efforts in this foolish plot accomplished nothing. As you can see, my granddaughter and I will be boarding a plane and heading home. Your last desperate act to try and win this war has ended in failure. I must admit, you did a fine job, and you are a very dedicated young man—foolish, but dedicated. We could use you on our side. When this is all over you must visit me in Hanoi."

Knowing the old man was trying to get under his skin, Courage looked at him and shrugged his shoulders. Taking a handkerchief from his back pocket, he wiped his forehead. "I don't know about working for you people," he replied, grinning. "Your health and retirement plans aren't that good, and I'd be willing to bet there isn't a bottle of Jack Daniels in the whole country. Now, how long would I last without a cocktail? Thanks for the offer, but I'll stick around here for a while."

Noticing that Huy's tie was not quite straight, Burt reached over and moved it to the left, and at the same time, grabbed the knot. "Now," he said softly, "as for not accomplishing any-thing, I wouldn't say that. You've been gone a long time, and when you get back your Russians friends are going to be ask-ing a lot of questions. You're going to have to account for every minute you spent with the Americans. When they see all of those needle marks on your arm, they're going to wonder where you got them. Some of them KGB boys are going to think you were drugged."

"I told you people nothing," Huy screamed suddenly, then stopped, realizing there were people close by. After looking around to assure that no one had heard him, he continued. "Those marks," he whispered, "were from needles used to feed me intravenously. I was too weak to hold any food, and this was the only way to nourish my body. You know that as well as I do. I told you nothing, and in fact, I was never interrogat-ed."

With his hand still on the knot of Huy's tie, Burt looked over at Thao and winked. "I guess if he really believes that, we're not going to be able to change his mind." Pulling up on the knot, Burt lifted Huy onto his tiptoes. "Let me tell you something, old man," he whispered, their faces only a few inch-es apart. "You may think you didn't say anything, but you did. We know all about the next offensive you had planned. And if you think you had your ass handed to you this time, it will be worse the next time. It won't be a surprise, and everybody will be ready."

Courage released the tie, and Huy's feet settled back onto the ground. By the sudden change on the old man's face, it was evident Burt had hit a nerve. Huy's lip began to quiver; there was sweat on his forehead, and he had that same hateful look as when they first met.

He glared at the American in front of him, disbelieving what he had heard. Only a handful of people knew of the next offensive. Not even the top Generals were told. How did the Americans find out? he wondered. Either there was a traitor in the high command, or they really did use a truth serum and he had told them. Or maybe he was just guessing. Ah, that's it, he thought, the Americans are just guessing. "You are just trying to trick me," he stuttered nervously. "You are making all of this up. You have lost. Why don't you admit it? You are beaten."

He was shaking so badly, Burt reached over and held him by the shoulders. "Calm down," he said. "You know your heart isn't that strong. You could have a heart attack, and then you wouldn't make it back home. That would be a pity."

"Take your hands off me," he ordered, stepping back. "You and I have said enough to each other. But before I go, I'd like to give you some advice." He again looked around to assure that he could only be heard by Burt and Thao. "If I were you, I'd leave Vietnam as soon as possible. I have agents in this city who would like nothing better than to kill you. You had better heed my words."

The translator called out that the plane was ready for boarding. Taking a final look at his previous captors, Huy waved. "Until we meet again, I'll just say good-bye."

As he started to turn, Burt called out. "Hey, Mr. Huy, there is one more thing before you leave."

"What is it?" he asked, obviously annoyed.

"Next time, don't make it so easy. Put some guards around your house."

Huy stormed off, disappearing into the maze of cameras and microphones that were following him again. When they were far enough away, Burt turned to Thao and nodded. "Well, we made our appearance like we were supposed to. Now let's get the hell out of here."

Walking towards the door, Burt noticed a number of American reporters running to catch up to them, sensing there was news to be had. "Excuse me, sir," someone called out, "could we ask a few questions?"

Knowing they would be followed and hounded until the questions were answered, Burt stopped and turned. "What is it you want to know?"

"It seemed to us that Mr. Huy was looking for someone. When you and your Vietnamese friend arrived, he stopped all interviews and went immediately to speak with you. It would appear that he knew you quite well. You also speak Vietnamese. Did you work with him in the past?"

"I really don't know the man that well," Courage replied after a short pause. "I speak Vietnamese because I've been here a long time and figured if I'm going to stay in a place, I should at least learn the language."

"What were you discussing with him? It seemed like you were talking for a long time."

"Oh, that," he blurted. "Is that what you're wondering about?" Burt put his arm around Thao's shoulder. "This here," he said, looking at Thao, "is Mr. Huy's nephew. The old man said that his nephew had picked up too many bad habits from the Americans, and he wanted him to go back to Hanoi. He asked me, since I'm such a good friend, if maybe I could encourage his nephew to go back. Hell, I'm the one who taught him all those bad habits like drinking, smoking and chasing women. If he went back, I'd be doing that all by myself!"

That drew laughter from some of the reporters. "You mean that was all you talked about?"

"That was it," he replied, shrugging his shoulders.

A few of the reporters looked at each other and shook their heads. "Well, thank you very much, sir," one of them said as they started to drift away.

Watching from the jeep as the Air France flight roared down the runway and lifted into the morning smog over Saigon, Burt reached into the glove compartment and pulled out a silver flask. "Have a nice trip, you old bastard," he yelled out, taking a drink and holding it up to the sky as the jet soared overhead.

Their eyes followed its path until the black smoke from the engines could no longer be seen and the plane was just a dot in the sky. Courage took another drink, wiped his mouth, and after screwing the cap back onto the flask, threw it on the floor.

"Well, there he goes," he said. "No sense sticking around here anymore. There's still a war going on."

# GLOSSARY

**105s** – American artillery pieces

**Air America** – The CIA Air Force in Southeast Asia

**AK-47** – Russian Assault Rifle – Standard issue for all Communist forces in Vietnam

**ARVN** – Army of Vietnam – South Vietnamese Army

**Charlie** – American nickname for enemy VC and NVA forces

**COS** – Chief Of Station - Head CIA man in the country

**Det. Cord** - Detonation Cord – Used to set off mines and explosives

**F-104s** – American fighter planes

**M-16** – American Rifle – Standard issue for all American and Allied forces in Vietnam

**MACV** – Military Advisory Command Vietnam–American Advisors

**NVA** – North Vietnamese Army

**NVIS** – North Vietnamese Intelligence Service–the CIA of North Vietnam

**S-2** – Military intelligence

**Starlite Scope** – A scope using the light from the stars to see in the dark

**Tet** – The Vietnamese New Year holiday. In 1968 the VC/NVA launched a number of attacks in the majority of the large cities. Because it was during the Tet Holiday it was known as the Tet Offensive.

**USAID** – United States Agency for International Development

**VC Viet Cong** – South Vietnamese Communists